Cache 72

Richard C Hale

Cache 72

By

Richard C Hale

This book is a work of fiction. Names, characters, places and incidents are either the product of the author's imagination or are used fictitiously. Any resemblance to actual persons, living or dead, or to actual events or locales is entirely coincidental.

Copyright © 2013 Richard C Hale. All rights reserved, including the right to reproduce this book, or portions thereof, in any form. No part of the text may be reproduced, transmitted, downloaded, decompiled, reverse engineered, or stored in or introduced into any information storage and retrieval system, in any form or by any means, whether electronic or mechanical without the express written permission of the author. The scanning, uploading, and distribution of this book via the Internet or via any other means without the permission of the publisher is illegal and punishable by law. Please purchase only authorized electronic editions, and do not participate in or encourage electronic piracy of copyrighted material.

Cover Designed by: Richard C. Hale

Copyright ©Richard C Hale 2013

Praise for the Thrillers of Richard C Hale

Frozen Past

"Hale captures emotion, seemingly effortlessly, and in turn this created reactions from me. During this read, I experienced a spectrum of emotion - anger, fear, and heartbreak to name a few. I even found myself "talking" to the characters more than once. When an author can elicit these reactions, I consider this a true talent"
~ *Carolyn Arnold, Author of the bestseller* Ties That Bind

"Mr. Hale's first thriller, *NEAR DEATH*, was an excellent debut novel but with *FROZEN PAST*, he's bounded to a new level of mystery and suspense. Don't let this one pass you by."
~ *Chuck Barrett, Amazon Best-selling Author of* The Toymaker

"What a ride! Richard does a great job of keeping the reader intrigued and constantly guessing. This was my first read of this author, it won't be the last."

"In his second book, Mr. Hale has a winner"

"My body felt shell shocked from the thrilling tension the author was able to convey in his highly charged writing. From beginning to end, Mr. Hale was able to keep me on the edge of my seat wondering what the demented, psychopathic serial killer was going to do next. I must say, this killer is one of the creepiest I've read about."

Near Death

"NEAR DEATH is a fast-paced, romance-laced, thought-provoking, and highly entertaining novel with an intriguing premise."
~ *Author Lisette Brodey*

"Blew me away! An approach I never saw coming. Well Done!!! I can't wait to read your next book."
~ *Author Fred Paxton*

"As I read the book, I couldn't help but think about a movie and who would play each part. I envisioned Matt Damon as Jake and Paul Giamatti as Bodey. What a fantastic read. I highly recommend it"
~ *Ryan Krohn Author of* OUR BELOVED RED

"Richard hooked me, pulled me in and kept me reading till the very end!"

"It was a romp that I finished in a couple of days, and I enjoyed almost every page."

"Wow, what an awesome read. I have not come across a book I could not put down like this since *"The Firm"* or *"A Time to Kill."* The subject and storyline is very thought provoking, and the twist and turns of the story catch you off guard."

Books and Short Stories by Richard C Hale

Near Death

Near Sighted

Frozen Past

Cache 72

Short Stories

The Camera

Flash Mob

The Sandbar

Richard C Hale

Please Visit the Author's Website at:

http://www.richardchaleauthor.com

Richard always answers e-mails. Drop by the website and say 'Hello!'

Richard C Hale

ACKNOWLEDGMENTS

I'd like to thank my wonderful wife and family. If not for their continued support, I may never have had the courage to continue on the journey. They inspire me in everything they do and my life would be incomplete without them. Thank you.

GeoCaching is catching on rapidly throughout the world and with new caches being hidden every day, it is an activity with endless possibility. Though many aspects of the GeoCaching world depicted in the novel are accurate, I have taken certain liberties to maintain the story and entertain. Any inaccuracies are solely my error and should not reflect on the GeoCaching community. They are a bunch of enthusiastic and fun individuals who are passionate about the hunt and I thank them for their wisdom and insight. If you would like more information about the real-world treasure hunt that is GeoCaching, please visit their website at:

http://www.geocaching.com/

For Paula, My Hope

Richard C Hale

CHAPTER 1

The severed finger fell from Jaxon's grip and landed on his boot where the sticky blood adhered to the leather.

He stared at it as he held the empty box in his other hand. His surprise at finding it here in this beautiful wooded area overshadowed the revulsion he felt. He looked back and forth between the box and the finger, shook his boot, dislodging the amputated appendage, and then unconsciously wiped his hand on his jeans. The pink fingernail polish gleamed in the sun as it rolled into a lighted area on the forest floor.

He looked back to the box and saw a white piece of paper crammed inside, a little blood smeared across its surface. He pulled it free and opened it, careful to keep from touching the drying blood.

It read: *Congratulations! You are the lucky recipient of the finger of one Bethany Hope. She's waiting to get it back. Should you so choose, you could be her savior. She's trapped in a place only you will be able to find, but you must hurry. The clock is ticking and I'm watching. I'll know when you find this note and I'll be watching your every move. Think of it as a game...only with a dire outcome should you fail. If you choose to ignore this or come to the conclusion this is a joke, she will perish just as surely as you will survive. If you call the police, she will die. Can you live with that? You*

have 72 hours. I'll be helping you along the way and for my first act of kindness here is your next waypoint. The rest may prove a little more difficult. Ready? Go!
N29° 58.91915', W081° 38.04077'

Jaxon read the note again, more slowly, and then looked around, searching.

He could make out no one watching or even a hint of how they would know he was here. He looked up and a glint of sunlight on an object caught his eye. He maneuvered to his left and saw what looked to be a camera high up in the tree, its lens facing down at him. A little red light blinked off and on.

Jaxon Jennings, retired cop, ex Army MP, and owner of Jennings' Investigations, dropped the box and paper on the ground and began to climb the tree. His six foot three, two hundred and forty pound frame didn't seem to cause the huge branches of the old oak any strain. At least until he climbed a little higher. Then he wondered if this little excursion was the smartest move for someone of his size and age. Forty eight was not old, but it was not young either. When he reached the camera, he tore it from its strap and stared into the lens.

"I'm coming for you, dipshit." He found the power switch and turned it off.

Back on the ground, he pulled his cell from his pocket and dialed a number from memory. It was answered by his wife on the third ring.

"Jennings' Investigations."

"Hey Vick. I need a little help," he said.

"What's up? I thought you were GeoCaching."

She sounded amused and he knew she didn't appreciate his hobby.

He explained the situation to her and she listened quietly, never interrupting.

"Shit," she said.

"Yeah, I agree. I need you to find out as much as you can about this Bethany Hope and then see if you can track anything down about this remote camera. Call the manufacturer and give them the serial number…"

"We've been here before," she interrupted.

"I know. I don't know why all the psychos find me. See if the serial number can get us an IP address or something. He has to be accessing the camera from the internet."

"On it."

"Don't call me. I'll call you. He may have some other means of watching me and I don't want him to know I've got help. We have 72 hours. No police right now until I know he's blind."

"Or she."

He contemplated that statement, "Right. I don't think it's a woman, but we can't rule it out."

"Be careful," she finally said.

"I will. You know me."

"That's what worries me."

He grinned to himself and then said goodbye.

It was amazing how she had fallen right in with him on this and they both knew exactly what needed to be done. It shouldn't surprise him, being that she was also an ex-cop and retired FBI agent, but it still made him feel better that they were in sync even after all they had been through. Working together they just might have a chance at saving this girl's life and taking down the bad guy. What a cliché, he knew, but it gave him comfort.

He opened the GeoCaching app on his phone and plugged in the numbers for the lat/longs the psycho had provided.

GeoCaching was a fun new hobby he had gotten into in the last few months. It was like a scavenger hunt you could participate in as much, or as little, as you wanted. It kept his investigative juices flowing and gave him an excuse to be outdoors. Who would've guessed it would lead to the ultimate scavenger hunt, where someone's life hung in the balance?

He stared at the map of North Florida and the blinking blip representing the latitude and longitude point he had entered into the phone. The GPS built into it said the new waypoint was to the south and approximately five miles away. The only problem was it showed it smack dab in the middle of the St.

John's River. He rechecked the numbers and confirmed they were correct.

"What the hell?" He didn't have time to question it so he used a leaf to pick up the severed finger and place it back in the box.

Trekking back through the wooded area, he scanned the note again to see if there had been anything he might have missed. It was scrawled in a looping pen, with purple ink. The handwriting looked very feminine and this bothered Jaxon. Maybe Vick had been right. Could this scumbag be a woman?

He emerged from the woods to the sight of his car being blocked by two local black and whites. Actually the vehicles were green and white, as Florida seemed to enjoy colorful cop cars over the traditional. Anyway, he was getting a ticket. Or a towing notice. Two cops stood by his car. One spotted him and they both waited for him to make the short walk from the woods to the car.

"This your vehicle?" one of the officers asked when Jaxon approached.

"Yes sir."

The cop looked him over and then to the woods from where he had emerged. He was medium height and slightly overweight, with brown to graying hair. He looked close to Jaxon's age.

Jaxon had tucked the box with the finger and note in his pocket and he hoped it would stay there. It would take quite a bit more explaining than he was prepared for at the moment. He was definitely not ready to involve the locals just yet.

"I need your driver's license and registration."

"Is there a problem, officer?"

"We've had numerous complaints of vehicles blocking the shoulder here and we're just following through."

"I'm not in the road."

"No, you're not, but you're on a piece of private property here and the owner doesn't like it. What exactly were you doing trespassing on his land?"

This was part of the issue with his new hobby. Many GeoCachers were hiding new caches on property that was not public. It was difficult to tell if the property belonged to another entity so the cachers just did their deed and went about the business of uploading the GPS coordinates and letting the games go on. The problem was that it was illegal to put a cache on private property and this wasn't found out until some poor cacher like Jaxon ran into a problem like this one. Jaxon hadn't checked it out before he got here. He had trusted one of his new GeoCaching friends, *PBIStalker*, from the forums, and had added the site to the list of places he was going to visit today. Mistake.

He really didn't have time for this so he decided to use his ex-cop trump card.

Jaxon pulled his old badge from Fairfax County in Virginia out and flashed it along with his driver's license. "Sorry for the problem. I'm an ex-cop from Virginia and I'm into this whole GeoCaching thing. Have you heard of it?"

The first cop looked irritated and nodded his head. "You folks are showing up all over the place, creating problems that are taking away from real police work."

"We were eating breakfast when we got the call," the second one said. He was tall, blond, and built well. Pretty close to Jaxon's own size.

"Didn't know we were that much of a pain to anybody but ourselves," Jaxon said. "I'll take care of this site and have it removed so you won't get any more calls."

The first cop finally smiled and said, "Yeah. Do that please. Old man Vincent is a pain in my ass and he'll keep calling for whatever else he can think of, but if you close this down, that will be one thorn extracted from my side."

"No problem. I'm Jaxon by the way," and he shook the first cop's hand.

"Fanucci. Robert Fanucci," the first cop said.

"Williamsen," the tall one said and clasped Jaxon's hand in a vice-like grip. Jaxon tried not to wince.

"You retired or just down on vacation?" Fanucci asked.

"Retired, but I run a private investigative firm with my wife." Jaxon handed him a card. "If you guys ever need anything outside of the normal channels. The wife is ex-FBI too."

Fanucci looked over the card and pocketed it. "Thanks. I may pick your brain in the future. Not too far from retirement myself." He waved, and got in his cruiser.

"Stay alert," Williamsen said, and put his fingers to his forehead in a half-hearted salute.

Jaxon waved as both cops drove off.

Jaxon sat in the car and brought up the GeoCaching app on his cell phone. He made a notation for this site that indicated it was closed and no longer safe to hunt. Private Property notated by a cache location was usually enough to keep most of the cachers away. He looked at the next waypoint on the GPS and started the car. Time to move.

CHAPTER 2

As Jaxon headed south out of Orange Park, Florida on US 17, he looked over the note again trying to find anything that might give him a clue as to what the real motive was behind this thing.

No one kidnapped a woman and held her life in the balance just for fun. At least no one Jaxon ever knew. The world was full of idiots and psychos and Jaxon had had his fill of those types during his lifetime, but usually there was something or someone creating a catalyst for the actions committed, even if they made little sense to anyone but the perp. He knew that in police work, motive was often searched for first. If there was no clear motive, then it was very difficult to win the case.

The note did not yield anything unusual.

The purple ink seemed to mock him as it stuck out on the paper like a sore thumb. There was a small stain at the bottom right corner, but without any forensic analysis at his disposal he could only guess at what it consisted of. Could just be a water stain. He sniffed the page and noticed a scent of perfume. Though unusual, it did not give any of the secrets like he hoped it would. It was just perfume. He put the note down and concentrated on the drive to the next town.

Green Cove Springs, Florida was the political seat of Clay County and had been a tourist attraction back in the 1800s. Everyone who had made the trip from up north to Florida back then had to stop and see the spring and bathe in its warm crystal clear waters.

When the spring had been discovered, there were those who thought it the fountain of youth and Ponce De Leon be dammed, they were going to capitalize on it. A huge resort was built and it catered to the well-to-do of the time. Even Presidents and foreign dignitaries had visited and bathed in the pristine liquid, hoping that some of the youthful legend would rub off.

As the progress of time so often did, the town lost its attraction and fell to the wayside as the interstate system built new towns and tourist attractions that were much more accessible. The big cities of the state, Miami, Tampa, and Orlando, were much more attractive and much easier to get to. Thus, Green Cove Springs remained a small hick town and though the spring head itself still fed into the St. John's River right at the center of town, it attracted little attention. In fact, Jaxon didn't even realize it was there until he passed the spring itself just off of the main thoroughfare through town while in search of a good cup of coffee. It just never occurred to him that the town with 'Spring' in its name actually had a real live spring.

The GPS in his hand told him to turn left off of US 17 onto State Road 16. He maneuvered the car to the turn lane and guided it left toward the old navy base, now named Reynolds Air Park. He drove past the installation which still housed an airport and dock facilities. It even had an old par three golf course.

He was approaching the Shands bridge which spanned the St. John's River far south of the city of Jacksonville and he wondered if he had made a wrong turn. The GPS told him a left turn was coming up and he bore left down the road with a sign that said Old Shands Pier. It was the original Shands bridge that had been replaced. The old wooden structure was now used by the locals as a fishing spot.

What remained of the bridge jutted out a good distance into the river and as he pulled into the parking space the mystery of the cache that put itself in the middle of the water was solved. The pier just didn't show up on the GPS map.

The parking lot was moderately full and he could see a dozen or more fishermen spread out along the length of the old wooden pier with their poles dangling line into the river. A toddler was running from his grandfather down the length of the structure and Jaxon wondered at the wisdom of bringing a little tornado onto an old, rickety, road of sorts, with little standing between him and the water. He was a fast tornado, too. Jaxon reached out and grabbed the tyke as he skittered past and held him tight while the little guy squirmed and protested. A man Jaxon assumed was the kid's grandfather caught up and took him from Jaxon.

"Thank you, sir. He's a little spunkier than I remember."

"I can believe that, my friend," Jaxon said and smiled. "Better tether him to a cleat or something."

"You got that right. I was actually thinking this wasn't such a great idea. He's pretty damn bored and the fish sure aren't biting. 'Bout time for us to head out. I thank you again for your quickness."

He touched the brim of his hat and turned with the boy wiggling to get out of his arms. He scolded the toddler as he walked back out toward the water where Jaxon hoped he was just going to retrieve his gear. The kid would probably end up in the river before long and Jaxon did not want to go swimming.

Jaxon held up the GPS and it indicated the cache spot was 127 yards to the north. Probably the end of the pier. He started walking. Even though GPS positioning had improved over the years, what with the government releasing some of the constraints on the technology back in May of 2000, the lat/long the GPS displayed was only accurate up to about twenty-five feet. It got you within that distance of the cache point, then it was up to you to do a little hunting and find the hidden treasure.

This is what appealed to the growing followers of GeoCaching, as it not only got them out into the wide world, and yes there were caches throughout the world, you had to put your thinking cap on to actually discover the little box, or tube, or Tupperware container that was hidden. The funny thing was that a lot of the caches were sitting right under most folks' noses and they either didn't see them or they didn't realize what they were. This was such a place, and Jaxon would bet that nobody on this pier even knew one existed here.

The GPS said he had arrived at the spot and Jaxon scanned his surroundings. Nothing jumped immediately out at him. He was at the end of the pier and there were three men spread out around the railing with poles and lines hanging into the still water. Nobody paid attention to him.

He looked for anything metallic as a lot of the caches were attached to sign posts or guard railings or anything that a magnet would stick to. Nothing metal out here but some old tie down cleats for boats and Jaxon saw nothing attached to any of those. He put the GPS in his pocket and started walking around the perimeter that would encompass the twenty-five foot radius inaccuracy built into the GPS. Nothing stood out. Not a box, a bag, a plastic bottle, or even a rubberized container. The only things that were within view were the fishermen's tackle boxes.

He looked over the rail and down into the water. The brown water of the St. John's River showed little beyond two feet into the murk. The bottom could not be seen and since it was high tide, Jaxon was sure it was probably a good ten to twelve feet to the sandy bottom.

He began to think that it might be attached to the underside of the pier itself and he got down on his knees and leaned over the edge trying to peer underneath. He dismissed this idea as no one would be able to reach the cache without the help of a boat or without getting in for a swim. He knew there were cache sites that had to utilize such things, but they were usually notated as such, and this one did not indicate the need to get wet or have a boat. He stood and paced along the railing looking for anything that might give itself up.

He was starting to attract attention.

One old woman sitting in a beat up folding chair with a cane pole hanging out over the edge eyed him and then went back to staring at the tip of her pole. Jaxon moved away.

He watched a fisherman move from his spot after reeling the line in and walk back to his equipment a few yards away, baiting the hook again. The man nodded at Jaxon, then bent to his tackle box where he rummaged around inside for something. He brought out a cigarette, lighting it. The smoke trailed away in the breeze and Jaxon watched it disperse.

He was missing something and though he was fairly new at this GeoCaching thing, he had figured out some of the tricks of the trade, but unfortunately they were not helping him now. He pulled out his phone and clicked on the GeoCaching app bringing up the page for this cache. The rating was three stars out of five so that meant it was moderately difficult to find. One star being the easiest.

He looked at his watch and saw that forty-five minutes had passed since he had found the finger and Bethany Hope was not going to save herself. He was already feeling the pressure and though he had a little over 71 hours, he planned on finding her much sooner than that. Jaxon was not going to make the girl suffer any longer than she had too.

He put the phone back in his pocket and took the note from his other one and read over the GPS coordinates again to make sure he had them correct. It was the third or fourth time rechecking them, he knew, but he was at a loss.

He turned toward the newer bridge, which stood white and tall in the afternoon sun, the few cars crossing its span whizzing by, their tires singing on the metal grating at the top. It was about one hundred yards away and there was no way the cache would be located there.

He did notice a DMV camera on a pole at the top of the span and wondered if the asshole was watching him through it right now laughing his ass off. He raised his hand to it and gave it the finger. A horn honked from a passing car and Jaxon put his hand down embarrassed.

Two of the fisherman stared at him and the old lady was glancing at him out of the corner of her eye, squinting in the bright sunlight. He stood out like a sore thumb. He was dressed in camouflage pants and shirt, and he wore a belt with a canteen strapped to it. He looked like a lost hunter and since he was not holding a fishing pole, he was sure these people were wondering what the hell he was doing. He glanced at each one, noted their sour, sunburned faces, their multiple poles in the water and their tackle boxes sitting by their feet, and decided he needed to talk to them.

He paused in mid-step as he headed for the first fisherman and looked back to the end of the pier as something nagged at the back of his mind. Each person standing in their spot had a little cluster of equipment next to them; tackle box, cooler, bucket. Even the guy who had walked away from his equipment possessed the same thing just not next to him.

But over to the side, where no one was fishing, a lone tackle box sat on the deck. It looked old and weathered, and the plastic, faded, as if it had been sitting in the sun for a long time. Jaxon glanced at each fisherman and counted their tackle boxes. Three. And then there was the lone fourth one with no owner.

Jaxon moved over to it and stopped.

He looked down the pier to see if anybody was walking back down to claim their forgotten tools, but everybody was either sitting in their chairs or standing with a pole dangled over the edge.

He bent to the box and picked it up. It was light. Like maybe there was nothing in it but paper. A paper GeoCaching log perhaps. He opened the lid and stared at the little plastic toys and coins of the cache and smiled. The log was there too. He breathed a sigh of relief.

CHAPTER 3

The woman woke and screamed.

The darkness that surrounded her was almost impenetrable as only a small sliver of light briefly made its appearance and then winked out. A few seconds later, it returned, then winked out again. She screamed more. Her voice echoed loudly and then trailed off. No one answered. She thought she could hear water nearby, but was unsure.

She struggled with her hands and realized they were bound to something behind her. She was sitting upright on the ground and though she could move her legs and feet freely, she was not going anywhere. Her hands ached, but she did not care. She needed to get out of here.

Panicking, she kicked her feet and legs and jerked her arms trying to break free. The darkness made her feel claustrophobic and she breathed rapidly as her chest heaved, trying to catch her breath. Adrenalin coursed through her veins and made her immune to the pain caused by her struggling. What the hell was going on?

How had she arrived at such a place? Who had brought her here (wherever here was) and tied her to this spot, she did not know. She only remembered going shopping at the mall, standing at her car as the mall was closing and dropping her keys. The next thing she knew she had awakened in this terrible place. No one with her and no one to help her. She screamed for help again and her throat burned from the effort. She was so thirsty.

A trickle of water found its way to her legs and she only noticed it because her pants felt wet. The trickle grew and after a few minutes, puddles formed around her calves. What was happening? The light winked on and off again and now she could hear water sloshing up against whatever she was inside of. Was it a boat? An old house by the sea?

The water began rising as her legs were slowly immersed in it. She could feel things skittering by her feet and hands, and she screamed and kicked continuously for what seemed a lifetime.

Her voice was starting to give out and no one was coming to her rescue. The water rose to her chest and the chill made her shiver. It must be the tide. She must be somewhere by the ocean. The tide was coming in and she was going to drown. Panic rose in her throat and then she vomited. Who had done this? Why was she here?

She tried screaming again but her voice was nothing more than a whisper. No one would be able to hear her now. The water seemed to slow in its rise and it stayed at about the level of her breasts. She shivered and waited. Waited for the water to rise more or for it to sink back again. She waited for death.

CHAPTER 4

Jaxon signed in to the GeoCaching app on his phone and logged the cache at the pier into the program.

As a cacher, when you found the 'treasure' you entered it into a website that tracked the visitors to each cache as they found the location and added it to their 'found' items. Some of the caches had prizes for the kids, just like the small toys in the tackle box, or coins, or trackable items, each with their own number on them so that the trackable item could be moved to a new location and tracked as it made its way toward its destination.

Usually, whoever placed the trackable item made a notation on the original cache site for the item as to where they wanted to see the coin end up. Sometimes it took months to get to its destination and others, days or hours.

Jaxon did not take the trackable item from the tackle box. He did not have time for this at the moment and he hoped that whatever game this sicko was playing didn't involve him retrieving and placing coins along his search. He couldn't imagine how they would play into it anyway.

After he made the cache entry, he waited.

Since there was no other message inside the cache itself, he expected to be given some kind of clue via another means as to his next position. At least he hoped so. If his clues ended here, he had no idea where to proceed next. His phone made a noise and he looked at the app. A message had been sent to his login ID. He touched the message and it was nothing more than a set of lat/longs. The next waypoint. At least the psycho was paying attention.

He entered the position and zoomed in on the location. It was an address in Mandarin, just across the river. The only problem was it was not a registered GeoCache site. Nothing showed up on the app and he wondered what he was headed for.

He started the car and accelerated away heading over the Shands bridge east. He flipped the DMV camera the bird again as he passed underneath and then made a left on State Road 13 on the other side of the bridge. His destination was about twenty miles away. He called Vick.

"Where are you?" she asked

"On 13 heading toward Mandarin. I just crossed the Shands bridge."

"You were in Green Cove?"

"Uh huh. The GPS position was at the end of the Old Shands Pier." He told her what had transpired and where he was heading next. "Any luck with Bethany Hope?"

"There are twelve Bethany Hopes in the area. I'm trying to narrow them down. So far three have answered their phones and are accounted for. I'm working on the rest."

"Ok. Anything on the web cam?"

"Haven't got to it yet."

"Ok. I'll call back in a bit."

He hung up and drove for a few more minutes looking for his destination. It came up quickly on the right and he had to brake hard, causing the car behind him to honk its horn as it passed. He waved. The other driver flipped him off.

He parked and looked at the GPS.

The spot was within fifty feet and he stepped from the car and looked around.

He was in the parking lot of some bar. The proprietor must have a sense of humor because the name on the establishment was Free Beer. From the looks of the parking lot, the gimmick no longer seemed to be working. One lone motorcycle sat leaning on its kickstand. He was sure that the place did not serve free beer.

He held the GPS in front of him and tracked it around. The destination was somewhere in line with the bar itself. He wandered around the side of the place thinking that the coordinates must be in the back since all GeoCaches were normally located outside. The locator arrow started to swing to the left as he passed the side of the building and was now pointing back to the front as he stood in the overgrown backyard of the place, facing it. The damn GPS position must be inside. This should be good, he thought.

Jaxon went back to the front and stared. The structure sagged in the center and the once red and white paint had deteriorated to a faded brown and gold color. One section of the eaves hung down close to the door and was held up with what looked like wire. The building was windowless. Maybe it was better inside.

He entered through a glass door that looked to have been broken years ago. The piece of plywood that took the place of the bottom panel of glass appeared faded and partially rotted. Either it had been there a while or the owner used any old piece of wood he could find to cover up the broken pane. The door made a horrible screeching sound as he pulled it open and he wondered how the patrons felt every time someone entered the establishment. It was like fingernails on a chalkboard. As his eyes adjusted to the darkness inside, he saw that the inside of the bar matched the condition of the door. This place was a dive.

The old juke box that sat just inside the door to the right was playing a Lynyrd Skynyrd song and the couple of pairs of eyes that were sitting up at the old, worn bar turned to him and glared. One had on a leather jacket that read 'Death Knell.' It probably belonged to the bike parked out front.

When they found nothing of interest, they turned back and nursed their beers.

Jaxon looked at the GPS and it showed the destination ten feet to the right. He looked in the direction and saw that the sign for the restrooms was in that general direction. He put the GPS away and headed for the bathroom. He felt the eyes of the patrons follow him as he passed. The bartender even looked at him funny.

The men's room was more of a men's closet.

One toilet stood to the right and a sink was to the left. Piss and shit were apparently the decor for this 'room' as no one had bothered to clean it since the glass door had broken in the front. Jaxon looked around hoping it would be obvious. It was not.

He pulled the GPS out again and it showed him within the twenty-five foot margin of error so he felt like this would be the most logical place. He bent and looked under the sink and then behind the toilet. Nothing.

The ceiling was solid without any type of panels, so it wouldn't be up there. Nothing else stood out. The soap was just that. A bar of grimy soap. And the towel dispenser lay busted on the floor. He picked it up and looked inside. Nothing.

He glanced at the toilet again and shook his head. He hoped that what he was thinking, he wasn't about to do, but instead, found himself standing in front of the toilet anyway. He lifted the tank's lid and almost dropped it as a couple of giant roaches skittered across his hands, running from the sudden exposure of their hiding place. He cursed and set the lid on the floor. It made a hollow ringing of porcelain.

In the tank was a waterproof container submerged under the water. He cursed again, stuck his hand in and grabbed it. Pulling it from its hiding place, he shook off the water and unscrewed the lid. A piece of paper lay inside. He unfolded it and read:

So far, so good, my companion. If you are willing to stick your hand into this toilet to do what needs to be done, then poor Bethany may just have a chance. Bravo! Why don't you grab a beer while you're here and relax for a bit. You have a long journey ahead. Here is the next spot. BTW. Don't get too confident. These were easy.

Jackson could hear laughing in his head as he stared at the new coordinates. The urge to smash his fist into the mirror was overwhelming, but he resisted it and stuffed the note in his pocket. Time to play cop.

Back in the bar he studied the patrons and the bartender, who studied him back. He walked up and decided Mr. Death Knell was as good as any.

Death Knell was about six foot two, 280 pounds and it was not all muscle. The man's beer belly made him look the brunt of some weird science experiment gone wrong. He looked about to give birth at any minute.

The other man sitting next to him was as old as dirt and the beer shook in his hand as he raised it to his lips. The foam on the top vibrated against his nose as he tipped it back. The bartender was probably the proprietor and he looked bored to death as he cleaned a glass with a dirty dishrag. It didn't seem to improve the appearance of the mug at all.

"Maybe you boys can help me," Jaxon said and his voice seemed to wake the dead. It just sounded too loud and he cleared his throat. They appeared not to hear him as neither of the beer drinkers turned to him. "You two look like regulars," he said, "and I was wondering if you'd noticed anybody unusual come in here the last couple of days. Maybe they grabbed a beer, maybe they didn't, but they used the bathroom."

Death Knell took a sip of his beer and looked at him out of the corner of his eye. He nodded. "Ayup. Fella just came in here dressed in camo and walked right to the head. He's now standing next to me asking irritating questions. Would that be the guy?"

The old guy next to him almost choked on his beer. The bartender smiled but did not make eye contact.

"No," Jaxon said. "That wouldn't be him. I'm talking about another guy. Or girl. Anybody like that?"

Death Knell shook his head and turned to him. "No. Wouldn't tell you anyway."

"Well I appreciate the hospitality," Jaxon said, dryly. "How about either of you? Anybody out of the ordinary come in here and use the restroom?"

"I don't know who you are mister," the bartender said, "but we don't take kindly to strangers asking a lot of questions. You're bothering my customers."

"Just looking for a little info. Sorry to bother you." He turned to go and Death Knell grabbed his arm.

"We don't like strangers."

"Yeah, I can tell." Jaxon tapped the man's hand with his finger and said, "Do you mind?"

"I do. Now you can answer a few questions of ours."

"Shoot."

"Why are you looking for this guy? Not that we've seen anybody like that."

"No. I'm sure you haven't. Well, I like to play for the other team, and there was this phone number on the wall in there. I'm kind of horny."

He smiled big and winked at Death Knell. The man's face fell and he started to move. Jaxon grabbed the wrist that was holding his arm and he twisted it to the left. The man was off balance as he tried to stand and the pressure from his arm bending in the wrong direction drove him to his knees. Jaxon pulled out his wallet and flashed his old badge. "Don't move," he told the other two. "Not unless you want to lose a kneecap. Now, I'll ask again…"

"We ain't seen nothing," the bartender said.

"You?" Jaxon indicated the old guy, who shook his head. He looked down at Death Knell, his face a grimace of pain as Jaxon applied more pressure. "You sure you haven't seen anybody?"

"Screw you!" Death Knell said, spittle running down his chin.

"I think I'm already doing that, my friend." Jaxon let up on him and Death Knell grabbed his arm in his good hand, standing slowly. "I'm leaving now. Any problem with that?" Jaxon said.

Nobody said a word so he turned to go. He put his wallet back in his pocket and kicked the door open with his foot. The piece of plywood disintegrated as his foot went through it. He turned to the bartender.

"You better get that fixed."

The bartender flipped him off.

The door closed behind him and he stared at the sky as the adrenalin pumped through his body.

"Assholes," he mumbled to himself. He hated violence. Unfortunately, his old job, and sometimes his new, required a certain level of it.

He sat in his car and pulled the note from his pocket. Plugging the lat/longs into his phone's GPS app he saw that the new waypoint was somewhere in Orange Park. Right off of Kingsley Avenue. At least it was registered in the system. Then he moaned. It was one of those Power Run caches.

Power Run caches were meant to be found rapidly in a sequence. It could involve as few as ten separate points or as many as two thousand. They were usually very easy to find and close to the road so they could be logged rapidly, the cacher building up a large number of locations quickly, usually within one day.

He pulled the associated cache locations up on the app and saw that they numbered twenty. At least it wasn't a hundred. They started at the beginning of Kingsley Avenue where Kingsley and US17 intersected, and ended at Kingsley and Blanding Blvd. A three mile run.

He thought about just going to the last waypoint and seeing what clue was left behind, but what if the psycho gave the next hint somewhere in the middle of the Power Run? He would miss it and lose precious time backtracking. Or maybe he would gain time by jumping ahead.

Jaxon tried to put himself into the mind of this idiot and think like him or her. The outcome was the goal here, not the game, and if he could make some shortcuts or think ahead, he might actually have a chance at saving Bethany Hope. If he played by the rules, Bethany would probably die. He needed an advantage.

Jaxon stopped at the first Power Run spot and found nothing. He wanted to make sure just in case. He bypassed the others and went straight to the last one. It was in a parking lot with a Burger King and a Lowes.

The cache was probably attached magnetically to a light pole in the lot and Jaxon concentrated on the closest one. Sure enough, a magnetic box was stuck to the side of the nearest light pole and he popped it off. Inside was the log so he wrote his cacher's ID, Jaxon, and logged the find in the app on his phone. He looked over the little box again and found some number scratched into the plastic just next to the magnet on the underside. It looked fairly new.

He had been right. The prick was not very smart. He wrote the lat/long down and then entered it into his GPS. It was two miles away in a neighborhood. It was not a registered GeoCache site.

Jaxon looked around the lot trying to find anything that would give the perp a clue he had been here. There was a DMV traffic cam on the corner of Kingsley and Blanding and he waved at it. A rider on a bike waved back, mistaking the wave for him. Jaxon ignored him. It was 1:00 in the afternoon. Sixty-nine hours to go.

CHAPTER 5

69 HOURS

Gil Fowler sat in his porch swing and chugged his beer.

He stared at the playground across the street from his house and watched. Specifically, he watched the rocking pig that sat on a huge spring in the center of the playground. It wasn't that it was terribly exciting or interesting to watch, but he needed to see. He wanted to know.

Gil was a diehard GeoCacher and at twenty-seven had found just about every cache that had been hidden in and around the Jacksonville metropolitan area and surrounding counties. He was kind of a legend in the local GeoCacher circles and if there was such a thing as a king of the cacher geeks, he would be it.

That's why the pig bothered him. The cache that was hidden there was one he had not been aware of until a few days ago and if there was one thing he was proud of, it was the knowledge of all the caches in the area. Something was definitely odd.

He pulled another beer from the Styrofoam cooler next to him and popped the top. He drank half of it in a swallow and stared at the pig. Melanie, his girlfriend, came out of the house and plopped her nice ass next to him on the swing, pulling a beer from the cooler. She sipped it slowly.

"How long are you going to watch it?" she asked. She set the beer down next to her, pulled her long brown hair into a ponytail, and secured it with a band. Gil knew she liked it pulled back when it was hot, but he liked it down. It was sexy down.

"As long as it takes," he said and turned back to the pig.

"Why don't you just let it go?"

"I can't."

"Why?"

He looked at her and then looked back at the pig. "I just can't."

"It's not that important."

"Something is up," he said and took another pull on the beer. He was starting to get a buzz and that made the pig watching a little more bearable.

"Have you called Ned?"

"No."

"He might know."

"He won't."

"You don't know that."

"If I don't know, then he won't know."

She rolled her large dark eyes at him and sipped the beer. She squeezed a little closer to him and put her hand on his thigh. It was warm and the weight of it had just the right effect. She apparently knew it would. She had a tiny smile on her lips and he wished she would find something else to do. He didn't want to be distracted, no matter how or why, and she was starting to distract him. He was about to say something that would really piss her off, when a car pulled slowly up to the playground and parked in front of it. A tall guy dressed in camo stepped from the vehicle and looked around. He saw them sitting on the porch and then his gaze moved on. It stopped at the playground.

Gil watched the guy pull something from his pocket. It was a cell phone and if he had to guess, he was sure the guy was using the GPS built in to it. Melanie squeezed his thigh and whispered, "Is he what you've been waiting for?"

"Shh," he said and stood up to get a better view.

When another car had pulled up three days earlier and a big guy got out with a GPS, he had watched him place the cache and then drive away. Gil had expected the cache spot to show up on the websites shortly afterward, but when it hadn't, he went over to the pig and pulled it out.

There were a set of lat/longs in the little magnetic box and he had plugged them into his GeoCache app on his phone. They were for another location across town and this did not register on any of the GeoCaching sites either. Something was going on. So he had waited and now it looked like he might get an answer.

The guy looked around and headed for the swing set.

"Rookie," Gil mumbled, stepping down off of the porch and heading for the park. He heard Melanie follow behind him. He walked up, stood at the edge of the park and watched. The guy hadn't noticed him yet. As the man bent to look under the slide, he caught sight of them and stood up.

"On a treasure hunt," he said and stooped again to the slide.

"I know," Gil said.

The man stood up straight and put his hand to his brow to block the glare. He was bigger than Gil first noticed and the muscles in his arm bulged as he used his hand as a visor. His hair was mostly brown with a little gray at the temples.

"You two GeoCache?"

"I do," Gil said. "She just tags along."

He looked around and then said, "How'd you get here? I don't see your car."

"I live right there," and Gil pointed to the house.

"Oh. So you know this cache?"

"No. That's what's bothering me. It doesn't exist…yet…but I've seen another guy here and now you. I know a cacher when I see one."

Gil stared as the man walked toward them. He looked a little excited.

"You saw the guy who placed the cache?"

Gil nodded. He wasn't feeling so sure now about all of this. Maybe he and Melanie shouldn't have told him where they live. Who knew what these people were up to?

"How long ago?" the guy said. "What'd he look like?"

"Three days ago. He was big, about your size. Wore a windbreaker in the summer. I saw him put the cache there and do something to his GPS. Weird that it hasn't shown up on any of the caching sites."

"I know."

"So, if it isn't on any of the caching sites, how do you know about it?" Gil asked and watched the man's face change.

"I found the lat/longs at another site and I'm following the path."

Gil nodded. He could tell the guy was lying. "I don't believe you, mister."

Melanie stepped next to him and took his hand in hers. She was scared. He could tell.

The man looked around as if trying to decide something. He seemed to make up his mind and he took another couple of steps closer. He was now standing three feet away. He looked tense and mean, his blue, penetrating eyes locked onto Gil's. Gil felt for sure the man could probably see through any lie.

"Listen," the guy said, "I can't go into it with you guys. Just believe me it's very important I find the cache."

"Why?"

"I can't talk about it."

"Are you in some kind of trouble?" Melanie asked and her voice surprised Gil.

"Not like you think. Someone else is in a lot of trouble."

Gil pulled out his cell phone and made a show of using it.

"I'm calling the cops right now," he said and pushed a few buttons. He had no real intention of calling them, he just wanted to see what the guy would do.

The man held up his hand and pulled something from his back pocket. It was a wallet. He opened it so they could see. Gil studied the badge and some kind of ID. It surprised him.

"I'd appreciate it if you wouldn't bother my brothers here in town. No need to involve them."

Gil lowered the phone and turned to Melanie. She shrugged. "Maybe we can help you, Mister, uh…Jennings. I'm pretty good at this caching shit." He could feel Melanie nodding her head next to him.

"Jaxon," he said, "and if you know where this cache is, that would be all the help I need. I'm kind of in a time crunch."

"The pig," Gil said, and for a second Jaxon looked confused. Then he turned and spotted the ride and headed for it. He found the magnetized cache in a few seconds. He held it up and smiled. "Thanks."

"No problem, Jaxon."

Gil watched him open the cache and study the slip of paper inside. He creased his brow, then pulled his phone out and punched in the numbers. He pocketed the cache and turned to go.

"You're going to need our help," Gil said.

Jaxon shook his head. "Not your responsibility," he said. "I got this."

"I don't think you do. I think you're a noob at this and you're going to blow it."

Jaxon studied him and then shook his head. "I can't involve you," he said. "It's too risky."

"Let us be the judge of that."

"I'm not worried about you," and he slipped inside the car, started the engine, waved, and was gone.

Gil turned to Melanie. "Something big is going on."

"You heard him. It's too risky."

"I don't care."

"He's gone, anyway."

"But I know where he's going." Gil pulled out his GPS and showed her. "I already loaded the position into my machine. I've even been there."

"When?" she said and smiled.

"Two days ago."

"What was there?"

He must have frowned for she creased her brow in concern. "Nothing," he said. "The spot was empty."

* * *

Jaxon pulled out of the neighborhood and called Victoria. She answered on the second ring.

"How's it going?"

"It's not," he said. "This is a wild goose chase."

"Did you think it would be easy? This guy's a psycho, remember?"

"Or girl." He could feel her smile even through the connection. "And no, I didn't expect it to be easy. I was just hoping."

"Hope—police work—they don't go together."

"Yeah. I know. We have to find some way to get ahead of him. It's just like in Virginia. We keep playing by his or her rules and we're going to lose."

"I know. That's why I'm here. I got some info. All the Bethany Hopes in the area checked out. They all are accounted for."

"That's a help?"

"It's a start. At least we know it's not somebody local."

"I take it you've expanded the search?"

"Yes, and I've got a hit."

"Where?"

"Savannah. One Bethany Anne Hope of 273 Brookville Ave. in Savannah, Georgia, has not been home in three days and does not answer her cell or home phone."

"Any more info?"

"She's a twenty-seven year old secretary working for a local law firm. She's been employed with them for the past five years, is a good employee and has never missed a day according to her boss. They are concerned about her."

"I bet."

"There's more. The law firm is Juliano, Juliano, and Anderson."

"Great."

"Yeah. The only law firm in the area that represents the mob's assets here in Florida."

"Could she have pissed somebody off?"

"It's a possibility. But why go to all the trouble? Why not just take her out?"

"Good question. Maybe they're making an example of her."

"Better than the first theory, but still, why not just take her out? Seems like an awful lot of trouble to play these games."

Jaxon sighed and said, "I'm at a loss. At least we have something. You did great. Can you keep digging?"

"Of course. When do you want me to join you on the hunt?"

"I don't know if I do. You'll be more help to me where you are."

"Are you sure? You know my talent is in the field."

"I know, but I have no one else right now. You ok with that?"

"Yes." She paused. "I got some info on the web cam. Do you want to know about it?"

"Ok."

"The IP address is located here in Jacksonville, but it's at a local slot bar/web café."

Jaxon knew of the places. They were scattered all over the state and any mom and pop could come up with a loan and open up one of the small gambling houses. It was legal here in the state to play slots as long as the winnings were dispensed in gift type cards like a gift Visa or American Express. They also disguised themselves as web cafés. The state did not like them and was working on shutting them all down.

"How did you get the info?" Jaxon knew what was coming but had to ask.

"I pulled a few strings."

"Holt."

She sighed. "Yes."

Emory Holt was her ex-lover and also her ex-boss. He was a division chief at the Hoover building in Washington, D.C. The

FBI. She had been involved with him when she and Jaxon had gone bad after the death of their son Michael. Jaxon had also been friends with Holt, but that relationship had ended a long time ago. Though Jaxon and Victoria had remarried last year, he still felt a twinge of jealousy whenever Holt came into the picture again.

"You didn't tell him what you needed it for, did you?"

"No," she said. "You know me better than that."

"Did he guess?"

"He tried."

"We don't want him poking around. He might attract the wrong attention."

"I told him that."

"Great. That probably made him more curious."

"He'll leave it alone. I made him swear."

"I'm sure you did." Jaxon sighed and she must have heard it through the phone.

"You're still worried about him aren't you?"

"We don't have time for this, Vick."

"I know. It just makes me feel…I don't know…like I'm important."

He smiled. He could see her slightly crooked smile in his mind and her long black hair pulled up away from her neck. He loved the curve of her neck and he showed her every day how much by kissing her there on the way out the door. She usually melted. "I don't like you two working together."

"Nothing for you to worry about."

"You always say that."

"I always mean it."

"Ok. Love you too."

He hung up and concentrated on his driving. It was rush hour now and the idiots in this town loved to surprise you. As if on cue, a new Mustang flew by his passenger side and cut him off as it zig zagged through the traffic. He honked but the driver ignored him. Where were the police when you needed them? He chuckled and kept moving. His next GPS position was still a good ten miles away.

* * *

"We can beat him there," Gil said.

Melanie smiled. "Then let's go."

He ran to the house and grabbed his keys to the Mustang and they sped off leaving a trail of rubber thirty feet long. A few miles ahead they saw Jaxon's car and passed him like he was standing still. He even honked at them and Gil thought he recognized them at first, but when he didn't pursue, he figured Jaxon was just angry at a maniac driver.

Gil turned left a quarter mile up the road and Melanie looked at him. "I thought we were going to Park Street?"

"We are. I just know a short cut."

She smiled then and put her hand on his thigh. He could tell this stuff turned her on. Hell, it was turning him on.

They pulled onto Park Street and accelerated to the small strip mall he had visited the other day. In it was one of those bagged ice machines. As a pro cacher, he could just about guess at the location of a hidden cache as soon as he arrived in the area. He was right 90% of the time because that was where he would normally hide things.

He pulled up to the ice machine and jumped out of the car. Two days ago nothing had been here, and when he figured he had misjudged the spot, he searched for another half hour and came up empty. It was then he decided that the cache was not there. This time he went straight for the back of the machine and reached under the portable building and felt along its underside. His hand immediately struck something that had not been there the day before and he smiled.

"Is it there?" Melanie asked.

He nodded and pulled it free. Another magnetic box just like the one in the park. He opened it and then dropped it to the ground in disgust. Melanie gasped. Inside, a bloody fingernail lay on top of a folded piece of paper. The blood still looked fresh.

"Let's get out of here," Melanie said, no longer having fun. "I don't like this."

"Wait." Gil picked up the box again and pushed the fingernail to the side with a stick. He pulled the folded piece of paper out and opened it. Two words were written in a looping hand in purple ink. *SOFTBALL BACKSTOPS.*

Melanie leaned over him and said, "What does SOFTBALL BACKSTOPS mean?"

He shook his head, confused. "I don't know."

He folded the paper back up, put it in the box and sealed it. He stuck it back under the portable ice building and grabbed her hand.

"Come on!" They ran back to the car, drove to the other end of the lot and backed into a spot.

"What are we doing?" She asked, worried.

"I want to see what he does."

"Why? Gil, we need to get out of here. We could be in big trouble."

"I want to see. I'll take you home when he leaves."

"Did you see that fingernail? It was real, right?"

He turned to her and touched her face.

"It looked fake," he lied. "Don't get too worked up, Mel."

"I thought it looked real."

Jaxon's car approached and circled a bit, then it parked a few feet away from the ice machine. "See—he's a rookie. He's just stopping wherever the GPS says the position is and then searching as if it could be anywhere."

Melanie only nodded and watched Jaxon get out of the car. He looked around and then headed straight for the ice machine.

"Maybe not so much the rookie you thought," she said. He shrugged.

Jaxon disappeared behind the machine and a few minutes later they saw him near the back where the cache was located. He bent down and started feeling along the underside.

"He's going to find it," Gil said.

"Good. Let's go."

"Not yet."

Jaxon stood up with something in his hand and then they watched him open it. He didn't seem to react to the fingernail like Gil expected him to. Maybe he knew it was going to be there.

Jaxon removed the folded paper and read it, then he stuck it in his pocket. He looked around and then seemed to focus on something to the left of where they were parked. Gil watched him move to the left to get a better view, then Jaxon did something strange. He raised his right hand and gave somebody the finger. Somebody high up.

Gil followed Jaxon's gaze and leaned down in the seat a bit to see higher up. A sinking feeling suddenly settled in the pit of his stomach as he saw what Jaxon saw.

"Shit."

"What?"

"There's a camera up on that light pole."

She leaned over his lap and stared up at the camera. "So?"

"Somebody may know we've been here."

"It's the store's camera, Gil. Only the store's security would know and they probably don't care. We're not doing anything illegal."

"Anybody can hack into those systems. Anybody with half a brain and a little expertise. I've done it."

Gil stared at the camera and watched it move. It turned directly toward them and stopped.

"Oh shit! Time to go."

Gil started the car, watching as Jaxon followed the camera's movement and spotted their vehicle. He started toward them, but Gil put the car in gear and drove off. Before Jaxon disappeared behind them, Gil saw him running to his car.

* * *

Jaxon watched the camera turn and then saw the same Mustang that had cut him off start up and drive off. He couldn't see who was driving it, but if he had to guess, it was probably the perp. He ran to his car and cranked it up. Slamming the gearshift in drive, he squealed the tires as he followed the Mustang. The car was fast and his little six-cylinder was going to have a hard time keeping up with the V8. His only hope would be the traffic.

He pulled out onto Park Street heading south and saw the Mustang make a hard left turn a few blocks ahead. He turned hard following it and barely missed a Honda Accord that was turning the same way. Its horn followed him angrily onto the back neighborhood road. The Mustang was pulling away.

He lost sight of it around a curve and when the road straightened out, it had disappeared.

The only possible turn he could make was up ahead so Jaxon took it and saw the car pulling away. The stop light was red at the intersection and he watched as the Mustang slowed, then ran the red light. It braked hard as a Semi almost took it out, then it turned left and he caught a glimpse of the driver.

"Shit," he said aloud and slowed down. No need to risk getting himself, or them, killed. He knew where the young guy and girl lived. He'd just go and wait for them to come home.

CHAPTER 6

Gil floored the Mustang and it put him in the seatback. He made another hard right, then left and was back on Blanding heading home.

"Is he still behind us?" he asked Melanie, who seemed a little shaken up.

She turned to look. "I don't see him. I think we lost him. Do you think he recognized us?"

"I don't see how. He doesn't know our car and he didn't get close enough."

"Still, he may have seen us at the parking lot."

"Too far away. We're good."

"I'm scared, Gil. What if whoever put that fingernail in the box was also watching us behind the camera? We're involved now and we have no idea what we're involved in."

Gil knew she was right and didn't know what to say. He was actually having the time of his life and he grinned without knowing he was doing it.

"You think this is funny!" she said and hit him in the arm. He started laughing then. He knew it was a combination of the adrenalin and the idea he may be involved in some kind of treasure hunt that would be the hunt of all hunts. He was pumped.

"No. I just…"

"I can't believe you." But she was smiling too, now.

"Ah ha. You're stoked too aren't you? This rocks."

She pretended to still be mad at him but she wasn't pulling it off very well. He could tell the wheels were turning in there. "What do you think this is all about?" She finally asked.

"It's like a treasure hunt. Maybe the ultimate treasure hunt. Maybe we'll be rich if we get to it first and I know I'm better than that guy."

"But it means more to him."

"Not anymore."

"I don't know. This could be dangerous."

"Life is a risk, babe. Sometimes you just have to know when to take the bet or fold. I think we take the bet."

"What now?"

"We need to go home and grab a few things then we plug in the lat/longs for SOFTBALL BACKSTOPS and we beat him to it."

She scooted closer to him and put her hand on his crotch. "You sure we don't have time to play a bit. I'm kind of all worked up."

He smiled at her. "Ok. Maybe just a few minutes."

But as they pulled up to the house, Jaxon was waiting for them in their driveway. He didn't look happy.

* * *

Jaxon figured they would bolt when they saw him in their driveway, but they pulled right up and shut the car off. He could hear them arguing for a minute and he walked over and banged on the window. The door opened and the guy got out. The girl followed on the other side and he wasn't sure if she was scared or pissed. Probably a little of both.

"Just what do you two think you're doing? I told you this was not something to mess with, but you ignored me. I should have you arrested."

"You can't," the guy said. "You're not a local cop. Your badge says Virginia."

"You caught that, huh?" and Jaxon shook his head. "All right. Why do you think I came back here and waited for you when I told you I was on a strict timeline? If you're so smart, answer me that?"

The guy looked at the girl and shrugged. "You like us?"

Jaxon couldn't help it. He chuckled and it seemed to ease the tension a bit.

"No. I'm pissed at you because now you're going to slow me down."

"Why do you say that?"

"What's your names?"

The guy looked at his girl again and made some kind of decision. "I'm Gil and this is Melanie. She's my fiancée."

"Well, Gil and Melanie, you two are in a shit-load of trouble now. Did you happen to see that camera back there in the parking lot? The one that intentionally turned toward you and got a good look at the two of you?"

Gil nodded but didn't say anything.

"I know you think this is a game," Jaxon said, "but unfortunately, it's not." He leaned back against his car and sighed. "You're going to have to help me now. I can't let you out of my sight. It's too risky for you."

He watched as Gil smiled and Melanie made some kind of face. He wasn't sure if she was happy about it or not. He figured Gil to be the driving force behind their actions, but the girl was still a mystery. If he were to guess, she was probably not very happy, though she played along like she was.

"Are you going to tell us now what is going on?" Gil asked.

"I'm going to have to. You're involved whether you like it or not."

He told them everything and they listened quietly. He watched Melanie's face change from non-committal to fearful. She was going to be a problem. He couldn't believe he was going to let these two tag along, but he had little choice. If the mob was involved like he and Vick thought, then they were in real danger.

"I can hide you guys away, and I'm beginning to think that may be the best thing, but I can't promise you'll be safe unless you're with me. I don't know if this guy is now accelerating his timeline because I've involved somebody else, but I can't let you two just fall victim to him without trying to protect you."

"I don't like this anymore, Gil," Melanie said and grabbed his hand.

Gil's eyes betrayed his excitement and Jaxon knew the guy was gung ho for this. He probably would have made a good cop.

"Maybe he can find a place you'll be safe," Gil said. "This isn't what I thought either, but I can really help him, even if he thinks he's just protecting me." He turned to Jaxon. "Can you guarantee she'll be safe hidden somewhere?"

"I can't," Jaxon said and he meant it. He had no idea if he could keep them safe at all, but he had little choice.

Gil turned to Melanie and said, "You need to stay with me. I can protect you."

She nodded and leaned up against him. Jaxon sighed and pulled his cell out.

"You guys get whatever you need from your house while I make a phone call and talk with my partner. She'll be overjoyed about you two."

Gil and Melanie walked to the house talking in low tones and Jaxon made the call.

"We have a problem," he said when Vick answered. He told her about their new partners.

"Jaxon. This is not good."

"Yeah, tell me about it. I didn't know what else to do. Do you have any suggestions?"

"Yes. Ditch those two. They're on their own. You mess in people's business and sometimes you get the head instead of the tail."

"You don't mean that, Vick. I know you're upset, but think about it. You and I couldn't deal with it if something happened.

Cache 72

Besides, this guy is really good at this treasure hunting stuff. He says he knows every single cache spot in this city."

Silence greeted him on the other end and he wasn't sure if he lost the connection.

"Still with me?"

"I'm always with you," she said, "This is just going to make things tougher."

"I hope you're wrong."

"Me too. Let me know what I can do."

"I will. We have to solve some kind of riddle now. I think it's another set of GPS lat/longs but it's just two words he gave us."

"What are the words? I can plug them into the computer and see what we get."

"SOFTBALL BACKSTOPS."

"I'll work on it. Call you when I have something."

"Bye."

He hung up and the kids were back with a bag they shoved into the trunk of the Mustang.

"Good idea," Jaxon said. "Your car will be faster. We'll leave mine here."

"Where are we going?" Gil asked.

"I was hoping you could help me with that. I'm assuming you saw the next clue."

"SOFTBALL BACKSTOPS."

"Right. We have to figure out what it means."

"It's a simple letter for number cipher."

"Ok. That means nothing to me."

"You have to figure out what number is represented by each letter and that will give you a set of lat/longs."

"Sounds like you have it figured out already."

The kid nodded. "It's a simple one." He walked over with a GPS in his hand and showed Jaxon a point on the map. "This is it. I figured it out on the way over here. Simple."

Jaxon shook his head and said, "Maybe for you, kid. Let me get a few things from my car and we'll go."

His phone rang. It was Vick.

"I got the words figured out."

"You're quick too," Jaxon said. "The kid figured it out already. What did you get and we'll confirm what we have."

She gave him the GPS position and it matched what Gil had done in his head. "That's it. Thanks Vick."

"Sounds like you didn't even need my help. Maybe you're right. The guy seems to know his shit."

"Yeah. I agree. Ok. Gotta go."

CHAPTER 7

He looked at the camera and slammed his fist into the table.

The stupid bastard was not following the rules. He watched the young blond guy and the girl in the Mustang drive off and he knew that his game player was not working alone. He panned the camera back and saw the player run back to his vehicle and accelerate away. The parking lot was empty. He clicked the exit button on the screen and it went blank. He sat in his chair and contemplated how to fix this.

The plan had been working flawlessly and he was sure the jackass would not be able to complete all the tasks he had planned, but now the players had tripled, and with help, he may be able to defeat his system. The girl would survive. Unless he changed the game himself.

He smiled then, and sat forward.

If the player wanted to cheat, so would he. He moved the mouse and clicked on the camera in the tank and watched the girl through the night vision camera. The tide was coming in and she struggled against her restraints as the water rose. Too bad he didn't have sound. He was sure her vocalizations would be highly entertaining.

He watched her struggle and then finally the struggling stopped. Exhausted, she realized she would not drown. He turned the monitor off and got up from the chair. He had work to do.

* * *

Jaxon held on as Gil took a turn sharply, the tires squealing. "You're going to get us killed, kid."

"I'm an excellent driver. Excellent driver. And don't call me 'kid.'"

"All right, Gil. You're going to attract attention, and we don't want that. And you're going to get us killed."

Jaxon watched Gil smile into the rear view mirror but he didn't slow down.

"He always drives like this," Melanie said and she leaned into the next turn like a pro.

"Maybe I should have stuck with my car," Jaxon mumbled and made sure his seat belt was secure.

"What?" Gil said.

"Nothing."

The sun was going down and the lights were coming on. It had only been ten hours since this all started and Jaxon was already exhausted. He was beginning to think he wouldn't make it 72 hours. If it lasted that long. He wasn't even sure he'd make it twenty-four.

Blue light suddenly filled the rear window and a spotlight illuminated the whole back of the car. Jaxon turned and squinted into the glare.

"Great, kid. Unwanted attention. This is exactly what I was talking about."

"Shit," Gil said and pulled over.

"Let me do the talking," Jaxon said and got out his wallet.

He watched the cop walk up to the driver's window and then Jaxon smiled. Gil rolled down the window and the cop said, "License and registration."

Jaxon leaned forward and said, "Officer Fanucci. We meet again."

The cop from earlier in the day reacted to his name and then bent over, shining a flashlight into the back of the car.

"Jaxon, right?"

"Yes."

"You seem to be popping up all over the place today," Fanucci said standing up straight. "Do I need to be worried about you?"

"No. Just doing a little work."

Fanucci nodded and looked at Gil and Melanie. "Employees of yours?"

"Yes—temporary employees. We're working a case."

"In a hurry aren't you?"

"My friend has a little bit of a lead foot, yes. Sorry. We'll keep it under 100mph from now on."

"Please," the cop said and shone the light on Gil and Melanie's faces. "Anything we can help with?"

"Not now," Jaxon said. "Just boring surveillance stuff. I'll call and ask for you if we need you guys."

"All right. I'll let you get back to work. Keep the foot light. You don't want me to have to scrape you off of the pavement."

"No, sir," Gil said. "I will. Sorry."

Fanucci nodded at them and then went back to his cruiser.

"Glad you knew him," Gil said. "I thought for sure I was going to jail."

"You don't go to jail for speeding, Gil."

"You do if your license is suspended."

"Great. Just great."

Jaxon shook his head and signaled for him to drive on. He'd just deal with whatever came up. If Gil got hauled off to jail, at least he'd be safe there. For a while anyway.

They pulled up to a softball field and there was a game going on. The lights were on and a small crowd was scattered around the bleachers. They got out of the Mustang and stood there staring at the game.

"Well, SOFTBALL BACKSTOPS makes sense now," Melanie said.

"How are we going to get to the backstop?" Gil asked.

Jaxon looked at the scoreboard and saw it was only the bottom of the second inning. "I guess we'll just have to walk out there during the game and get it. What could they do? Beat us up?"

Gil shrugged and they walked toward the home plate area.

"Have you seen it yet?" Jaxon asked.

Gil shook his head, but he was searching and Jaxon followed his gaze.

"There!" Gil pointed. Just to the left of the backstop area, there was a pole with a flag run up on it. Stuck to the metal about ten feet up was a small box.

"I can't reach that," Jaxon said.

"No shit," Gil said. "Somebody is going to have to climb."

"I'm forty-eight years old," Jaxon said.

Gil gave him a look and said, "All right. I'm on it."

Melanie smiled and then started giggling.

"What?" Gil said.

"I just can't wait to see what these people do when you climb that pole. You'll stick out like a sore thumb."

"You want to do it?"

"No!"

Jaxon pointed. "Time's a wastin'. You wanted to help."

Gil grinned and moved away.

A few of the onlookers noticed him but went back to watching the game. Jaxon scanned the crowd and could find no camera or video surveillance systems that might clue the perp in to their position, but that didn't mean there weren't any out there.

Gil walked straight to the pole and started climbing. The pitcher noticed right away and paused in his wind-up. Then the ump called time and turned around as the catcher followed the eyes of the pitcher. The small crowd started to buzz. A man with a Florida Gator t-shirt and hat stood and pointed to Gil.

"What the hell, man! You're screwing up the game."

Gil grabbed the cache and slid down.

The ump said, "What are you doing?"

"It's already done," Gil said and saluted the ump. He watched Gil walk away and shrugged.

Florida Gator man wasn't so forgiving. Jaxon watched as the man jumped from the bleachers and stopped Gil with a beefy hand. "What are you doing?"

"None of your business," Gil said and pushed at the guy's arm. "Excuse me."

"It is my business," Gator said. "My kid was about to hit and you just messed up her concentration."

"Not my problem."

Gator man turned red. "I'm making it my problem," and he bunched up Gil's shirt in his hand and pulled him closer. "You need to learn some manners."

"Uh oh," Jaxon said, and grabbed Melanie's arm. "Come on."

Everyone in the bleachers and the game was watching the altercation and one guy even yelled, "Give 'em hell, Joey!"

Jaxon pulled his old badge out and shoved it in Gator man's face. "What's the problem here?"

Gator man seemed to deflate a little, but didn't let go of Gil's shirt. "This guy's disrupting our game."

"You need to let him go," Jaxon said.

"But…"

"Now."

Gator man released his grip on Gil and took a step back. "I wasn't gonna hurt him."

"Didn't look that way from over there," Jaxon said. He turned to Gil. "Do you want to press charges?"

Gil looked at him in shock. "What?"

Gator man's face fell and his mouth dropped open. "Are you serious?"

"Do you want to file assault charges against this man?" Jaxon asked Gil, ignoring the other man. Melanie was trying to keep from laughing.

"No," Gil said. "I just want to be left alone."

"He's messing up my daughter's game and I'm in trouble?" Gator man asked.

"You physically assaulted this man," Jaxon said.

"I grabbed his shirt."

"That's assault in the state of Florida."

"I don't believe this."

"It doesn't matter," Gil said. "I don't want to press charges anyway. I just want to go."

"You're not going anywhere but downtown to answer some questions," Jaxon said.

Gil just stared at him.

Gator man grinned. "You're going to jail, punk."

Gil flipped him off.

"Enough!" Jaxon said, and grabbed Gil's arm to escort him away. The crowd cheered.

"I didn't do anything," Gil whined, playing the part. Jaxon almost burst out laughing himself.

"You disrupted the game and you smell drunk. Public intoxication is also a crime."

"You tell him officer!" Gator man yelled after them. "Take that punk to jail!"

Jaxon stopped and turned to the man. "Go sit down, sir, before I take you along with him."

Gator man frowned and did what he was told. His buddy in the stands clapped him on the back as he climbed back to his seat. Jaxon could not hear what was said, but did catch laughter from the people around them.

"Play ball!" The ump cried as Jaxon pulled Gil toward the Mustang.

"That was fun," Gil said under his breath.

"What? No thank you?" Jaxon asked.

"For what? You made me look like an idiot."

"I saved your ass from a beating."

"Bullshit! I could've taken him."

"Right."

Melanie watched the two with a smile and then said, "He's right." She pointed to Jaxon. "He saved your ass."

"Whatever," Gil said and got in the car. Jaxon slid in the back and Melanie went to the passenger side. Gator man was still watching. He stood with a funny look on his face.

Inside they opened the cache and saw three sets of lat/longs.

"Which one first?" Melanie asked.

"Let's plug them in and see which is closest," Gil said and got his GPS out of the glove box. He punched the first set in and saw they were in Gainesville.

"Shit. That's a trip," he said, and plugged in the second set. The map moved to Lakeland, Florida. "Damn!" The third set proved to be even worse. "How do they expect us to make it all the way down to Naples after we go to Gainesville and Lakeland? This will take all night."

Jaxon nodded and fidgeted. He had expected something like this. Some trek to use up time. Gator man was standing now and watching the car. "We can skip some and just see what's at the first stop in Gainesville. Maybe the next clue will be there."

"I'm sure they've thought of that. Are you sure we're supposed to follow all of these? Maybe we're only supposed to pick one?"

"But which one?" Melanie asked. "Is that it? We're supposed to guess and then see if we're right? That's stupid. Of course we're going to pick the closest."

Gator man pointed at the car and said something to his buddy who stood.

"Then maybe we should pick the farthest and go from there. If that's not the right one then we back track and go to the next one," Gil said.

"But what if the next point is closer to Naples than Gainesville or Lakeland?" Jaxon said. "Then we're backtracking anyway. I say we start at Gainesville and follow the path."

"We need to find a way to get ahead of these people," Gil said. "You know we're not going to get to her in time if we follow their rules."

"I know. I'm just waiting for something to give so we can jump ahead. So far, that hasn't happened."

Gil nodded. Jaxon was impressed the kid had seen the futility in this chase. Maybe they were going to be a help after all.

Gator man and his friend had climbed down from the bleachers and were coming their way.

"Whatever we do," Jaxon said. "We need to do it now." He pointed at Gator man walking quickly.

"Oh shit." Gil said.

"We split the difference," Jaxon said as Gil started the car.

"Lakeland it is," Gil said and squealed the tires as he pulled out.

Gator man and his friend shook their fists after them. Gil rolled his window down and flipped them off.

When they got to Lakeland it was just before midnight and they had to use flashlights to find the cache. It was hidden in the stump of a fallen tree at a rest stop on I-4. Even Gil had been confused for a bit and they spent fifteen precious minutes searching the picnic areas, bathrooms, snack machines and out buildings. Melanie had actually been the one to find it and she smiled, proud of herself. Jaxon liked her and he hoped he would be able to keep her safe.

The jump proved fruitful as the next waypoint messaged to Jaxon's ID after they logged the cache was the point in Naples. At least it wasn't the Gainesville waypoint. Jaxon just hoped that when they got to Naples, they'd get some new information. The clock was ticking.

Gil let Jaxon drive for a bit while he and Melanie climbed in the back and took a little nap. Jaxon glanced back at them from time to time. They were cute together. Once, he found Gil staring at him as he glanced back and he asked if everything was all right.

"Yeah," Gil whispered. "Just hope we haven't made a mistake bringing her."

Jaxon only nodded. What else could he say?

Gil took over at two in the morning and Jaxon climbed in the back with Melanie who slept through the stop. She was not a light sleeper. When he was just about to doze off, she startled him by snuggling up next to him with her head on his shoulder. She was still asleep and he tried not to wake her. He looked up to see Gil grinning in the mirror.

"She's a cuddler," he whispered. "She can't sleep without something to hold on to. It's all right. I don't mind."

Jaxon nodded and relaxed. He fell asleep and dreamed of severed fingers. He awoke with a start as the car swerved. Melanie sat up and said, "What?"

"Sorry," Gil said. "I kind of dozed off."

"Pull over," Jaxon said, and Melanie looked at him like he was an alien. "I'm Jaxon. Remember?"

Her eyes finally focused and she sighed in relief.

"Oh yeah. I guess I didn't remember. Hi."

"I'll drive for awhile," Jaxon said. "I don't want to die in my sleep wrapped around some tree."

"Thanks," Gil said. "I need a break. Or some coffee. Want to stop for a minute?"

"Yeah. Sounds good. I need to call Vick anyway."

"It's four o'clock in the morning."

"She'll be up."

They pulled in to an all-night gas station and Gil filled up while Jaxon got coffee. He updated Vick on everything and she told him to be careful. He told her to get some sleep. She said she would and they ended the call.

Back on the road again, Jaxon drank his coffee and thought of Michael. His dead son always seemed to pop up at times like this and he realized it gave him comfort. He missed him terribly.

He and Vick had never had another child and he knew she regretted it. They had spent so much time hating each other after Michael had died that they missed the opportunity and now they were too old. At least he felt old. She could still get pregnant, he knew, but late age pregnancies were always risky. For the mom and the infant. Still, they had talked about it and he was sure they would talk about it again.

They were only an hour out of Naples and he let the kids sleep while the flat expanse of I-75 flew by. Traffic was light at this hour and he made good time. Besides, the Mustang was fun to drive. Even if it was just cruising on the interstate.

Bethany Hope. The name meant nothing to him but he was sure it meant something to the psycho. Most of the time, these people, who had lost touch with reality and decided to take things to a level that most of the world considered heinous and insane, knew their victims. Either by a chance meeting and something clicked, a little research on the internet, a run-in at some mall, or a coworker, but they usually knew them to some extent, or the person had some meaning that only the psychos could comprehend. Jaxon wondered what Bethany Hope meant to this one. If anything, the name was beautiful and Jaxon presumed the woman was too. Most of the time, he was correct.

As soon as this asshole messed up and they could get a little something on him or her, then the pieces should start to fall in place. Jaxon knew that all they needed was just the tiniest of breaks and the ball usually started rolling down hill. It picked up steam as it went and by the time the ball was at the bottom, it was huge and damaging. At least to the perp.

"Are we there yet?"

The voice floated up from the back and Jaxon shook his head. Melanie was staring at him in the mirror and her face glowed in the lights of the interstate. Every time they passed a light, it would brighten and make her seem real, then it would fade and she would become just a ghostly glow. "About an hour out," he whispered. "You ok?"

"Yeah. I'm just a little worried."

He nodded. "Everything will be all right."

"I can't help thinking of the girl. Bethany. Is she my age? Does she have any kids? Where is she? Is she suffering some horrible torture or just alone and afraid waiting for God knows what?"

"Most of the time kidnapping and hostage situations are not as bad as the movies make them out to be. She's probably comfortable, locked in some room where the perp can keep her under control."

"You said, 'most of the time.' What about the other times?"

Jaxon didn't answer and that was answer enough. He watched her turn to look out the window and as the next light passed them, he could see a wetness on her cheek. He knew how she felt.

"We'll find her."

"Do you promise?"

"Yes. I promise."

* * *

The woman had realized hours ago that one of her fingers was missing. She had been surprised that this realization hadn't happened sooner. It was probably because her hands had felt numb from the bindings and the cold salt water. She shivered in the darkness and wondered if she was running a fever. She knew that it was a good possibility the amputated site was infected. Both of her hands tingled, but the one with the missing finger ached too. She also discovered one of her fingernails was missing from the other hand. She didn't know if her struggling had ripped it off or something else had happened.

She stared at the light that winked on and off above her and could feel whatever she was trapped in moving with the water she now knew held her afloat outside. Where the body of water was she did not know. She had no idea how long she had been out or even if it was day or night. The winking light gave her no clue and she figured it was either moonlight, or sunlight, shining through some crack. The light became a beacon for her and she watched it, holding her breath, waiting for the next wink. It came every ten to fifteen seconds, and when she finally saw it, she would let the air out in a sigh and breathe again. Though it was exhausting, she clung to it like a life raft.

She was twenty-five years old and her life had been easy. Until now.

She rarely wanted for anything and she had a great job. She loved her mom and dad and her brother was even ok at times, if he wasn't stoned or drunk. Her fiancé had swept her off of her feet and they had fallen hard for each other in a matter of weeks. She wondered what he was doing right now and if he was trying to find her.

It was weird that she hadn't heard from him for a whole day prior to all this happening to her and she now wondered if something had happened to him. There was no way for her to know, so she kept the hope in her heart that he would rescue her. He would be worried, she knew, especially if it had been some time since she had seen him.

She closed her eyes and pushed the winking light from her mind. She needed to rest and with her thoughts on Dirk, her fiancé, she drifted off to sleep.

CHAPTER 8

Jaxon exited I-75 at Golden Gate Parkway and though he knew it was Florida, the name brought up visions of his honeymoon with Vick in California.

The Golden Gate Bridge was something they would always have together and he didn't want to associate this nightmare with such a good memory. He pushed it out of his mind and concentrated on the road.

Gil and Melanie were awake in the back and the sun had yet to show itself over the horizon. Traffic was still light for this time of the morning and Jaxon made good time through the streets. The GPS indicated he was to turn left on Goodlette-Franklin Road and their waypoint would be just up ahead. When he made the turn, he saw what it was and moaned.

"I hope that's not our destination," Gil said.

"You should know," Jaxon said. "It's the only place it could be."

"I know. I was just hoping."

Jaxon pulled into the Naples Zoo and Caribbean Gardens and parked in the lot. They were the only ones in it. He looked at the ticket gate and saw that it didn't open for another two hours. "Maybe we should go eat while we wait for it to open."

"I'm starving," Melanie said. "Can we get pancakes?"

"You can have whatever you want." Jaxon said and pulled out of the zoo.

They found an IHOP and everyone ordered pancakes. Jaxon found he was much hungrier than he thought and he had a second order. He watched the two smile and talk softly to each other and he felt like he was a third wheel. He excused himself and stepped outside to call Victoria. She answered on the fourth ring.

"I woke you, didn't I?"

"It's ok. I was just dozing. Are you there?"

"Yeah. Well, we were, but it doesn't open for another hour so we're getting something to eat."

"Everything ok?"

"No. It's in a zoo."

"You're kidding."

"I wish. The Naples Zoo and Caribbean Gardens. It was a shock to us. It will probably be a nightmare trying to find the next cache."

"Maybe you'll get lucky. The Gil guy seems smart."

"And I'm not?"

"That's not what I meant. You're just old."

"So you get stupid when you get older?" he said, but was smiling.

"Speak for yourself. Only YOU get stupid as you get older. Like getting involved in GeoCaching."

"Hey. It's fun."

"Are you having fun?"

"Ok. It was fun. But what if some Joe Blow had found the finger instead of me? With me, at least Bethany Hope has a chance."

"True." Silence settled between them for a moment and then she surprised him. "Could this be something more than a coincidence? Have you considered that it wasn't just some random thing?"

"No," he said, but now the wheels were spinning. "I don't see how it could be anything but. How would you control that kind of thing?"

"I don't know," she said, silent again. He knew her wheels were spinning too. "I guess it's not possible. It's just when you said the Joe Blow thing, it kind of made sense that you would find it. Am I making sense?"

"Yeah. You are. And that scares me."

"Right. Let's just keep that in the back of everything. I'm just saying."

Silence again between them and then he said, "Hey."

"Yeah."

"Miss you."

"Me too. Come home safe to me."

"As soon as Bethany Hope reveals herself, I will. Gotta' go."

"I know."

"Go back to sleep."

"Like I'm going to be able to do that now."

"Try."

"Bye."

"Bye."

He went back in and found Gil and Melanie looking at him with grins on their faces. "What?" he asked.

Her eyes betrayed her and she glanced down at his plate. His pancakes were gone. "Sorry," she said. "We couldn't help it."

"You owe me," he said but grinned. "That means you get the bill."

"What?" Gil said.

"It's only fair, right?"

Gil mumbled something and took out his wallet. Jaxon winked at Melanie and she smiled big at him. At least she was in a better mood at the moment. Two kids on a big adventure. He hoped it didn't get any worse than what they'd seen already, but he had a feeling it would. He sat in the booth and sipped his coffee.

"What do you guys do?" he asked.

"You mean work?" Gil asked.

Jaxon nodded over the rim of his cup.

"I'm a restaurant manager and she's a waitress. Matter of fact, that's where we met. I was a waiter then though."

"So you both work at the same place?"

He nodded. "Texas Roadhouse. You know it?"

"Yep. Vick and I go there quite a bit."

"I thought you looked familiar," Melanie said.

"You're just associating familiarity with the situation. I'm sure you don't remember your patrons."

"Not true," she said. "I have people I recognize all the time. They even ask for me. You two must be quiet and polite or else I'd really remember you." She smiled.

"Well, I don't remember you guys. It's probably because you have so many employees. I don't know how you make money. I mean, how many hostesses do you really need to take patrons to their table? There are always six or seven up at the entrance standing around while one seats us. What's up with that?"

"I know," Gil said. "I'm always arguing with the owner about that but he's adamant about customer service. He doesn't want anybody waiting to be served."

"If that's the case, he needs to fix the wait times on Friday."

"Can't help it if we're popular."

Jaxon nodded. "True." He sat silent for a moment and then said, "It's funny that you guys are engaged after meeting at work. What are you going to do when you get married?"

"What do you mean?" Gil asked.

"Nepotism. You're going to be married to her and be her boss all at the same time. They usually frown on that kind of thing."

Gil looked at Melanie and shrugged. "Nobody's said anything to us."

"You might want to find out. You don't want to be surprised."

Jaxon watched their faces fall and he couldn't help feeling like he just crushed their dreams. Even if the dream was just two restaurant employees working together forever.

"I'm sure you guys will be ok. The owner probably won't even care as long as you don't show favoritism. You'll be all right." Jaxon stood and threw a couple of dollars on the table. "I got the tip. Come on. It's time to go."

The sun had come up while they ate and the day was going to be steamy. It was already in the 80s at seven in the morning so Jaxon figured it would be 97 degrees by noon. South Florida in the summer was not a cool place. Even on the coast, and the beach was only a short distance away.

Gil got behind the wheel with Melanie in the front passenger seat and Jaxon crammed in the back. He was surprised he had been able to sleep back here last night, but with the road vibrating beneath him, he guessed anybody could doze under those conditions.

In the parking lot, Gil broke out the GPS and looked at their position in relation to the waypoint.

"It's a hundred yards to the north." He pointed in the direction of the park itself.

"This will be fun," Jaxon said.

"I love zoos," Melanie said and got out of the car.

"We're not on a fun day, Mel," Gil said. "This is serious."

"I know. I was just saying."

The parking lot was starting to fill up and the day looked like it was going to be busy. A few school busses were in the lot now with church groups and foreign exchange students all out for a day of hot fun. At least there would be a crowd to mask their searching.

They passed a group of kids all wearing red shirts with white lettering spelling out their school in Spanish. The head of the group carried a bright yellow flag on a pole so that they would all stick together. Jaxon remembered groups like this from the theme parks they visited with Michael when he was alive. He had always said, "Come on Dad! We can't let that group of geeks get ahead of us." He had known what he was talking about because another group was waiting in line to buy tickets in front of them now and it was taking forever. The leader did not speak very good English and was having a hard time talking with the ticket agent.

Jaxon stared at his wristwatch and counted the seconds ticking by. They needed to move faster.

The group finally cleared out and Jaxon paid for their tickets. Gil was holding the GPS up and following its directions. He looked like he was searching for radioactive spots with a Geiger counter. People were staring at him.

"It's right up here," Gil said and hurried around a big hedge of hibiscus that was in full bloom. When they rounded the corner, Jaxon's heart sank as Gil and Melanie stopped in their tracks. A few people mumbled things as they sidestepped around them to get past.

Directly in front of them was a huge pond and swampy area that encompassed a large part of the park. An employee was standing just inside the fence, leaning over a dock area dangling pieces of chicken in the air as a twelve foot alligator stretched up to snatch it from the pole the employee was using. A good sized crowd had gathered to watch the feeding.

"Don't tell me it's in there," Jaxon said.

"Ok. I won't tell you." Gil turned and gave him a look.

"Shit."

There were probably fifty or more alligators and crocodiles within the confines of the area and they looked very active.

"At least they won't be hungry now," Melanie said and Jaxon was glad somebody was positive about the situation.

"What now?" Gil asked.

"We try and narrow it down. You're the expert. I thought you'd be able to sniff it right out."

"This is not a normal cache site," he said. "It's not registered and for a good reason. This is illegal."

"Doesn't matter. Use your head. Where would you put it?"

Jaxon could tell Gil didn't like him shaming him like that and he watched as the wheels started turning in there. He looked at the GPS again quickly, and then put it away. He moved to the left where the path meandered around the swampy area as it traveled completely around the pond rejoining the other path that went to the right. Jaxon figured he must have seen something.

Gil kept his eyes glued to the park employee as he worked his way around to the nine o'clock position of the pond. This was directly across from the employee. He stopped and then knelt down to get a better view. He gestured for Jaxon and Mel to join him.

"Look at the platform the guy is on," Gil said. "Do you see that little silver-like extension of the steps down into the water?"

Jaxon looked and did see it. The stairs were gated off from the platform and went straight down into the water where the last couple of steps lay submerged within the pond. On the last visible step there was something that was sticking out on the underside, just above the water line. If you weren't looking for it you wouldn't even notice it, but Jaxon nodded and felt for sure it was out of place.

"I've seen those silver boxes before. They're used by a certain Geo group that goes by the name of Cock Cachers."

"Cock Cachers?" Jaxon repeated. "Great name."

"Mark's one of them," Melanie said, shocked. "They're doing this?"

"No," Gil said. "I'm sure they're not involved. I just recognize the box coloring. I could be wrong too. It's hard to tell from this distance. It could have been stolen from one of their sites though."

"How are we going to get to it," Mel asked.

"Come on," Jaxon said. "I have an idea."

He led the way around to the little platform where the employee was feeding the crocs and gators. The crowd here made it difficult to see, but Jaxon forced his way to the front with Gil and Melanie squeezing through while people made angry comments and glared at them. Jaxon didn't care. They could all go screw themselves.

"Hey!" a large woman in spandex purple pants and a t-shirt that did little to flatter her ample figure bumped Jaxon and pushed him back. "My Malcom can't see. Wait your turn."

"Your Malcom needs to grow a little taller," Jaxon said and nudged her out of the way.

"Hey!" She said again, but did nothing but gripe to the people next to her. "Did you see that? Asshole."

"Excuse me," Jaxon said to the employee. "Excuse me!"

The man finally turned with a piece of chicken hanging from the pole he was using to feed the reptiles and raised his eyebrows at Jaxon.

"How much to feed the gators?"

"We don't allow that, sir," the man said.

"I'm sure you don't. But if someone insisted, how much?"

The employee looked around as if searching for help from some manager or other employee, but he was the only one around. Jaxon gestured to him to come closer and the man hesitated. "It's important," Jaxon said.

The man put down the pole and the crowd grumbled. One guy shouted, "What the hell?"

The employee looked tense.

"I need to feed the gators," Jaxon said. "Actually, she needs to feed them. She's dying of cancer and this is her last chance. It's what she wants."

The employee looked at Melanie and she smiled, shyly. Gil looked away trying not to laugh. Jaxon hoped he wouldn't blow it.

"How much?" Jaxon repeated.

"I don't know…"

"Just for a few minutes. Think of how you'll feel if you deny her dying request. She only has a few weeks the doctors say."

The man stood up and looked at the angry crowd. They were getting restless and a few were leaving. He seemed to come to some conclusion and said, "I might get fired."

"It will be worth it. How much?"

He looked at Melanie again and fidgeted for a second. Then he unlocked the gate and waved them in. "Quick. Before I get in trouble."

Jaxon clapped him on the back and let Melanie and Gil go first. Melanie leaned in and kissed him on the cheek. "Thank you!" He blushed. Jaxon grinned. She was a great actress. Gil just laughed.

"Hey!" the woman in the purple spandex yelled, "What are they doing? That's not fair."

Jaxon turned to her. "Shut up or I'll shut you up."

She looked shocked and took a step back. Then she seemed to regain her courage. "You can't talk to me that way. Who the hell do you think you are? I'll report you."

Jaxon pulled out his badge and flashed it. "Shut up or I'll arrest you and you can pick your son up at social services tomorrow or the next day. In the mean time, I'm sure he'll enjoy a sleep over where all the teenagers are horny and just love a little fresh meat."

She blanched and grabbed her son's hand. "You're a bad person."

"You're an obnoxious bitch. Now behave."

She turned and dragged her son through the crowd as he wailed for her to let him go.

When Jaxon turned around, Melanie had the pole in her hand and was being helped by the employee. Jaxon moved to the gate where the steps were and Gil nodded his head. He lifted the latch and took a step down toward the water. It was swirling with alligators and crocodiles. One thirteen footer eyed him as its head surfaced just two feet away. Jaxon could only imagine his hand disappearing into the jaws of that monster. He bent over and started feeling under the bottom step. He couldn't seem to find the box.

"Hey! Sir! You need to come back up here! Sir!"

The park employee's voice had risen in pitch and Jaxon figured he would blow a gasket here in a few seconds. He ignored him. The crowd behind him murmured and shuffled as they saw what was happening.

"To your left," Gil whispered. "Left."

Jaxon shifted his hand to the left and it struck the metallic shape sticking out from the stair. He grasped and gave it a tug. It didn't budge.

The thirteen footer continued to eye him and it rose a little higher in the water exposing its teeth. It opened its mouth slowly and hissed. Just next to it, another snout surfaced and a croc decided to join the party. It moved closer to the steps.

"Sir! That is not allowed. You need to move back immediately!"

Jaxon gripped the box tightly and yanked with all his might. The box must have a very strong magnet because it only slid sideways an inch or two.

"It's a magnet," Gil said. "Pry it sideways. Don't slide it."

"Do you want to do this?"

Gil shook his head.

The park employee had dropped his chicken and was heading straight for Jaxon. He only had a couple more seconds. He tried prying the box downward at an angle and it finally came free. He stood and stepped back up on the platform.

The croc lunged as he moved and missed his foot by mere inches. The crowd gasped and then a few clapped and laughed. They apparently thought it part of the show. The park employee stepped to him and looked about to knock him down. He saw the box in his hand.

"What is that?"

"Nothing you need to be concerned with. Thanks for granting my daughter's wish. She sure looks happy."

The park employee stood there with a dumb look on his face as he watched Gil and Melanie move away. She waved and smiled at him as she left the platform.

"Thanks," Jaxon said and walked away. The guy stood there with his mouth open for a moment but then said, "Hey!" as Jaxon opened the gate. He ignored him. Jaxon quickly melted into the crowd. The park employee didn't follow.

When Gil and Mel joined him, he found his hand shaking a bit. "That was fun," he said.

"Man—that was awesome! Did you see that croc? He almost got you."

"Yeah. I noticed."

Mel smiled at him and grabbed his hand. "I'm glad you're ok. That was scary."

"You did great," Jaxon said to her. "You should be an actress." She blushed but said nothing. "Let's get the hell out of here before we have the manager on us."

They left the park and went straight to the car without anyone even acknowledging them. That was fine with Jaxon. In the car Gil and Melanie stared as he took the silver, decorated box and popped the lid.

It was empty.

CHAPTER 9

Rayford Maningham the Third sat in his truck and sipped his coffee.

It had been a quiet night and the last couple hours of his twelve hour shift had crawled along. He was bored. The only thing that had kept him awake all night was the occasional trucker hauling ass or drifting off to sleep at the wheel.

As a State Wildlife Officer, he liked having the same power as any law enforcement agent in the state of Florida. His jurisdiction was limitless, yet he mainly dealt with speeders in the Everglades and unlawful transportation of goods and wildlife. He had lots of power but rarely used it.

People liked to buy exotic pets and then when they outgrew them, brought them to the 'Glades and set them free. Unfortunately they did not belong there and the indigenous populations of Florida often suffered at the hands, or claws, of a more aggressive species.

Because he also dealt with wildlife issues outside of the state park system, his radio came to life and it told him there was a situation at the zoo. He sighed. "Why aren't the locals handling it?" he asked the dispatcher.

"It involves the alligators."

"So?"

"They don't do alligators."

"Shouldn't this fall to a park employee?"

"A theft is involved."

"What? Did somebody steal a gator?"

"No. They stole something from the gator area."

Ray sighed again. "All right. I'm rolling. Out."

He started the large SUV and backed out of the spot. He was only a couple of miles away. As he accelerated, his cell phone rang.

"Hey."

A sleepy voice that was smooth as silk even at this early hour said, "Hi. When are you coming home?"

"I just got a call."

"Darn. I was going to stay in bed and wait for you."

"Tease," he said. The vision of his girlfriend in his t-shirt always got him going. "Are you wearing my t-shirt?"

"Why don't you come home and find out."

He sighed. "I can't just yet. I have to go to the zoo first."

"That sounds fun. Did the elephants stampede?"

He chuckled. "No, somebody flipped a monkey off and it wants to file assault charges."

"That's even better. Ok. I'm going back to sleep. I'll be here when you decide you want me."

"I'll hurry."

"You better." She hung up.

He pulled into the zoo and parked at the back entrance near the gator exhibit. He'd been here before. The manager was a woman in her early forties with bright red hair and a waistline that needed a little attention. She was munching on a granola bar as she spoke and he couldn't help but wonder if that was her fifth one or something. There was no way she put this much weight on eating just one.

There was another large woman in purple spandex pants scolding a young boy of about five. He had taken his mother's Coke Zero and shook it up. Then he opened it and it sprayed everywhere. He thought this was hilarious until she smacked him in the behind. Now he was screaming. Apparently she was some kind of witness.

"She says the guy flashed some kind of badge and then threatened to have her arrested and her kid hauled off to social services." The manager took another bite of the granola bar. "Pete says the guy took something off of the steps in the pen and left with it after some story about his daughter dying of cancer and her last wish was to feed the gators."

"What did he take?" Ray asked, not quite sure where this was going.

"We don't know. It wasn't anything that we have inventoried. Pete said it looked like a small, silver box. He'd never noticed it before."

"So what's the problem?" he asked.

She just stared at him. "I don't know. We thought it was unusual and you should know about it. Besides, Mrs. Shelling is pretty upset. She thought that was a horrible way for a police officer to act."

"Did she get his badge number or name?"

"No. He didn't give her a chance."

"All right, I'll talk to her."

He approached Mrs. Shelling and the bratty kid, and introduced himself.

"Are you a real police officer?" she asked.

"Yes, ma'am."

"Your uniform says you're some wildlife officer."

"Yes it does. I actually have more power than your average every day cop. I can arrest anyone for anything. My jurisdiction is not just with animals. I'm here because this happened in the zoo."

"Well, one of your counterparts was very rude to me and I'd like to file a complaint."

"The manager told me what happened, but if you don't have a badge number, or name, I really don't have anything to go on."

"He was tall. Dark hair that was graying. He looked about forty-five years old. Stocky."

"That still doesn't help. I'm sorry, but there is nothing I can do."

He turned to go and she stopped him, "Wait! His badge. It looked different than yours. It had blue letters instead of green."

"Did you notice if it had the state of Florida in the background, like this?"

"No. I can't remember."

He nodded. "I've got your name. I'll call you if anything turns up."

"Thank you," she said and went back to her child. He was complaining that she never took him to see the monkeys.

Ray went back to the manager and Pete. He turned to the guy. "Anything else you can think of? Was he with someone else? You mentioned a daughter who had cancer."

Pete nodded. "Cute girl too. She didn't look sick, but who am I to judge? There was another guy too. He seemed like he was close with the girl. Like maybe her boyfriend." Ray noticed that he seemed a little disappointed at this. "She kissed me."

"But you don't know what they took?"

Pete shook his head.

"Show me where all this happened."

Pete led him to the platform and entered the deck. He pointed to the steps leading into the water and said, "The guy just opened the gate and stepped down there. He leaned over and pulled something from under the steps. The croc almost got him too. He didn't seem afraid."

"Or maybe what he wanted was more important," Ray said.

Pete nodded his head vigorously. "Yeah. He wouldn't listen to me and was pretty worked up about his daughter feeding the gators."

Ray went to the steps and opened the gate. None of the gators were near so he went down a couple of steps and leaned over to look under the stairs. He could see nothing. As he straightened up, a set of eyes rose from the dark water a few feet away and looked him over. He backed away up the stairs.

Ray had a lot of experience with gators and he knew when to keep his distance. Besides, that one was a croc and they were even more unpredictable.

"Have you looked at the security tapes?" Ray asked.

"No," said the manager. "We were waiting for you."

"I'd like to see them."

"I'll have Ted meet us in the security office. He knows the equipment better."

In the security office, a balding, middle-aged man with thick, black rimmed glasses stood in front of the monitors, and as they walked in, he froze a video he was watching.

"I'm Ted," he said and extended his hand. "We haven't seen one of you guys in here in a long time."

"That's probably a good thing," Ray joked. "We're not very good with the monkeys anyway."

"They're my favorite," Ted said, pushing up his glasses. He looked like a cross between Buddy Holly, and Gallagher, the comedian. Where he wasn't bald, he had long wavy hair to his shoulders. He sucked on a lollipop as he talked. "I'm sure you don't have much time so I'll show you what we got." He turned and played the frozen video. "Here's the three you are looking for. The girl, the young guy, and then the older one who took the box."

Ray watched the video and was surprised at the quality. "This is pretty good."

Ted nodded, popping the lollipop out of his mouth. "We just got this new equipment. It's HD."

"How much hard drive space does it take up to record in HD?"

"We've got a lot, but you're right. It uses it up pretty quickly. We have a high rotation because of it. The videos are saved for only seven days and then the data is overwritten."

Ray nodded and went back to watching the screen. The big guy was on the steps now and he could tell Pete was trying to get him off. He knelt and worked at something under the steps, then he seemed to free it and step back just as the croc rose up out of the water and lunged for the steps. It was weird without sound.

"That was close."

"That guy is lucky to still have his hand," Ted said.

"Can you zoom in on his hand?" Ray asked.

Ted manipulated a few keys and used the mouse to zoom in. He froze the frame and they could see something silver in it. It looked to be about three to four inches long and rectangular. "And you say that this item is not part of anything the park would have under the steps?"

Pete and the manager both shook their heads.

"All right. Can you save this for me?"

"Already have," Ted said. "I can mark it on the hard drive and it will be retained until I delete it manually." The lollipop went back in, then popped back out again. "I saved something else for you too. I think you'll find this very interesting."

He clicked the mouse on another section of the screen and the next monitor over began playing a video. It was night time and the cameras had now switched to night vision.

"This system is pretty high tech," Ray said.

Ted just nodded and watched the screen. He was smiling.

A man dressed in what appeared to be a dark color with some kind of mask crept along the high hedge of the alligator pond and went directly to the platform. He entered and went to the steps where he bent and looked to place something under the steps right where the mystery box was in the previous videos.

"I'll be damned," Ray said.

The lollipop popped back out of Ted's mouth and he grinned. "I thought you'd like that."

"What day is this?"

"Six days ago. If we had waited one more day, it would have been deleted." Ted seemed proud of himself. Ray would never have taken the time to look at all this recording.

"What kind of security do you have at night?"

"Minimal staffing. We usually carry three. Two stationed here and one to roam periodically. They missed this guy, though, as you can see. I only found it when I did a search of motion activity on the after hour tapes."

"These are motion activated?"

Ted nodded. "It also helps with disk storage space. We run motion sensing at night and full time during business hours."

"You saved this too?"

The lollipop was back in his mouth and he nodded.

"Good job, Ted. This may come in handy. How about the parking lot? Any cameras out there?"

Ted frowned but nodded. "I didn't check those. They're not HD though. Only the cameras in the park."

"Can you pull up the parking lot around the time frame they exited the alligator area or a few minutes after?"

"Sure."

The lollipop went back into the mouth as Ted manipulated the system. He stood up straight when he found what he was looking for and they all watched the screens as the parking lot was displayed.

Shortly, three people were seen exiting the park and heading for their car. They were the only ones leaving. Everyone else was coming in. It was the tall guy, the girl and the young guy. They walked directly to a new Ford Mustang and got in. They sat in the car and did not move. Eventually it started and moved off. The back end of the car showed itself to the cameras briefly and Ray said, "Freeze that."

Ted hit pause and he nodded, knowing what Ray would want. He zoomed in on the license plate and wrote the number down. Ray used his radio and called dispatch, relaying the plate number. He had information on the owner in a matter of minutes.

"Registered to one Gilead James Fowler. Mr. Fowler has a propensity for fast driving. His license is currently suspended."

Ted beamed. "What do you think it is?" Ted asked. "Drugs?"

"Could be, but it's too vague to tell."

"Let me know what you find. I'm curious, and since it happened in my park, I want to know."

"You'll be the first. Here. My card. It has my cell if you find anything else. You've been a big help."

Ray made his way to his SUV and put the call out for the Mustang as he walked. His next call was to Michelle.

"I'm still hurrying but I got caught up."

"Monkeys pissed?"

"Yeah. Something like that. Sorry."

"Your loss."

"You're telling me."

He hung up and cursed. One Gilead James Fowler was going to be very sorry when he caught up with him. Very Sorry.

* * *

Jaxon handed the silver box to Gil and cursed. "Shit. Now what?"

Melanie was in the back and she leaned forward looking at the box. "Is there any writing on the box itself?"

Gil shook his head as he turned it over in his hands. Jaxon couldn't believe it. He had made a bad choice and now some innocent girl was going to pay for it. They had bypassed Gainesville and when Lakeland had proved fruitful, they thought they were off the hook. But apparently, they had missed something by skipping the first waypoint and now they were going to have to backtrack and waste valuable time. It was coming up on twenty-four hours and Jaxon felt no closer to finding Bethany than he did standing in the woods holding her severed finger.

"We've missed something," Gil said.

"I know," Jaxon said. "We missed it in Gainesville. Now she has to suffer because I screwed it up. Dammit!"

He drove his fist into the dash. Melanie and Gil looked away embarrassed, but they remained silent.

"Maybe we're missing something else," Melanie finally said. "Why would he put an empty box for us to find? It doesn't make sense."

"To throw us off," Jaxon said. "In case we tried to skip something. Just like we did. He or she is paying us back."

"No," Gil said, looking at Melanie excitedly. "She's right. It doesn't make sense. If we had gone to Gainesville first, what would we have found?"

Jaxon thought about it and could only come up with one thing. "Another clue, of course. Something we need so we can move on."

"Or just a confirmation that Lakeland was next. What did we find in Lakeland?"

Jaxon sat forward. In Lakeland, it had just been the set of coordinates that they already had for Naples. Nothing new or nothing that would tell them they had made a wrong choice. It was like a double negative. They were sending them in circles when the obvious was right in front of them.

"Ok. I'm following," Jaxon said, "but we have an empty box. Did we miss something inside? Do we need to go back in?"

Jaxon looked back at the zoo entrance and thought once was enough. The staff would not tolerate being taken advantage of again.

"Unless the box itself is our clue," Gil said and smiled.

Jaxon remembered Gil saying something about some group that had certain boxes decorated just so other cachers would know it was the group's hide. "What was the name of the group who uses these boxes?"

"Cock Cachers."

"Does that mean anything to you? It means nothing to me."

"Would they use the letters as a cipher again?" Melanie asked.

"That would be too obvious, but let's try plugging it in."

Gil took a pen and quickly scribbled some numbers down and said "No. This isn't it," as he entered the numbers into the GPS. "They're too far away for us. See?"

He held the GPS up and it showed a position somewhere in the middle of the Indian Ocean. All the way on the other side of the world.

"Maybe we're supposed to go there," Melanie said, but Jaxon could tell she was just grasping like they all were. No one even bothered to answer her.

"Wait a minute," Gil said and pulled out his smartphone. He opened up the GeoCaching app and typed something into the phone. He talked as he typed. "We've been given locations that are not registered on any of the caching sites, right? Well, what if our next point has been made inactive from the site?"

"What do you mean?" Jaxon asked.

"Sometimes, caches get stolen. Kids find them, or somebody who doesn't know what it is, and they take it, or mutilate it, something that negates the site from further use. It will still be registered on the website but it will show as inactive. Look."

He held up the app and Jaxon read what was on there. Then he understood. "Somebody took this box from its cache point and then the group reported it as inactive."

"Right. I just did a search for all of Cock Cachers caches and this one is the only one that is inactive. It has to be the next point."

"Where is it?" Melanie asked.

Gil punched in the coordinates and held up the GPS. "The Everglades."

Jaxon sat back grinning. "I knew I brought you along for a reason."

Gil shrugged but grinned big. Melanie gave him a kiss.

"Well, what are you waiting for? Let's go."

Gil cranked the car up and headed out. They had a little drive ahead of them and Jaxon was not looking forward to more alligators.

The Everglades waited for them.

CHAPTER 10

48 HOURS

Twenty minutes into the drive on Tamiami Trail, a tire blew. Gil had been driving and didn't see a tortoise crossing the highway. He hit it doing 75 mph and the shell of the creature punctured the tire. It was 10:00 a.m. and the heat was already sweltering.

They were pulled over on the side of the highway with the car jacked up and the blown tire off when a Wildlife Officer vehicle pulled up behind them with its lights on. Jaxon thought the guy was there to help. He was wrong.

The officer stepped out of the vehicle and stood with the door acting as a shield. Jaxon recognized his posture right away and realized that they were probably in for some trouble.

"All three of you," the officer yelled. "Hands on the car, feet spread!"

"Shit," Jaxon mumbled and moved to comply. No use getting shot by not cooperating. Gil froze and Melanie looked like a deer in the headlights.

"Do it! Now!" The guy meant business.

"Do what he says," Jaxon said and placed his hands on the car. Gil and Melanie followed next to him. The officer came up behind them and kicked their legs further apart.

"What seems to be the problem, officer?" Jaxon asked.

"Shut up."

"If you'll look in my back left pocket, you'll find my wallet. Inside is my badge."

The officer stopped and stared at Jaxon. "You're some kind of cop?"

"Retired," Jaxon said. "I'm an investigator now."

The officer didn't look convinced. He stepped to Jaxon and withdrew his wallet. He looked it over but said nothing.

"Can I stand now?" Jaxon asked.

"Stay right there."

He radioed his dispatch and waited for confirmation of Jaxon's credentials. When he got them he walked up to Jaxon and handed him the wallet.

"You can relax. You check out. What about these two?"

"They're with me," Jaxon said standing straight up and getting a better look at the man. He was in his mid-thirties, brown hair, brown eyes, muscular build. He wore the uniform of a Wildlife officer and the nameplate said Ray Maningham.

"Well, this one," Ray pointed to Gil, "has a suspended license. He isn't driving is he?"

Jaxon shook his head. "No, I'm driving. Or I was. I'm Jaxon." He stuck his hand out to shake but the man ignored it.

"What I want to know is what in the hell were you three doing in the zoo this morning and what was it that you took from the alligator display?"

Gil hung his head and Melanie looked away. Shit. They were no longer under the radar.

"It's like a scavenger hunt," Jaxon said, and the officer looked at him like he was crazy.

"I take it she's not really dying of cancer."

"No."

"You threatened a woman and her young son."

"She was being a total bitch."

The officer actually grinned at this, but then grew serious. "She wants your head."

"I'm sure she does."

"What kind of treasure hunt? It doesn't sound like something a DC cop and private investigator would do."

"A lot is at stake."

"That doesn't answer my question."

"It's for a lot of money."

The officer looked them over again and turned back to Jaxon.

"I don't believe you. I think you better come down and answer a few questions."

"We don't have time."

"You'll make time."

Jaxon sighed. "All right. This is what's going on." And he told Ray Maningham the story.

* * *

Ray was tired.

It was the end of his shift and the last couple hours had been exhausting. He had felt lucky when he came upon the broken down Mustang, the same Mustang that he was looking for, and when he decided to handle it without backup, he was wondering if he had made a mistake. Now, the story coming from the mouth of this ex-cop was bizarre. Probably some truth to it, but still bizarre. He wasn't sure if he could believe him. He had a few questions of his own.

"Who is this guy? The one sending you across the state in this so called game?"

"I don't know," Jaxon said.

"Who is the guy at the zoo? The one that planted the box?"

"Probably the same guy. Or girl. We don't know yet."

"I've got him on tape."

Jaxon came up off the car he was leaning on and said, "His face?"

Ray shook his head. "No. It's covered."

Jaxon leaned back against the car. "Still, I'd like to see it."

Ray tapped his notepad with his pen and looked at all three individually. The ex-cop seemed sincere. The young guy hadn't said a word and the girl looked nervous. Normal responses as far as he could tell. This really wasn't his field of expertise, he normally dealt with fisherman, hunters, and smugglers, yet he believed them. He made a decision.

"I should take you in, but I can't seem to find anything to charge you with since you really didn't steal anything that wasn't meant for you, and you didn't harm any animals. You did scare a lady and her kid but it's not a crime that I know of." He paused. "Finish the tire. We'll go back to the zoo and you can look at the tape."

Jaxon nodded at him and turned for the jack. They had the tire changed in record time.

"I'll follow you. Stay in front of me," Ray said and he watched the kid get in the driver's side. "Hey! He can't drive. You know that."

The kid got out and Jaxon took his place behind the wheel. As they drove, Ray called dispatch and asked Sally if she'd search for anything on a DC detective named Jaxon Jennings. She got back with him in five minutes.

"Jaxon Jennings, forty-eight years old. Retired early last year. Married. 1 child. Deceased. Oh wow. Apparently the child was murdered. Oh I remember this! He was the lead in the swimming pool killer who was stalking young teenagers up in Virginia two years ago. Do you remember that?"

Ray remembered hearing something about it but hadn't really paid attention. "Not really."

"His partner was killed in an explosion in Indiana related to the case and a couple of young kids were killed too. The killer would put the bodies in a neighborhood pool. Jaxon and his ex-wife, an FBI agent at that, were wounded. It was on the news for a few days."

"Sounds like a movie."

"Yeah. He's famous."

"Or infamous."

She agreed and signed off.

Some hotshot detective from DC was on a hunt for some missing girl. Sounded too convenient for it to be random. Ray wondered if he realized that.

At the zoo, the manager was reluctant to let Jaxon and the kids back in, but Ray assured them he had it under control. Pete was not too happy, but Ted was more than helpful. He seemed ecstatic that Ray was back. They all crammed into the security room and Ted played the video.

"This is good stuff," Jaxon said and Ray nodded.

"That's what I said."

The screen displayed the recorded video again and Ray watched as Jaxon studied the monitor. Jaxon asked to pause it and he looked closely at the head. The face was in shadows. He told Ted to continue, but when he clicked the mouse, the picture stuttered, grew grainy looking and then went to snow. Ted stopped it and backed it up. When he hit play, only snow was displayed.

"That's weird," Ted said.

"It's gone," Jaxon said and turned away.

"No. It's just locked up," Ted said manipulating the system with the mouse.

"It's gone," Jaxon repeated and he gave Gil and Melanie a look. Ray was surprised.

"How can it be gone?" Ray asked.

"They've hacked into the system. Just now. I'd be surprised if any of the recordings were left."

"That can't be," Ted said. "This system is secure."

"Check it, if you want," Jaxon said. "But I'll bet it's all gone."

Ted worked the mouse and as display after display showed only brief glimpses of the park through various cameras, they all eventually turned to snow.

Ted looked at Jaxon and said, "Just what are you into here?"

"You don't want to know."

Jaxon pointed to Ray and motioned outside. Gil and Melanie stayed inside.

"They know we're here and they know I've been talking to you."

"You keep referring to him as 'they.' Do you think it's more than one guy?" Ray asked.

"I don't know. We think it's mob related, but we're not sure."

"We?"

"My wife and I. She's back in Jax working the details for me while I'm in the field. She's ex-FBI."

"I know."

Jaxon grinned. "Checking up on me?"

"Wouldn't you?"

Jaxon nodded. "We have only a few leads, like the name of the girl and an IP address of a small internet café where he accessed a remote web cam. Now I've seen him, but it's not much to go on."

"Is your wife working the girl's name?"

"Yes. What she found only confuses the issue and that's why we're not sure of the whole mob connection. The girl works for a law firm whose sole clientele is the Florida connection for the mob."

Ray thought that sounded just too farfetched.

"That doesn't make sense. Why not just knock her off if she's a problem?"

"That was our thought too. The mob thing is pretty flimsy."

"Have you considered that you've been singled out for this?"

Jaxon looked at him. "The wife brought that up too. Am I too close to this to see?"

"When I look at it from what you've told me, it doesn't feel like just some random act. Who've you pissed off lately?"

"Who haven't I pissed off? The list is a long one."

"You better start narrowing it down. That girl isn't going to survive for the whole 72 hours. I can guarantee it."

"My thoughts exactly." Jaxon grew silent for a minute. "These two that are with me, I feel like I'm dragging around extra luggage. They've been helpful, but they aren't law enforcement."

"What are you getting at?" Ray wasn't sure he liked where this was heading.

"I could use some help."

"Why did I know you were going to say that?"

"This perp knows everything. He uses anything and everything he can get access to, to track my movement and stay on top of the game. He warned me not to involve others, but I had to take the kids on because they fell into the game. I felt responsible for their safety. If I had someone in the system, someone with access, without the perp knowing, it sure would give me a hand up and maybe I could get ahead of this game."

"I'm not your guy."

"You're all I've got at the moment."

"I'm not your guy."

Jaxon nodded. He seemed to understand. "Look the other way then. We were never here."

"I don't have a problem with that. Dispatch is the only one that knows what I've been doing. Sally will do anything I ask."

Jaxon stuck out his hand. "I owe you."

Ray took it and shook it. He felt like he was letting the man down. "Be safe."

"I don't think I'll get it done being safe, but thanks."

Jaxon turned, signaled Gil and Melanie, got in the Mustang, and drove off. Gil was driving. Ray couldn't help but think Jaxon did that on purpose.

CHAPTER 11

Bethany woke to find a little more light making its way inside.

Along with the light came heat. She was sweating and the box she was in was getting hotter by the minute. The sun must be up and she was definitely somewhere tropical. Looking around, she could see some bottles of water a few feet away and paper and trash scattered around. She was so thirsty. She stared at the water and couldn't believe she would be tortured like this, the water just a few feet away and her unable to reach it.

She struggled against her bindings and they felt a little looser. Maybe it was her imagination. The sweat was dripping in her eyes as she worked her hands back and forth, and she hoped she wasn't imagining things, but it felt like she was making progress.

Her hand with the missing finger ached, and the other hand felt raw, but she ignored it and pulled harder. An audible pop found her hands free and she held them up in front of her, shocked. She cried. Her hands and wrists were a wreck and the sight of her missing finger sickened her, but the relief at being free was overwhelming. The tears flowed freely and she sobbed at her good fortune.

She got herself under control after a minute and stood. Immediately, her world spun and she found herself on the ground again, banging her head painfully on the metal floor. She was so weak. Dirk filled her head, and she found some strength from him and sat up. Vertigo took hold again, subsiding slowly. As the room stopped spinning, she felt liquid in her right eye and reached up to touch her head. Her fingers came away red. She sagged against the wall and cried more. It would be just her luck to finally get free and then bleed to death before getting out of here.

She eyed the water again, just sitting there a few feet away. Her thirst came raging back and she leaned forward until she was on her hands and knees. Only a little spinning accompanied this and it passed quickly. Crawling across the dirty floor, she focused on the water and willed herself to move. Her arms gave out once and she found herself face down on the gritty surface of the rusted metal floor, but she pushed herself up again and continued to the water.

She grabbed the first bottle, struggled with the twist top, sobbing in frustration, and then finally switched to her good hand and the top came free. She drank in giant gulps, choking as the water ran down her throat and overflowed to spill down her neck and chest. She finished the bottle in a matter of seconds.

Her stomach revolted and she threw it all back up.

Collapsing on the ground, she felt as if the whole world were against her. She just wanted a drink. Her throat burning and her head throbbing, she sat up again and opened another bottle. She sipped it slowly, the cool, clean, liquid soothing her raw throat and mouth. It stayed down. The bleeding had stopped on her head and even though the heat continued to build within the little room, she felt better.

She leaned up against the wall and soon drifted off. She awoke with a start, unsure of her surroundings and when she realized where she was, the tears started again. She cried for a few minutes, and then she tried to stand. She felt stronger, but the heat was suffocating up near the ceiling. She reached up with her hand, touched the surface of the ceiling, and pulled her fingers away quickly. It was scorching.

Shuffling along slowly, she maneuvered along the wall, looking for a way out. She found the doors at the other end of the box that she estimated at ten feet by twenty feet. It was darker at this end and she had to feel along the doors for a way out.

She searched for what seemed like an eternity, but she could find no way to open the doors. She could feel the seams, but the latch and hinges must be on the outside. She banged repeatedly on the doors and walls, a hollow metallic ring to them, shouting until her voice gave out, but no one responded. She fell into despair again, and the elation she felt at being free of her bindings became a deep, lonely ache that she believed would be the end of her. She could not get out.

She shuffled back toward the water, kicking trash and debris beneath her bare feet, the light getting a little brighter as she moved closer to the small crack in the corner of the ceiling near the water. She kicked something slick and it stuck to the bottom of her foot. She reached down to grab it. It was a picture. She went to the light and stared at the photo.

It took a moment to register, and she was confused that she would find something familiar in this isolated and unfamiliar place. As recognition spread through her, she sagged to the floor and moaned. She knew the girl framed against the backdrop of the ocean. She mouthed her name slowly as the world started to spin again. The dead girl's face followed her into the darkness and the nightmare she was in deepened.

CHAPTER 12

As they headed East, Jaxon got on his cell phone and called Victoria.

"I was just about to call you," she said.

"You won't believe what we've been through."

He filled her in on the morning's events and told her where they were headed and what Ray had suggested.

"I think it's something we should consider. Has anybody popped into that head of yours that might be capable of something like this?"

"There's a shit load of people who would want me suffering, but nobody who's this sick. At least who's not in jail."

"Maybe I should check and see if anybody you put away is out on early release."

"Good idea. Nobody told us we'd have to watch our backs for the rest of our lives as a result of being cops. Nice perk."

"I messed up," Vick said then, and he heard her own disappointment.

"What's wrong?"

"The Bethany Hope we were investigating is not the Bethany who's missing."

"I take it you've found the one who's missing."

"Yes."

"Then how is that a mess up? That should help us."

"I know, but I should've had this yesterday. When I was going through the Florida list, I called all the phone numbers and asked for Bethany Hope. I talked to each and every one. Or so I thought. There are two Bethany Hopes in a single household in Palm Beach."

"How can that be?"

"One is the grandmother, the one I spoke with. The other is a twenty-five year old nurse who was named after her grandmother."

"I would've missed that too," Jaxon said. "Don't beat yourself up over it."

"I know. I just shouldn't have missed it. I usually catch those details."

"How did you find the mistake?"

"The Bethany Hope in Georgia came home. She spent the night in Savannah with a friend. Then I went back to our list in Florida because I had a feeling I missed something and there it was. Grandma and granddaughter were listed right next to each other and I thought it was just a duplicate result in the search."

"I think it was a good catch. Anything that might help us?"

"Yes. Couple of interesting red flags that pop up in her life. She's engaged to a Dirk Samuels and he is also missing according to the grandmother. He hadn't been over to the house in a few days and Bethany was wondering where he was."

"Could they have eloped or something and this is another false positive?"

"I don't know. I've considered it, but this next little tidbit is very interesting. As a teenager in high school, she was part of a group of teens that bullied another girl and that girl eventually committed suicide. It was a big scandal eight years ago in the community, but Bethany was never charged with anything and the thing just kind of blew over."

"What about the parents of the suicide?"

"Both dead. The father died when the girl was young. The mother killed herself shortly after her daughter committed suicide."

"Nice."

"Yes. Pretty tragic. I'm still working all the angles, but nothing is jumping out at me."

"How about some pissed off boyfriend back eight years ago, or some relative?"

"Checking all that now. There's lots in the media about it, but the family seems to be rarely mentioned."

"What was her name?"

"Danielle."

"Means nothing to me. Keep on it. You did good. This could be our first big break."

"If it's related."

"Seems awfully convenient not to be related," Jaxon said, and thought, just like him finding the finger. Convenient. Definitely not a coincidence. "All right, get back to work. We're on our way to some airport in the middle of the Everglades."

"The next point?"

"The only thing we have at the moment. We're playing the game and he keeps staying a step ahead."

"So you're positive it's a he?"

"The video sure looked right for the build. Couldn't see the face, but he was pretty big. My size."

"Be careful."

"No."

She laughed but then sighed. "I know you won't but I can ask. Love you."

"Love you too." As he hung up, he saw Mel staring at him with a little smile on her lips. "What?"

"You're cute," she said. "I mean you and your wife. You care for her a lot don't you?"

He nodded. "She's all I have left."

"No kids?"

"We had a son."

"What happened?"

"He was killed. It was a long time ago."

"Oh, I'm sorry. I didn't know."

"How could you? No need to be sorry."

"We still on track for the airport?" Gil asked.

"Yes. Some new developments, but right now it doesn't help us find her."

"What did your wife find?"

He told them about Bethany and Danielle.

"That's messed up," Mel said. "We had a guy in our school kill himself because he got picked on. He was gay. It was a big deal. I liked him."

She looked away and Jaxon could tell it was a sore spot with her.

An hour later, they arrived at the Oasis Ranger/US Government airport and pulled in. There were only a few cars in the lot and as they drove through, Jaxon watched a gator cross the road behind them. They were all over the place. Personally, he was tired of gators.

They drove onto the airport property, heading for the waypoint. There were very few aircraft. An old Korean era helicopter sat on the tarmac. A few hangars were spaced along the pavement, but no people could be seen. Either they were busy inside or the airport was deserted at the moment. Jaxon was relieved. He was tired of making shit up so people would leave them alone.

Gil stopped the car near a hangar that looked fairly new. "This is it."

Jaxon watched as Mel looked around like he was doing. "There's nothing here," she said.

"The building," Jaxon said and they got out.

There was a door on the side that was locked. Around the front of the building, they found the hangar door down and sealed tight. Maybe it was around back. They searched the other side on the way to the back of the hangar and found nothing. Out back, there was a small lean-to type shed up against the back wall and Gil lifted the lid.

"Here!"

Jaxon and Melanie walked over as he was pulling a camo covered container out. It was the size of a small toolbox.

"This is probably it," Gil said and opened it.

A flash of black struck out from the box and Gil pulled his hand back, dropping it. A medium sized snake reared up and then slithered away in the direction of the brush. Mel screamed.

"Dammit!" Gil said, holding his hand. "That hurts like a mother."

"It bit you?" Jaxon asked and grabbed his hand.

Two small marks were visible on the padded area between his thumb and index finger. They were growing redder as he watched.

"Burns," Gil said.

"What kind of snake was that?" Jaxon asked.

"Hell if I know."

Jaxon kicked the box and nothing else came out of it. He bent and picked it up. Inside was a piece of paper. It was covered in some yellow and brown stains that had a strong ammonia smell. Probably snake piss. He opened the page and read the note out loud.

Say hello to the Black Mamba. Hope you were careful, but since it is one of the deadliest snakes in the world, if you happen to find the business end of it, you may want to hurry to your next number point. You could call it your Color Personality Anti-waypoint. Oh...depending on how much venom the Mamba pumped into you, you probably have very little time. Maybe an hour. Have fun! Orange blue blue yellow indigo indigo blank yellow yellow / rose red red indigo violet blank blank gold green.

Jaxon looked up to see Mel with her hand at her mouth, her lip quivering, a tear trickling down her cheek. Gil was not looking good. His face was turning ashen and he was sweating.

"Shit," Gil said and then bent over the bitten hand in pain. "Where is the next waypoint?"

"We don't have a waypoint. There's just a bunch of colors."

"Crap! This isn't the time for a puzzle. I'm gonna die. Shit!"

Gil sat on the ground and held his hand out in front of him. It was swelling.

"Think Gil," Mel said. "What would colors represent?"

"I don't know. I can't think. It hurts too much."

"Come on," Jaxon said and helped him up. "We have to get you to a hospital."

"They won't have Black Mamba anti-venom. Not here in the US. We have to figure out the next point. Read it to me again."

Jaxon read the note out loud.

"There's nothing there," Gil said.

"What's a number point?" Mel said.

"He just means waypoint," Gil said.

"Are you sure? That's a weird way to put it. And what did he mean by color personality?"

Gil looked up at her. "How should I know?" he snapped. "The guy's a psycho. His brain just doesn't work like ours."

Jaxon could tell the pain was pretty intense. The kid had guts. He had heard snake venom was one of the most painful things to endure.

"Isn't there some chart or something that will give you your personality traits based on colors? You know? Like your favorite colors." Mel's face was frantic. She snapped her fingers. "Numerology!"

She pulled out her smartphone and tapped the screen. "Here." She held up the phone to Gil. "Every color has a number associated with it as well as letters. Substitute the colors for the numbers and I bet we have the waypoint."

He looked up at her, a little grin on his lips through the pain. "Mel, that's awesome. You figured it out."

She broke out in tears and handed the phone to Jaxon. Jaxon took the GPS from Gil's pocket and plugged in the numbers. The GPS map tracked east rapidly and centered over Asia.

"This can't be right," Jaxon said.

"Where is it?" Gil asked through clenched teeth.

"India."

"That can't be," Melanie said in a panic. She grabbed the GPS from Jaxon and stared at the screen. "The note said it was here. How are we supposed to get to India in an hour?"

"We're not," Jaxon said. "We're missing something."

He paced and read the note to himself again.

"Is there a 'W' in front of the second set of numbers?" Gil asked.

"No."

"That's it. Put a 'W' in front of them."

Jaxon did it and the map skewed west until it centered over a spot in the Everglades just west of them on the Tamiami trail.

"Got it! Come on, kid. We have to move."

Jaxon reached to help him up and Gil stumbled as he stood. He leaned over and vomited all over the ground.

"Sorry," he said weakly. "I couldn't help it."

"Don't worry about it. I got you."

Jaxon grabbed him under the shoulders and Mel got on his other side. They helped him to the car. There wasn't much time.

CHAPTER 13

Ray lay awake next to Michelle.

She had been good on her promise when he got home and though he had been late, she didn't seem upset. He stared at her sleeping face and couldn't believe how lucky he was.

They had met at his best friend's wedding. The bride was her sister and they hit it off right away. At the reception, she had caught the bouquet and though Ray didn't believe in fate or any kind of spiritual guidance, he did feel like she could be something more in his life than just a fun date.

That had been three years ago, and though she promised she would always be with him, he had yet to give her a ring. He knew it was time, he had even been to the jeweler and held the ring in his palm. He just hadn't pulled the trigger. He didn't know what was keeping him from this last step, he just knew that things kept getting in the way.

That's not what was keeping him awake, though.

He kept going over what Jaxon had asked him. The guy was definitely a piece of work, but he had been sincere to him and that was something Ray respected. The problem wasn't that he didn't want to help him, he just felt that Jaxon was working outside the law and he couldn't condone that. Everything Ray did in his life was to uphold the delicate balance between the idiots in this world and those who behaved. The law was there for a reason, and in Ray's eyes, was not meant to be messed with. Even if it seemed warranted.

He reached for his phone and started to punch in some numbers but he stopped. If he called the FBI, would he actually endanger this girl's life, or help? That same question was what had prevented him from calling right away. He didn't have enough information.

Jaxon had provided him the gist of the situation, but Ray had not asked enough questions. Maybe he had been protecting himself from further problems in the future should they arise and he was questioned. He wasn't sure of his reasoning, Ray just knew he had somehow made it convenient to avoid further knowledge of the specifics. Now, he wondered if that had been a mistake.

He put the phone back down and stared at the ceiling. Michelle suddenly spoke and it startled him. He hadn't realized she was awake.

"What's bothering you?"

He turned to her and touched her face. She smiled but he could tell she wasn't going to be put off that easily. He sighed.

"I had a crazy morning."

"What happened?"

"You sure you want to hear this?"

She nodded.

"I had a run in with an ex-cop. From DC."

"Was he breaking the law?"

He paused. "In a way."

"Tell me."

He told her. When he was done, she had a funny look on her face. Normally she was blasé about his work and rarely showed interest in what went on.

"Why didn't you help?"

"I don't think what he's doing is right."

"He's trying to save a girl's life. You feel that's not worth it?"

"No. He's going about it all wrong. He's acting above the law and I don't agree with it."

"But he's being prevented from doing so because of the rules imposed by this psycho. He's doing it the only way he can. What if it was me and you were put in the same situation? What would you do?"

He looked at her and didn't see anger in her eyes. Just concern. She wasn't testing him. She was genuinely concerned for this girl. He turned away from her and stared up at the ceiling. She had a point.

"I would do what he's doing," he finally said.

"Help him." She reached out and caressed his neck. "He needs your help."

* * *

Jaxon drove back west as the GPS directed and he pressed the pedal down hard, the car pushing them past the speed limit and beyond. They were flying.

Mel was in the back with Gil, holding him and trying to soothe his pain. He was rocking back and forth, breathing hard and sweating up a storm.

"Pull over. I'm gonna puke again," he said and Jaxon braked hard. He threw the door open and Gil gave up what was left in his stomach to the sand and grass of the Everglades. There wasn't much left, but he heaved for a good five minutes, his body trying everything it could to kick out the poison. When he sat back up, he was ghostly white. Jaxon floored the accelerator and the car leapt onto the road. His cell rang.

He picked it up, thinking it was Vick. "Yeah."

"Jaxon?"

"Yeah. Who is this?"

"It's Maningham. Ray Maningham."

"I'm kind of busy right now, Ray."

"Can I help?"

"I thought you weren't the guy."

"I changed my mind."

"Well, I got a problem. The kid got bit by some Black Mamba and we're trying to get to the anti-venom. Apparently the perp has it hidden."

"What? You're kidding right?"

"No time for kidding. We're flying down Tamiami back toward the west. The GPS says I'm still twenty-eight miles away."

"I know a herpetologist."

"A what?"

"A snake expert. I'll meet you there with him. Give me the coordinates."

"I'll hand the phone to Melanie. She'll give them to you. I have to drive."

He handed the phone to her and told her to give him the waypoint in the GPS. She did it and then hung up.

It started to rain then and thunder rumbled as lightning flashed. The road became slick and Jaxon had to slow down or risk losing control of the car. He kept glancing in the rear view mirror and Melanie's face would look up, stricken, her eyes red and worried, pleading with him to go faster, to get there before it was too late.

He pushed the car harder again, but the tires came up off the pavement, hydroplaning in the water, and he fought it, almost wrapping them around a tree in the process. He couldn't go any faster.

Twenty minutes later they were coming up on the waypoint. The GPS said it was two hundred yards ahead. A turnoff appeared in the vast wilderness of the Everglades and Jaxon read the words on the sign. Skunk Ape Research Center.

"You've got to be kidding me," he mumbled as he applied the brakes hard.

The rain had slowed but the tires still didn't want to bite quite like they should. They slid into the grass and he yanked the wheel hard back toward the entrance. The place looked deserted.

It was basically a shack in the middle of nowhere, gaudy tourist trinkets hanging from racks on the porch, a giant gorilla statue standing sentinel over the property, its yellow eyes glaring at the vast expanse of the Everglades. Jaxon was positive that a skunk ape, if it existed, looked nothing like this creature, nor did gorillas live in the swamps of Florida.

The GPS said they were within fifty feet. The anti-venom must be within the shack. He stopped hard in the only parking spot, the rest was dirt and mud. Putting the car in park, he turned to Mel.

"You stay with him. I'll find it."

Gil was leaning against her, his head against her breast. The skin around his eyes was gray and his breathing came in sporadic gasps. His hand had swollen to three times its normal size.

She nodded. "Hurry!"

He stepped from the car and heard a siren. A few seconds later. Ray's SUV came into the entrance and slid to a stop. Ray and another man jumped out.

"He's in the car," Jaxon yelled.

The man that Jaxon presumed was the snake expert said, "Did you find the anti-venom?"

"Not yet. We just got here."

"Hurry."

"No shit."

The man went to the car and climbed in. Jaxon could see him working on Gil and Melanie was freaking out.

"Mel, it's all right. He's a snake expert. Let him do his thing."

She calmed down and cried silently as the man worked on Gil.

"Where have you looked?" Ray asked.

"I haven't. It's probably in the building. It's definitely within twenty-five feet of the car."

"Let's go."

They rushed inside.

A woman was behind the counter smoking a long cigarette and watching a small portable television that appeared to be a relic from the 70s. She looked up and put the cigarette in an ashtray shaped like a foot.

Ray flashed his badge and said, "We're going to have a look around."

"Do you have a warrant?" the woman asked, her voice hoarse and ragged. She looked as if this was a regular thing.

"Don't need one, Wilma. You've done nothing wrong."

"Can't let you look without a warrant," she rasped.

Jaxon pulled his gun from his holster and shoved it in her face.

"How's this? This warrant enough?"

She raised her hands and nodded.

Ray scowled at Jaxon but said nothing. He started at one side of the small shack and Jaxon the other.

The woman finally found her voice again and asked, "What the hell are you looking for?"

"Has anybody strange been here in the last couple of days?" Jaxon said. "Someone who looked around, maybe, and then left without going in to your park, or buying anything? Maybe he even asked to use the rest room?"

"That's just about everybody who comes in here," she said.

"Have you found anything in here that doesn't belong? A box or small container?"

"No," she said and puffed on her cigarette.

The smoke that she exhaled looked yellow. Jaxon ignored her and concentrated on the shop.

The shelves were full of crap. Shells, gator heads, flip flops, mugs, plastic gorillas, plates with Skunk Ape Research Center emblazoned on their surface, toys, incense, and all the other junk you'd find in a tourist trap. It could be anywhere.

"We're never going to find it in here," Ray said. "Are you sure it's in the shop?"

"No. The GPS only gets us within twenty-five to thirty feet and then we have to do the rest."

He nodded, picking up a stuffed gorilla and then putting it back down. "I'll keep looking in here, you go outside. Maybe it's around back or on the side."

Jaxon agreed and he stepped outside. The rain was still coming down and he sloshed through the mud to the side of the shack. A water meter and gas meter sat up against the wall but nothing else was around.

In the back, a small fenced in area designated the back yard. He opened the gate and found a trash can and various other gardening tools. Nothing else. He slammed the gate closed, frustrated, and went back out front. He stood under the overhang and looked around. The trinkets on the porch were just like the crap inside and he rifled through them, quickly, finding nothing.

He went to the car and stuck his head in. "How is he?"

"Bad," the guy said. He had Gil's arm in a tourniquet and was monitoring his blood pressure. "We need that anti-venom. Now. The Black Mamba can inject large amounts of its very powerful venom within a matter of a split second. He's been given quite a large dose as the condition of the surrounding tissue is quite inflamed. The toxin is spreading as we speak and he doesn't have much time."

"What about a hospital?"

"They don't have that specific anti-venom. The snake is not indigenous to Florida and the anti-venom is very expensive. They would not stock it."

Jaxon closed the door to the rain and looked around again. The giant gorilla glared down at him but nothing else moved.

The gorilla.

Jaxon ran to it and circled its feet. In the back a small hatch lay recessed in the heel of the statue and he pulled out his pocket knife and worked the screw. It turned slowly and then the hatch popped open. A small box lay inside and Jaxon grabbed it. Inside were two vials, a syringe, and alcohol swabs. He jumped up and ran to the car. Throwing the door open, he thrust the box at the herpetologist.

"Oh. Thank God," he said, and went to work.

"What if it's some kind of poison or something," Mel said. "He could die."

"He's going to die anyway if we do nothing, honey," Jaxon said. "It will be all right."

Ray must have seen the commotion. He came out and stood by the car and watched. "He'll be all right, now," he said.

"This guy's going down," Jaxon said. "If it's the last thing I do. He's going down."

CHAPTER 14

Gil sat up in his hospital bed and smiled.

Melanie was lying in the bed with him. She put her head on his shoulder and wrapped an arm around him. Jaxon stood at the door, unsure if he should come in.

"You don't have to stand there," Gil said. "I'm all right."

He walked in and glanced at Gil's arm. It was bandaged from his elbow to his fingertips, the bulk of it around his hand. He had been lucky not to lose it. The emergency room physician at the hospital in Naples had seen lots of snake bites, but never one like this. He had all kinds of questions and Gil had done a good job of keeping things quiet. According to Gil, he had run across the snake in the Everglades and didn't know what it was. He had tried to catch it, like an idiot, and the thing had bitten him.

The anti-venom was a problem though. Gil had given the lame excuse that the herpetologist had some in his stock and Ray had called him. They got the stuff in him and then brought him to the hospital. The emergency room physician eyed them, but didn't say anything. Jaxon could tell he didn't believe them.

More than likely the doctor thought they were all rare reptile smugglers who carried anti-venom just in case. Jaxon knew there was quite a bit of money made on black market animals.

For some reason, people thought it cool to own a very rare or very dangerous animal.

"You're alive."

"Yep. Thanks to you. I owe you."

"I don't think you owe me a thing. I got you into all this mess, remember?"

Gil shook his head. "I got myself into this mess. I was the nosy son-of-a-bitch who stumbled into your little problem."

Jaxon nodded and glanced at Mel. He felt like he had let her down and it made him feel like shit. She didn't seem fazed by it, though, and only had eyes and smiles for Gil.

"What's next?" Gil asked.

"You sitting your butt in that bed and getting better."

"We have a girl to find."

"This is my thing. You've done enough. Besides, they aren't going to let you out of here."

"I'll leave on my own." He went to sit up, but his eyes kind of glazed over and he sat back against the bed. His smile had disappeared.

"See. You're not ready to go anywhere and I can't wait around. I know it seems harsh, but you're right. I have a girl to find."

Gil slowly nodded his head. "Will Ray be helping?"

"Yes. He has some things to tie up, but he'll join me in Miami."

"Is that where the next waypoint is?"

Jaxon nodded. "No tricks this time. The lat/long was in the box with the anti-venom. I guess he figured we'd been through enough. The GPS puts it in the city of Miami. I'm leaving now."

Gil stared at him. "I'm sorry I let you down. I know you could use my help."

"I'll be all right."

Mel got up from the bed and came to him. She stood in front of him staring and then she grabbed him and hugged him hard. "Thank you for saving him," she said. She stared up into his eyes. "You be safe."

"I won't," he said, but grinned. She smiled back, kissed him softly on the cheek, and then separated herself from him. "I'll check up on you later."

Gil raised his good hand in a wave and said, "Find that bastard for me."

Jaxon nodded and then left. He didn't look back.

* * *

Bethany woke with sweat in her eyes.

The little chamber had become a steam bath while she was out and she found it hard to breathe. She sat up, woozy, the picture still in her hand. The dead girl swam in and out of her vision until the wooziness passed. She stared at her and a tear tracked down her face.

Danielle Newsome. Eight years ago she had taken her own life. A life that had just begun. She had been a senior at North Palm Beach High School, petite, red hair, green eyes, quiet, a member of the math club.

She had also been a lesbian and Bethany and her group had never let her forget it. Bethany had killed her, just as surely as Danielle had taken all those pills. No, Bethany hadn't shoved the pills in her mouth, made her gag them down with a soda, and stood by her in that lonely room until she passed out, but she might as well have.

Bethany laid her head back against the metal wall and thought of her old friends. Becca, Sloan, Taylor and Ellie. Her best buds all through grade, middle and high school. Nobody could have separated them. Not with a crowbar. But she hadn't spoken to any of them in over eight years.

Not that they hadn't tried. Bethany just refused.

She couldn't stand the thought of even seeing them, much less speaking to them. What they had done all those years ago was something she could never forgive them, or herself, for. She had killed Danielle Newsome and nothing she did would change that.

Water.

She leaned over and grabbed a bottle of water and twisted the top off. It was hot, but wet. She was losing water rapidly in this heat and she was probably moderately dehydrated. She looked at her severed finger in the low light and saw it was swollen and red. It throbbed and oozed blood, but it didn't seem infected yet, though it should be in this horribly hot and dirty place.

Moisture touched her foot and she looked down at it to see the floor filling with water. The tide was coming in again and she panicked. What if it was higher this time? At least she wasn't tied to the wall in a sitting position. Unless the chamber filled completely she should be all right.

The water entered rapidly and she was sitting in waist deep water in a matter of minutes. It felt cool and refreshing. All the trash in the room was floating around as the container rocked gently in the tide. She could hear it sloshing up against the sides outside.

She held on to the picture of Danielle. As the water rose higher, she made sure it did not get wet. No matter what, she would not let the picture get wet. Danielle's image needed to stay clear for her to see. She would not let it fade away. Not this time. Not ever.

* * *

Jaxon's body was buzzing.

He could feel it. It vibrated beneath his clothing, a faint pulsation that he felt all along his skin. The caffeine he had been drinking for the last two hours was coursing through his veins, yet he was exhausted. The pieces of ground glass in his eyes scraped against his lids every time he blinked. At least that's what his imagination said they were. It sure felt like glass. He'd never been this tired and not been able to sleep.

Two hours ago Ray had dropped him off at Alamo where he rented a car. He had shaken his hand and said, "I'll be there two hours behind you. Keep me informed of where you are.

Sorry I can't come just yet. I've got some actions I have to answer for."

"Thanks for sticking your neck out for me. It's important."

"Get moving and find that girl."

Find that girl. If it was possible.

This game had taken a deadly turn and much sooner than he had foreseen. When was this son-of-a-bitch going to make a mistake? When would something go Jaxon's way? He picked up the phone and dialed Vick's number. Even if it was just to hear her voice. He needed something to keep his sanity in check and she was the best thing for it. She answered quickly.

"The dead girl's stepfather's a cop."

"What?"

"The dead girl. The one that committed suicide."

"Shit."

"Yeah. A cop in Clay County. Right here in our town."

"Shit."

"I agree. That's why I'm pissed at myself for missing this."

"What's the dead girl's name?"

"Danielle Newsome. But the stepfather's name is Fanucci."

"Robert Fanucci," Jaxon said, slowly.

"Do you know him?"

"I met him yesterday. At the cache site where this all started. Damn. He pulled us over yesterday afternoon too after I hooked up with Gil and Melanie. I thought that a strange coincidence. Vick, you need to call the sheriff."

"I'm on it. I wanted to talk with you first."

"Go. Call me back when they've got him. He's got to tell us where she is."

Jaxon kept going back to Bethany Hope and the dead girl. What had she and her friends done that would cause a girl to kill herself? He knew kids were teased every minute of every day. It was just a part of growing up, but some took it a little too far.

There was always the group that thought they were better than everyone else, prettier, stronger. Hell, even Jaxon had picked on kids when he was younger. He never considered his actions back then as something that would hurt anybody. It was just a spur of the moment thing, done without thinking.

Did Bethany cause the girl to take her life? Or were there other circumstances involved? How was it living with the knowledge you may have been the reason somebody decided their life was not worth living? It must be a horrible burden. Jaxon only hoped it wasn't a burden that she would eventually pay for with her life.

CHAPTER 15

The killer watched the monitor.

Bethany was still in her place, the camera still functioning and giving him the soundless picture. It was a wonder she hadn't found it yet. She had managed to break free of her bindings at the appropriate time. If not, she would surely have drowned. He could only control so much, so the guess at her ability to free herself had been somewhat of a calculated risk. Still, it had paid off.

If she had drowned, oh well. Her death was a necessity anyway. He just wanted it to be as planned, and as the moon slipped ever closer to full, the tides cooperating with the pull of gravity, her death would arrive on time. And if the player somehow managed to discover her location, he'd take care of both of them together.

If things were progressing correctly, the player was traveling east toward Miami. The snake had done its job, he had seen to that, and the nosy guy and girl were in the hospital. He'd have to take care of them. No loose ends. The player had pretty much stuck to his plans by not involving the police or law enforcement, but the two he picked up to protect had definitely been a violation. He'd have to dish out some punishment.

Soon. And he knew just what he would do. He'd kill two birds with one stone. It would be easy.

∗ ∗ ∗

Jaxon's phone rang and Ray asked where he was.

"I'm about an hour out. You?"

"Just leaving but I've got the lights on. I'm doing about ninety on this piece of shit road. I should catch you about the time you arrive."

"The kids?"

"They're fine. I called the hospital just before calling you. He should get to go home in a couple of days. He was lucky."

"I don't know if I'd call getting bitten by an extremely deadly snake, lucky."

"True. He's lucky that he survived it. He owes you for that."

"And your friend. Thank him for me."

"Any new developments?"

Jaxon filled him in on Robert Fanucci.

"Shit. Sounds like a no-brainer. He's your guy."

"It is pretty obvious. That's what's bothering me. He wouldn't be that obvious. As good as he is at this game crap, it seems too easy."

"You know what they say. Usually criminals are idiots."

"Yeah. I've met a bunch of them. Some crafty ones too." His phone beeped. It was Vick. "Hey, gotta go. My wife is calling on the other line."

"See you in an hour."

Jaxon switched over to Vick's call. "Tell me you've found him."

"They can't locate him. He took sick leave today and he isn't answering his phone. They're on their way over to his house, but I've heard nothing yet."

"Dammit! He was working yesterday."

"Is there any way you would know this guy? Did you recognize him when you first met him?"

"No. I've never seen or heard of him before. Still thinking I'm somehow connected with this?"

"Just thinking out loud I guess. It all seems too convenient."

"I keep hearing that, but I'll be damned if I can make a connection. You're right about it being convenient, though. He made it pretty obvious with a motive. Since he's a cop, he'd have to know we'd check her out and come up with this connection."

"I know. Like we were supposed to figure this out easily."

"We're missing something, Vick. I know it. I just don't know what it is. He's keeping us busy with this stuff while he maneuvers elsewhere in the background. We're going to have to start thinking ahead of him."

"I know, you keep saying that, but I have nothing. Do you?"

He sighed. "No. Damn. I'm not angry with you. I'm just frustrated."

"You're exhausted too. I know you're not thinking straight. When's the last time you slept?"

"On the way to Naples. In the back of their car for about an hour."

"You're working on fumes. You need to recharge."

"I don't have that luxury, Vick. Time is ticking. She has less than forty hours before time is up. I'll sleep then."

"Even a short nap will help. When is Ray meeting up with you?"

"He'll catch me in Miami. He's flooring it with his lights running. The road is slowing him down though."

"Maybe you should pull over and sleep for thirty minutes while he catches up."

"Then we'll have lost thirty minutes. I'll be ok."

She sighed, frustrated with him he knew, but she understood. "Promise you'll sleep as soon as you can. Let Ray drive to the next place."

"I will."

* * *

Gil awoke from a restless nap, his hand throbbing and his eyes unable to focus.

When the room finally grew clear, he saw that Mel was not there. She must be down getting something to eat. He wished she'd go and get a hotel or something so she could rest, but she refused. She didn't seem to want to leave his side. He was even surprised that she was gone now.

His door opened and a male nurse walked in pushing a small cart with some equipment on it. The nurse was wearing a mask and though Gil knew they were all about infection control in these types of places, this was the first employee who was wearing one. Maybe he was sick.

"Time for your medication Mr. Fowler," the nurse said and he stepped to the side of his bed.

"What kind of meds?" Gil asked. "I'm tired of being drugged up. If it's a pain killer, I'll pass."

The nurse hesitated as if unsure, but then busied himself with something on the cart. "You're not having any pain, then?"

"It hurts. But I can tolerate it."

"Well, the doctor has ordered some antibiotic for the Mamba bite and we need to start that now. You don't want it getting infected."

"True."

He watched the nurse fumble with some things in the cart and then looked at his bandaged hand. Ray had told him that the hospital staff were only informed he was bitten by a poisonous snake, not a Mamba. They didn't want the media getting hold of the Mamba bit as people would freak out. He looked at the nurse again and noticed that the uniform was just a little different than the others. Not quite the same shade of pink. There was no name badge either.

"Yeah. That rattlesnake was a mean one," Gil said.

"That was no rattlesnake," the nurse said, looking at him over the top of the surgical mask. "The Black Mamba that bit you is one of the most venomous snakes in the world."

He handed Gil a handful of pills and a glass of water.

"What did you say your name was?" Gil asked.

"I didn't. But it's Collin."

Gil looked at the pills, then looked at the nurse and something must have shown on his face, because as he went to jump from the bed, the nurse grabbed him in mid leap and slammed him back into the bed.

"Not so fast, asshole. You should learn to keep your nose in your own business."

Gil went to yell, but a pillow was shoved in his face and the full weight of the man was pressing down on him.

He struggled, striking the man's back and arms, but he was incredibly strong. He suddenly heard a scream and then Mel yelling at the top of her lungs. The pressure came up off of the pillow and Gil flung it off of him. The man fled the room, knocking things down and pushing Mel out of the way in his haste and then he was gone. Mel came to him as he heard a commotion in the hall. A nurse he recognized ran into his room.

"What happened? Are you all right?"

"That male nurse just tried to kill me," Gil said. "The one running out of here."

The nurse went to Gil's phone, picked it up, listened, and then hung it up.

"Stay here. Your phone is dead. I need to call security." She left.

Gil got up and grabbed his pants.

"Are you all right?" Mel asked. Her voice shook and she had to sit down.

"We're getting out of here."

"You can't leave," she said. "You need attention."

"I'm not staying and neither are you. I won't wait around for someone to slip me something in my sleep or kill you while you're getting something to eat."

He ripped the I.V. from his arm and it started to bleed. He ignored it. Grabbing his shirt, he tried to put it on, but struggled with the bandage. "Help me, Mel! Come on!"

She jumped up and helped him get the shirt on and then he grabbed her hand and led the way out of the door. The nursing station was to the right, so he went left and headed straight for a sign that said 'Stairwell.' He pushed the door open and pulled Mel through. The stairwell was lit by one four foot fluorescent bulb on every other landing, casting shadows on walls and in the corners.

"I'm scared, Gil. Maybe we should go back."

"We're not staying. That guy is probably long gone, but he'll be back."

He led the way down and tried to listen as they went. He heard commotion from behind them and wondered if the nurse discovered they were gone already. It didn't matter. They couldn't stop him. He could leave if he wanted.

A door slammed open below them and footsteps rushed up at them from below. Gil paused, waited a beat, and then a door opened again and slammed shut. The footsteps trailed away. He continued down, the stairs seeming to rush up at him. He was still a little woozy and he stumbled, but Mel caught him and kept him from falling.

"Gil, you're still not doing well. We should stay."

"No."

He kept on going and they reached the bottom without anyone else coming into the stairwell. He pushed the door open into the parking garage and glanced around. It seemed deserted.

"Where's the car?" he whispered.

She pointed and he saw it in the distance. Looking left and right again, he saw nothing. He stepped from the cover of the stairwell and moved toward the car. A shadow leapt from the left and hit him hard. He slammed into the cement, the full weight of the guy on him as Mel screamed. He couldn't seem to catch his breath.

He felt fingers wrap around his throat and squeeze.

Mel was shouting, but her voice seemed to fade as the pressure increased. He thought his eyes were going to pop from his head. The world was turning red around the edges and the guy's eyes bore into him as everything faded.

Suddenly the pressure released and the garage slowly came back into view. Mel was standing over him holding a piece of metal in her hands and the male nurse was limping off in the opposite direction. She dropped the metal tube and bent to him.

"Come on!"

She helped him up, but the world spun crazily and he found himself back on the pavement again. He shook his head, trying to clear the cobwebs and took a deep breath. The air made a whistling noise as it tried to get past his swollen throat. He stood and was able to maintain his balance.

"Thanks," he squeaked, but he could barely hear his own voice. He coughed and wheezed as she pulled his hand along toward the car. They made it to the Mustang and she beeped the doors open. She helped him into the passenger seat and went around and cranked the car up. The roar of the engine was deafening inside the garage, but the power of the engine gave Gil strength. They may just make it out of here.

Mel dropped it into gear and punched the gas. The car leapt from the parking spot and she spun the wheel left toward the exit. She lost control as the car slid and he put a hand on her hand.

"Easy," he whispered. "It's all right. We'll be all right."

She eased up on the gas and exited the gate without paying the fee. An alarm sounded behind them, but no one followed. She sped away into the early night and breathed a sigh of relief.

Gil leaned against the window and worked the air in and out of his lungs. His ravaged throat was easing off. Maybe he would live after all.

CHAPTER 16

Jaxon met up with Ray at a Publix grocery store parking lot just off of Tamiami and I-95 in downtown Miami.

Jaxon hadn't waited very long as Ray had made good time all the way over. Gil had called him shortly after he had hung up with Vick and informed him that they had left the hospital and were on their way to them.

When Jaxon hit the roof, Gil told him what had happened at the hospital and he had grown quiet as he listened. He told them to be careful, keep their eyes open and they would wait for them. He knew it would cost them an hour or more, but if the psycho had tried to kill them twice now, actually three times if you counted the snake, there was a good chance he would try again. At least, if they were with Jaxon, they'd stand a better chance.

While they waited, Jaxon and Ray got a bite to eat at a McDonalds a block over. Jaxon told him about what happened at the hospital to Gil and Melanie.

"This guy is taking some risks now," Ray said. "He may make a mistake soon."

"That's what I'm hoping for. He's been able to keep us where he wants us so far, but as soon as he makes the mistake we've been waiting for I'll nail him to the wall."

Mel and Gil arrived at the Publix parking lot at 9:00 and Mel hugged Jaxon as soon as she saw him. "You were right. He's after us now too. All this time, I thought you just needed our help, but it looks like we really need yours."

"We stick together, we'll be all right. Is he ok?"

She shook her head. "He's still hurting, but he won't complain. I can just tell. He won't go to another hospital though. I've tried."

Gil came up, hand bandaged, smiling. He was putting on a pretty good show, but she was right. Jaxon could tell he was hurting.

"You're in no shape to be out here," Ray said.

"I'm fine. I'm not going back to the hospital. It's safer out here."

"I'm not worried about you," Ray said. "I'm worried you'll weigh us down."

"I can hold my own."

Ray shook his head, but said nothing more.

"All right, let's go. We'll take the SUV, Ray, since we can all fit in it."

"Do you have an idea where it is?" Gil asked.

"The map says Virginia Key."

Gil groaned. "Not another animal park. The Miami Seaquarium is there. Shit."

"Are there alligators there?" Mel asked.

"I would say yes," Jaxon said. "Let's go."

They loaded up and headed out.

It wasn't very far and as they paid the toll for Rickenbacker Causeway, Jaxon could see the lights of the aquarium in the distance. The GPS was showing a position further north and he showed this to Gil.

"I don't think it's the aquarium."

Gil nodded but said nothing.

After the causeway, they took Arthur Lamb Junior Road to the north and watched the beach as it floated by on their right. They passed a big gated sewage treatment plant and continued north until they reached the beach's public access. They pulled into the park and stopped. It was close. Within a hundred yards.

The lot had a few cars parked in it. Low riders. Older American made cars decked out in loud paint jobs and gleaming chrome, the suspension systems jacked up so that the car rode real low or super high. Latino music boomed from the stereos of the cars and Jaxon could feel the bass beat through the skin of the SUV. He had been hoping the place would be deserted.

They all stepped from the car and looked around. Eyes fell on them, and Jaxon could tell they were not welcome. He was used to it. Most of his career he felt this way. It was the same every time he arrived at a situation that required his attention. Cops dealt with it. Sensed it in even the minutest of places. It had bothered him at the beginning of his career. The anger and resentment directed his way, throwing him off. He was the law. A savior. Someone who restored order to the order-less and helped those in need. So when he arrived at a scene and felt a totally different vibe than the thankfulness he expected, it had surprised him.

After a while, though, he got used to it and even expected it. If he was in a place that appreciated him, then he wasn't needed. It was just the way of it.

Apparently, this place was one where a little law enforcement was lacking and he suspected that a little illegal trade was going on at the beach after sundown. Maybe even a lot of trade.

"I don't think they want us here," Mel whispered to Jaxon.

"No. They don't. But that's tough, because we're here and we aren't leaving."

A little burst of laughter from one of the scattered groups pulled Mel's attention away for a second and then she said, "There are a lot of them."

"We'll be all right."

"Great place," Ray said as he walked up. He looked nervous. Jaxon guessed he hadn't dealt with this kind of thing much in the Everglades.

"Ignore them. We'll only be here a few minutes. Which way?"

Gil pointed toward the picnic area and they headed that way, staying in their tight little group. A bonfire was burning to their right, toward the beach, and Jaxon could see the faces in the firelight. They were all looking their way.

Gil held the GPS up to his face and stopped. "This is it. Close as we're going to get."

A bathroom was sitting about twenty feet in front of them and little covered picnic areas surrounded them within that same radius. Metal barbeque grills accompanied each picnic table and a garbage can sat between every other one.

"Ray, you take Gil and search the bathroom area. Mel will stay with me and we'll look around the tables and stuff."

"What are we looking for?" Ray asked.

"Gil will explain."

They headed off to the bathroom and Mel turned to him, her eyes huge in the light of the bonfire.

"Everybody is staring at us," she said.

"Ignore them. You look in this area and I'll look here. I'll be right here."

She nodded and went to work. Jaxon glanced at the people around and noticed that they all sported a certain kind of bandana. Some wore them on their heads while others had them wrapped around their upper arms. Even the women. Most bore numerous tattoos all over their bodies and stood with that swagger Jaxon recognized as trouble. He counted them as he glanced around. Twenty-three. Not good.

The picnic tables and grills held nothing in his immediate area. He climbed up on a table and got a closer look at the eaves for the covering over the tables but nothing was hidden or attached except mud dobber wasps. One buzzed around his head and then flew off. He turned to look at Mel and noticed she was just standing there looking at him. He jumped down off of the table and said, "You all right?"

She nodded at something behind him and he turned.

Three Latino men in their early twenties stood a few feet behind him. A tall one with earrings in his right ear and a wife beater t-shirt spoke. "Who are you?"

"Nobody," Jaxon said. Mel came up next to him and stood close. He could feel the fear radiating off of her.

The guy chuckled and took a step closer. "Well, Nobody, why are you here?"

Jaxon glanced around the park and then met the man's eyes. "We're enjoying our summer vacation. We like dark, smelly places to hang out."

"What? You and your daughter?" The three laughed. Mel moved closer.

"What do you want?" Jaxon asked. "We're kind of busy."

"We noticed. We want you to leave. We don't like visitors."

"Last I heard, this was a public beach."

"Only for a certain kind of public. I'll ask you again and then we won't be so pleasant. Why are you here?"

"We like the music."

"Problem?" Ray and Gil had walked up and Ray was standing next to him. In his uniform, he was attracting even more attention. The three Latinos were no longer laughing.

"No problem," Jaxon said. "Our friends here were just welcoming us to the neighborhood. They seem awfully nice."

"I bet." Ray pulled out his badge. "Problem gentlemen?"

"Who the hell are you?" the tall one asked. "Are you even a real cop?"

"As real as they get. Now, move along. Official business here."

Ray dismissed them and showed Jaxon a box. They found it. "What the hell is that?"

The three hadn't moved and Ray acted like he hadn't noticed.

"You three still here?" He took a step toward them and put his hand on his gun. "Do I have to tell you again? Move along."

"I want to know what's in the box. Then, maybe, we'll move along."

"Not gonna happen."

"I don't see it that way. I see you four handing us what you have and then you get back in your pansy ass car and get the hell out of here. The way I see it, you don't have a choice. Not too many of your brothers around here."

Jaxon stepped forward. The three watched him but did not move. He walked right up to the tall one, stopped in front of him and leaned in close.

"I don't like you."

"Tough shit, asshole."

"We're leaving," Jaxon said, "and the box is going with us."

He straightened up and then without so much as a word, sprang forward and head butted the tall one. His nose crumpled underneath Jaxon's forehead and he went down. The one on the right hadn't even flinched and before he could even move, Jaxon slammed an elbow into his larynx and the man staggered backward grabbing his throat. A strange gargling sound came from him as he went to his knees, his eyes bulging from his head.

The one on the left was moving now and Jaxon saw the elbow coming in toward his face. He ducked and it grazed the top of his head. Crouching now, he drove his knee up into the exposed abdomen of number three and the guy bent over, the air leaving him in a violent cough. Jaxon brought both fists down on the back of his neck and the guy collapsed to the ground.

"Shit!" Ray said and grabbed Mel. "Move!"

He shoved her toward the SUV. The other twenty people stood in shock for a second and then they came to life.

"Hey! Shitheads!"

Guns started coming out from beneath shirts and pant legs.

Jaxon pushed Gil toward the car. "Time to go, kid." He pulled his gun and ran.

Shots rang out and he could hear bullets whizzing over his head. Ray was at the car and Mel jumped in as bullets starting pinging off of the metal. Ray returned fire and Jaxon watched one of them go down. He fired as he ran and the Latinos scattered for cover, their weapons hitting nothing but air as they fired wildly. Jaxon and Gil reached the car and leapt in.

"Punch it!" Jaxon shouted and the car lurched forward, the tires squealing on the pavement. Gunshots were going off all around and the side window blew out. Jaxon hoped they wouldn't shoot the tires.

The shots faded as they sped away and Jaxon was surprised no cars followed them. He guessed they had second thoughts about a shootout with all the cops that they suspected would be showing up shortly.

Mel sat up in the front as Ray pushed the SUV around the curves of the small island road. They hit the Rickenbacker Causeway and accelerated across the bridge. Jaxon told him to slow down, no one was following and Ray eased up on the gas.

"Anybody hit?" Jaxon asked, and they all answered no.

"Why the hell did you hit that guy?" Ray asked angrily. "You blew that situation all out of proportion."

"Bullshit," Jaxon said. "They weren't going to let us leave with the box. And we need it."

"How bad did we need it? Bad enough for me to shoot and possibly kill somebody? Doesn't sound like much of a tradeoff. Take a life or save a life? Come on man."

"You know for a fact those thugs will live and die by the gun. We only helped them along. They asked for it anyway."

Ray shook his head. "How the hell am I going to answer for this? Dammit!"

"You've never shot anyone have you?"

"Eat shit, Jaxon."

"You just winged him anyway. He'll be fine. I saw him grab his leg and go down."

"You're on your own," Ray said. "I can't work with you. You're as bad as the psycho sending you on this wild goose chase. I'm out."

"Fine. I don't need your help anyway. You'll just get in my way later."

"I know everybody is stressed right now," Gil said, "but you two need to calm down and think this through."

"You don't know what you're talking about," Ray said. "You don't just go into a gang's hangout and start shooting."

"Jaxon didn't. They shot first."

"You don't know what you're talking about," Ray said again.

"Please," Mel said. "I'm really scared right now and I need you two to stop fighting. Aren't we supposed to be saving a girl? Please."

Jaxon shut his mouth and looked into the rear view mirror. Ray was staring at him. Jaxon shook his head and sat back. "That's the point," he said. "Saving this girl."

Ray said nothing.

CHAPTER 17

Jaxon was losing it. He wasn't himself.

The exhaustion was causing him to make stupid and rash decisions and his patience was very thin. Normally, he would not have head butted an asshole unless he had no other choice, and as he looked back at the situation, he could say the choice had been made for him. Give the thugs the box, or head butt the guy. Still, it had escalated way beyond anything he had imagined and now Ray didn't trust him. Not a good thing. Even in short lived partnerships, if your partner didn't trust you, the outcome was probably not going to be good.

On the police radio, calls were coming in of shots fired somewhere in Key Biscayne and units were mobilizing. They weren't really at any risk of being detained, but Jaxon still didn't like all the activity in the area.

Gil was sitting quietly in the back holding his bandaged hand and Melanie sat up front staring out into the night. They had looked in the box and found another note. The message cryptic, but Gil had known what it was right away.

It had read, *Night time is a lonely time. A time for reflection, a time for thought. This night, you must reflect on what you are after. Is it salvation? Redemption? Entertainment? You'll have to be a trooper and a tracker. Many things will get in the way, but you've come this far. Come a little farther… 2 2 8 / 8 3 7*

"It's a night cache," Gil had said.

"I take it that means one we will only find at night. What? Does it glow or something?" Jaxon asked.

"Actually, yes. The site is identified by special reflectors called FireTacks that can only be seen with a flashlight. A lot of times they form a trail to follow directly to the cache."

The rest of the message had only a few numbers with some left blank. Or so Jaxon thought. Apparently the rest were written in invisible ink or lemon juice or some other reagent that reacted to heat. Gil had taken his lighter and run it under the paper and the rest of the numbers appeared. The waypoint was in Kissimmee.

After some more discussion which involved Ray leaving the group and going back to Naples, Jaxon had made amends and convinced him to stay. He needed him. The kids were great at solving these puzzles, but they were useless if they ran up against anything like what happened in Miami. He reluctantly agreed, but didn't like the next decision. His vehicle was shot up and when they got back to the Publix parking lot, they discovered the radiator had a hole in it. He didn't want to leave it but they had no other choice.

They climbed into the Mustang, leaving Ray's SUV and Jaxon's rental car, and headed north. Gil was not driving. Since Ray had had little sleep, Jaxon not too far behind, and Gil without a license and still suffering some affects of the snake bite, Mel was driving so they all could rest.

Jaxon watched the lights of the highway flash by and thought of Vick. He had talked to her briefly and brought her up to speed. She was feeling the exhaustion too and Jaxon told her to get some rest while they drove. Nothing she could do in the middle of the night anyway. She agreed and said she would try.

"Call me if anything happens," she said.

"I will, but I'll probably be asleep myself. How are the locals doing up there? Are they muscling in?"

"I've kept them in the loop, but have told them the FBI is investigating."

"That's not like you, Vick. Using your brothers as a convenient excuse. Could backfire on you if they call Holt."

"I know. Just trying to keep it quiet. Fanucci probably knows we're on to him anyway. Nothing we could do about it."

"I think he's having way too much fun with this game. I think she's still alive."

"I hope so."

Jaxon watched the lights and his eyelids grew heavy. Thirty-six hours left. The clock was ticking. He slept and dreamt of snakes.

* * *

Three hours later they were at a rest stop.

Jaxon was shaken awake, his dream following him into the harsh lighting of the parking lot. He jumped and reached for his gun but caught himself before scaring Mel to death.

"You all right?" she asked as she stepped back from the car door.

He shook his head awake. "Yeah. Just a dream. Where are we?"

"We're at the next spot. We're parked in a rest stop but the waypoint is in a field next to it. Ray and Gil are in the bathroom. You were sleeping like a rock."

"What time is it?"

"One a.m."

Jaxon climbed out of the back seat. "I need to use the john. I'll be right back."

He passed Gil and Ray on the way and Gil said, "You look like crap."

"Thanks. I'll be all right. You look like crap too."

"But I was bitten by the world's deadliest snake."

"Not the deadliest."

"In the top ten."

"Whatever. I gotta piss. Mel is waiting at the car."

Gil chuckled at him and Jaxon felt himself grin. At least Gil was doing better.

Back at the car, Gil took the GPS and Ray's flashlight and they climbed the fence to the field. "All right," he said, "this works just like you think it will. We get close to the waypoint and then we shine the flashlight around until we find the first reflector. It will be bright orange or red. With the brightness of this tactical LED flashlight, it should be very bright when the light hits it. Then we find the next FireTack and follow the path. It should take us to the cache."

"Let's go," Ray said looking around in the dark. "Keep your eyes peeled for anything weird."

"Us in this field in the middle of the night isn't weird enough?" Mel asked.

They moved as a group into the field following the GPS. When they got within the twenty-five foot area, Gil stopped and panned the light around. The first FireTack shone bright to the left of their track. Gil moved to it quickly. It was stuck in the ground with grass growing all around it. Even though it was mostly hidden, the flashlight had exposed it like a beacon in the dark.

"We would have never found this in the day," Jaxon said.

"That's why it's a night cache only."

"This is fun," Mel said.

Jaxon chuckled. "I'm glad one of us is having fun."

Gil tapped some keys on the GPS and Jaxon noticed a small graph pop up on the screen.

"What are you doing?"

"Sometimes these night caches have you follow a trail of FireTacks and plot each tack on a GPS that can plot points. Mine can. When we've found all the tacks it can spell out a phrase or numbers. I'm plotting all the FireTacks now in case we need to look at the plot to find the cache. A lot of people do this as an added level of difficulty because the FireTacks are usually pretty easy to find. It's the cache that will be difficult in the dark."

"Got it."

The next FireTack showed up about twenty feet ahead and they moved toward it. Gil plotted it and they found the next one. This went on for about a half hour. Finding FireTacks and plotting the position, searching for the next one and then moving on.

At one point, they lost the trail and had to search around for a few minutes until the tack showed itself half buried in a cow patty.

They moved through the rest of the points rapidly, and when they came to a spot with three FireTacks lined up next to each other, Gil said that was the end. He held up the GPS and showed them the plot. It was the outline of Mickey Mouse.

"Great," Jaxon said.

"I love Disney," Mel said.

"How are we supposed to find a cache in all of Disney World without any GPS position?" Jaxon said. "We could spend days on it."

"There are only two GeoCaches in Disney World," Gil said. "And one of them is a virtual cache."

"What's a virtual cache?" Ray asked.

"You just have to prove you were there to log it. Like taking a picture of yourself and posting it to the servers. It's in front of Cinderella's castle at the end of Main Street."

"I take it you know where the other one is?" Jaxon said.

Gil nodded. "It's officially sanctioned by Disney. It's a pain in the ass."

"Why?"

"Because it's at the bottom of a lagoon."

"How the hell do we get to that?" Ray said.

"You have to sign up at the main gate and pay a fee for scuba equipment."

"Who knows how to scuba?" Jaxon asked.

"I do," Ray said. "I got a certificate."

"That's all fine and good," Gil said. "The problem will be getting to it on short notice. They have a waiting list that's like a month long."

"Shit."

"And the park doesn't open until 10:00."
Jaxon started walking back to the car.
"Where are you going?" Ray said after him.
"To break into Disney World."
"I was hoping you weren't going to say that."

CHAPTER 18

"It can't be done," Gil said. "By the time we figure it out and get what we need to break in, it will be time to open anyway. We might as well wait."

Jaxon stared at the satellite view of the park and shook his head. "I can't believe that security is so tight for an amusement park. What the hell do they have in there?"

"Just the most beloved theme park in the whole world," Gil said. "It attracts millions of worldwide visitors a year with the promise of fun and joy without the worry of injury or safety issues. They take it pretty seriously."

"You sound like a brochure. We are wasting valuable time," Jaxon said. "I know he planned it this way, but dammit, we need to find a way around this."

"I don't see any other way," Ray said. "We'll get in there at 10:00 and then we'll start throwing our weight around to get us in a scuba suit and to the bottom of that lagoon."

"I think we can get in through this hotel, commandeer a boat here and get to the cache site. All we need is some snorkeling equipment. You know where it is, Gil, right?"

Gil nodded. "I've done it."

"We're going to need more than that," Mel said. "We're gonna need luck."

"That's what you're here for," Jaxon said and smiled.

"I'm going to get fired," Ray said. "I've probably lost my job already after shooting that guy."

"Then you have nothing to lose," Jaxon said. "I could use another investigator anyway."

"You're in a pretty damn good mood," Ray said. "This won't work."

"It won't if we sit here. Look. I'll take all the risk. Just help me get in there and I'll do the rest."

"Have you ever snorkeled before?"

"Can't be that hard. You just breathe through a tube, right?"

Ray shook his head. "That water is probably murky too. You won't be able to see five feet in front of you."

"I'll figure it out."

Ray sighed. "I'll do it. I'm the only one who's even come close to doing anything like this."

"Didn't think you'd be doing anything like this, did you? It'll be fun."

"I can't wait."

"Where do we get snorkeling gear?" Mel asked.

"Walmart," Gil said. "They're open 24/7. I'm sure they have it."

"Walmart it is," Jaxon said and they loaded up.

They pulled into the Super Walmart on Vineland road and went in.

At this hour of the night, the aisles were filled with boxes and stock items and the shoppers were sparse and strange. These were definitely night people. Women in slippers, men in bathrobes grabbing anti-diarrheal medication or Tylenol for their kids, late night partiers in need of some cheap entertainment. They really were Walmart people.

They found a snorkel set that included fins and a mask and they paid quickly and got out.

They followed Vineland Road north until it became Winter Garden and then eventually turned left on Vista Blvd. At Fort Wilderness entrance they turned right. The road was deserted. It wound through the Fort Wilderness resort area for a few miles and they eventually stopped when it ended at Trail's End on Bay Lake in the Walt Disney World resort.

The area was quiet at 3 a.m. Ray pulled the car into an empty slot under a big tree and they got out. Ray had also bought swim trunks and he went behind a small outbuilding and changed. He came out from behind looking like a tourist with the mask and snorkel on his head and the fins in his hands. Mel giggled in the quiet night and he glared at her.

"Sorry," she said.

"You know the plan," Jaxon said to Gil and Melanie. "If somebody questions you, you're out for a little midnight tryst in the park. Move along and then come back to get us as soon as you can. Ray and I go to the cache site. We should be no more than thirty minutes."

"Got it," Gil said. "Remember, look for something different down there. This is a public cache site and he probably planted something when he was down there. It could be anything."

"That will be the hard part," Jaxon said. "Figuring out what he's left us."

"Good luck," Mel said.

Jaxon and Ray made their way to the shore area. There were cabanas and picnic areas to their right, and lounge chairs directly in front of them. A large pier stood at the end of the cabanas with a few boats moored and two large ferries for park goers. Surprisingly, no security was present. Jaxon did see a boat moving slowly in the bay, but it was a good distance away.

"Must be a patrol of some sort," Jaxon whispered. "We'll need to avoid it."

Ray nodded.

They moved to their left. A smaller dock was nestled up against a wooded area and it held paddle boats and small johnboats. On the dock, Jaxon saw that they were tied with a kind of alarm system that would go off if they were disconnected from the line. Jaxon expected as much and pulled out the rope they had purchased at the store. He tied one end to the johnboat next to the one they were going to take and then secured the other end to the security line and then cut the line to their boat. It still had pressure on the line so it did not alarm. They quietly got in and pushed off.

The water was dark and quiet as they rowed toward Discovery Island. The cache point was just on the other side. They made good time with Jaxon rowing and he watched Ray shiver in the night air.

A boat rounded the island to their left and Jaxon pointed. It had lights on it and they could see two men in uniform sitting at the controls. It trolled slowly around the island heading for them. Ray pointed to a dock on the island and Jaxon changed course heading for it. At the dock, Jaxon grabbed hold of the wood and stopped them.

The johnboat banged against the mooring and the sound echoed across the water. The two men on the patrol boat heard it and stood, looking toward the sound. A spotlight came on and its beam shone directly toward them, but they had ducked down in the boat and the light passed overhead, searching. The crew looked for a few minutes more, then the light was doused and the boat slowly moved on.

Ray sat up and Jaxon resumed rowing. They stayed behind the patrol boat, following it to the other side of the island. It moved off to the right toward the opposite shore and Jaxon and Ray circled left toward a pylon that stood thirty yards offshore of the Discovery Island. As they came up to it a sign read *Discovery Island Cache. Welcome GeoCachers of the world.*

Jaxon tied the johnboat to the pylon and Ray slipped into the water silently without a word. Jaxon watched his light come on under the water and he worried it could be seen from a distance, but as he sank to the lagoon floor, the light grew dim. The water was pretty murky.

Ray surfaced after a minute and a half and took a few breaths through the snorkel and then he was down again. He worked the light on and off whenever he came to the surface. He stayed down for two minutes this time and then came up and hung on to the boat.

He caught his breath and said, "I don't see a thing. I found the cache, but it's basically a rock with a number on it. I'm assuming it's one of those virtual caches Gil talked about. Where you have to take a picture next to it. I don't know."

"Is there anything else in the area?"

He shook his head. "Just sand and water grass. Visibility is only a few feet."

"Dig around in the mud and see if there is a box or container there. See if the rock will move and check under it."

Ray nodded and was gone. Another three minutes passed and then he surfaced gasping for air.

"Got it."

He held on to the side of the boat and caught his breath. After a few seconds he handed a Tupperware container to Jaxon and then climbed in.

"It was under the rock," he whispered. "I had to dig a little."

Jaxon untied the rope and started rowing. Ray shivered in the night air and tried drying himself with his hands. He grinned in the gloom and Jaxon nodded at him.

As they rounded the island on the east side, they could see the lights of the shore and even the car parked in the distance. At least no one had bothered Gil and Mel. They'd be back in the car in ten minutes.

Leaving the island behind, Jaxon rowed faster as they crossed the open water between land areas. They heard a motor before they saw it and Jaxon cursed. The patrol boat was back and it was making good time directly toward them. The spotlight was not on. It grew closer rapidly and Jaxon looked at Ray. It was headed right for them. There was only one thing to do.

Ray was in the water quickly and Jaxon followed holding on to the side and putting the boat between him and the patrol. Ray held on right next to him.

"Where's the cache?" Ray asked.

"Shit!"

Jaxon jumped back up leaning into the boat and grabbed for the cache. It slipped away out of his grasp and he sank back in the water. He climbed back up into it and grabbed the cache.

He could see the faces of the boat crew in the light of the instrument panel. They were that close.

As he sank back in the water, the patrolmen saw the johnboat. Slowing, the patrol boat's spotlight came on and light bathed the johnboat and water around Jaxon and Ray. They were hidden behind the boat in the water, but he didn't know if they could stay that way.

The patrol boat idled up alongside the johnboat and the light swung back and forth over the craft. Jaxon could hear the two talking.

"Looks like a johnboat broke loose from the mooring."

"That's weird. I wonder why the alarm didn't go off."

"Maybe the battery is dead. It's happened before."

"Tie it off. We'll tow it back in."

Jaxon looked at Ray and he signaled down. Jaxon nodded.

The boat rocked as one of the guys climbed on board and tied it to the patrol boat. It rocked again as the guy stepped off. The patrol boat's motor increased in RPM and then the johnboat was jerked out of their hands.

Jaxon dove down as did Ray and they hung there in the water for what seemed an eternity. The light above slowly dimmed as Jaxon thought his lungs would burst. Finally he surfaced and watched the patrol boat moving away at a good clip. Ray came up next to him breathing hard. He pulled the snorkel from his mouth.

"I guess we get to swim."

Jaxon grinned and they started swimming. After the patrol boat dropped the johnboat off at the dock, tying it back up, it drove off to the west and continued its patrol. Jaxon and Ray reached the shore a few minutes later, exhausted and wet, but glad it was a success. Jaxon was still in his camo outfit of course and it sloshed as he walked through the sand. They strode up to the beach and looked in the Mustang. It was empty.

* * *

Gil shivered in the night air and wondered if he was getting a fever. He hadn't been feeling too well the last couple of hours and though he knew it would take a while to recover from the snakebite, he was disappointed in himself. He wasn't functioning at 100% and he didn't like it. He and Mel were leaning against the car watching Jaxon and Ray row away into the night when a car engine signaled its approach and they watched a security vehicle pull into the parking lot. It moved slowly through the lot, cruising up and down the rows.

Every once in a while it stopped and a flashlight beam shone from within the vehicle, inspecting whatever they were supposed to inspect. Gil motioned for Mel to get in the car. He slipped in beside her and shut the door.

The patrol vehicle approached the Mustang and then stopped. The flashlight came on and illuminated the inside of the car. After it found them in the back, the light clicked off and then two men got out. They approached the Mustang and knocked on the window. Gil thumbed it down and a man with bottle bottom glasses and a very thin mustache spoke.

"You folks need to retire to your room. We don't allow loitering in vehicles."

"Yes, sir," Gil said. "We'll head right back. Sorry." He opened the door and he and Mel got out.

The man's partner, a short, older gentleman who chewed on a toothpick and leered at Mel, said, "Enjoying your visit?"

Bottle bottom glasses guy looked away and tried to keep from laughing.

"Yeah," Gil said. "It's great here. Again, we're sorry."

"No problem," toothpick said. "Have a special night." He waved.

Gil blipped the car locks and grabbed Mel's hand. They started walking toward the resort area and Gil could feel the two patrolmen's eyes following them. They entered a covered walkway and then turned right, leaving the parking lot behind. Gil stopped.

"That was close," Mel said. "I can't believe they didn't even ask to see our room key or anything."

"Yeah. I think they were too busy thinking about what we were doing. Let me check if they are gone."

Gil peeked back around the corner and saw the two walking around the Mustang. Short, toothpick guy stopped at the back and wrote down the license plate. Bottle bottom glasses shone the flashlight inside the car and then they both got back in and drove off.

"They took the plate. Shit."

"Do you think they'll check it?"

"I don't know. But we better not waste any time getting out of here. Come on, Jaxon. Hurry up."

Gil looked out toward the water, but could not make them out. He did see a boat slowly cruising around the bay. That was not good.

* * *

Jaxon tried the door and it was locked. "Where the hell…?"

Ray bent over, peering inside the Mustang. He stood. "I wonder what happened."

"We need to get the hell out of here."

A sudden noise behind them caused them to jump as Gil and Mel came running up.

"You're all wet," Gil said to Jaxon.

"No shit. Everything ok? Where were you?"

"Security found us and sent us back to our room."

"They didn't ask for ID?" Ray said.

"No, but they wrote our license plate down. We need to get out of here, now."

"I agree."

Gil unlocked the doors and they all climbed in quickly. Lights shone in the distance and Gil cranked the car up and headed in the opposite direction toward the resort area's exit.

"Did you get it?" Gil asked.

"Yeah," Jaxon said. "We had our own run in with security."

"That boat?"

"Did you see it?"

"We saw it cruising around out there. What happened?"

"I'll tell you in a bit. Just drive and get us out of here before security returns."

Gil accelerated and moved through the curves of the road expertly. No one else joined them on the road. At Vista Boulevard they turned left and headed back into town. Jaxon told Gil and Mel what had happened.

"Man that is awesome! I can't believe you didn't get caught," Gil said. "I bet you shit your pants."

"Just find a gas station or something," Ray said. "I want to get back into some dry clothes."

"Only for a minute," Jaxon said. "We have to get moving to the next point."

"What was in the box?" Mel asked.

"We haven't opened it yet."

"I hope it's what you needed," she said.

"Me too. We didn't have time."

Jaxon opened the box and pulled out a piece of paper. He read it out loud.

I'm amazed. I assume that since you're reading this, you have somehow gotten to the bottom of Bay Lake and retrieved this cache. Congrats. A little bonus for you. I'm not what you think I am. You may just figure this out. In that case, I'll be waiting for you. Enough about me, here's the next stop. Bethany is waiting. N30° 9.51792', W81° 43.90974'

Jaxon plugged the lat/longs into the GPS and stared at the map.

"Shit!"

"What?" Mel asked.

Jaxon ignored her and picked up his phone. He dialed quickly. Vick answered on the fifth ring.

"You need to get out of the house. Now!"

She sounded half asleep. "Why? What is it? Where are you?"

"Just go, Vick. Don't pack, don't shower, don't do anything, just put some clothes on, take your phone and get out. He knows who I am."

"What? How?"

"The next waypoint. It's our house. Call me when you're out. Move!"

CHAPTER 19

Bethany stared at the picture.

Danielle was in her band uniform, next to a palm tree, smiling, holding a clarinet, with the ocean behind her. In the glow of the moon, she looked happy. Then the tide shifted the box she was in and the light winked out. Danielle disappeared. Bethany held her breath and waited. The box shifted again and the moon shone through the crack. Danielle was still there. She breathed.

Every time Danielle disappeared, Bethany's heart sank and she went back to that horrible place where Danielle died. Not the day she took her life. But the day when Bethany and her friends took away everything she had. The day they made her ashamed of what she was. The day they killed her spirit. The day she began wishing for death to take her away.

It had all started normally, then went to hell quickly.

The locker room was always a place of rumors. If you had something to spread there was nothing like being naked in a public place to remove any inhibitions that might hold you back. At least for some.

Bethany's best friend on the squad was Rebecca Murray, but everybody called her Becca. That day in the locker room, Becca came running up to Bethany, looking like something was about to burst from her.

She sat on the bench and whispered, "I saw them."

"Who? What are you talking about?"

"Mary."

"No way."

Becca nodded, the smile growing on her face.

The rumors had been flying around the campus that two girls were hot for each other and one of them was Mary Masterson. Mary was a junior who wore biker clothes, had her hair cut short and generally tried to look like a dude. She had been easy to spot and didn't seem to care what people said about her. And there was always a lot being said. She took shop, worked on cars, and did basically anything a guy would do except play football. And that was only because the guys didn't want her around.

"I saw them behind the lockers in the math wing," Becca said. "They were kissing. It was gross."

"Who was the other girl?"

"That's what's so funny. You know the geeky little thing in band? She's plays clarinet, I think. She always has stupid stuffed animals in her backpack."

"Danielle Newsome?"

"Yeah. That's her. They were kissing and Danielle looked like she liked it. We know Mary did."

Bethany couldn't believe it. Two lesbians in her school.

Bethany had even talked to Danielle a few times in geometry. She had seemed nice enough, just a little shy. Not the kind of girl Bethany would hang out with, but at least someone she would talk to now and then.

"When was this?"

"Just a few minutes ago."

"Oh my God. I have to see. Let me get dressed and show me."

Bethany threw her clothes on and they ran to the math wing.

Becca put her finger to her lips as she opened the door and they slipped in quietly. Becca led the way, tiptoeing to the back of the lockers and peeking around. She pulled back and nodded her head, grinning. She moved out of the way and let Bethany in.

She didn't know what to expect, but what she saw surprised her. Mary was holding Danielle's hand and her arm was wrapped around her. She was staring into Danielle's eyes and Bethany almost didn't recognize her. Her face had changed. It was so soft and caring and the look she had on her face was one she wouldn't recognize herself for a few years. Then Mary leaned in and kissed Danielle. On the lips. Danielle kissed her back and it grew more passionate.

Bethany had kissed a few boys in her life and she had liked it of course, but this was something different. It was like a movie. The kiss was so deep and so passionate, Bethany just stared and wished in her heart that she had something like this. Something this strong and this special. And that's when the flash on Becca's camera ruined everything.

Mary's face pulled away from Danielle, and Bethany watched it change immediately to one of shock, and then rage. Then the camera flashed again.

Danielle's face had turned toward them and she looked like a deer in the headlights. Bethany would never forget that look. It was what she saw in her mind every time she thought of that day. The face that broke her heart. The fear that tore at her soul and left her feeling empty and lonely.

"Hey!" Mary had shouted and then Becca pulled on Bethany's arm. Giggling she said, "Come on!" and ran.

Bethany took one more look at the two and saw something in Danielle's face that haunted her still. It was a plea. For her to let it go. Her face said 'Please' and Bethany ignored it. She ran.

Later that night, Bethany, Becca, Sloan, Taylor, and Ellie were all at Becca's house looking at the two pictures on Becca's camera. They laughed and made up names for the two, pointing to the second picture where Mary's face was turning to the camera in surprise and Danielle could be seen half turned toward the lens. But you could tell who both of the girls were.

Becca was uploading the pictures to her MySpace page and the other girls were giving her things to put for the caption. Bethany had stayed mostly quiet, until Sloan had said to her, "I can't believe them. How gross. How could someone do that?"

Bethany had nodded and said, "I know. I can't believe it. But don't you think it's bad to put those pictures up on MySpace? Everybody will see them."

"That's what we want," Becca had said. "We need to expose these two for what they really are."

Under the pictures on the web, they had put 'One time at band camp…' and hit submit.

The world now knew and there was no taking it back.

Danielle killed herself two weeks later.

Bethany stared at the picture in the sliver of moonlight and held on to the image as the box shifted with the tide. She closed her eyes as the picture went dark, but instead of the smiling Danielle Newsome with her clarinet in front of the ocean, wearing her band uniform, she saw the face that would haunt her for life. The pain and shock behind those lockers when the flash went off on Becca's camera. And in her mind, Bethany could even hear the girl's voice in her head.

"Please."

CHAPTER 20

Victoria didn't listen to Jaxon.
There was no way she was leaving her house without a few precious things. She grabbed a bag in the closet and threw in some clothes, then went to the study and took the pictures of Michael off of the mantle and put them in the bag. The last thing she had to have was the laptop computer on her desk. Then she ran from the house. As she opened the front door to run out, a blast of heat and pressure threw her forward into the yard and then the sound of her house exploding behind her filled her ears. She lay on the lawn, ears ringing, head swimming, thinking that at least she had saved Michael. At least she had saved Michael. Then the world went dark.

* * *

Jaxon ran in to the hospital and screamed at the receptionist.
After she told him she would not tolerate him treating her like that, he finally got himself under sufficient control to learn his wife was in room 2432. He ran to the room and showed some ID to the uniform standing at her door and he let him in.

She was lying in the bed, a bandage on her forehead, her eyes closed, holding a picture of Michael in her hand. He touched her softly and her eyes opened. She started to cry.

He held her gently and said, "I'm sorry, Vick. So sorry. I should have been here."

She shook her head and pulled away. "I'm all right. I'm just angry."

"So am I. I'll find this guy. I promise."

"We'll find this guy. We got careless. I won't let that happen again. This is the second time a house has blown up on me. I'm not about to let this asshole get away with it. It was my house."

"I don't want you near this thing."

She grew even angrier.

"What? You do remember that I was a cop and an FBI agent too. Don't treat me like some little scared girl you can cuddle and make all better. We work this together. You and me. You need my help anyway."

He hung his head. He knew she would be this way. She was right, of course, but it was hard to put her in harm's way. He wanted nothing more than for her to be that scared little girl he could cuddle and then hide away from the monsters. Only she wasn't and he was thankful for that too.

He took her hand in his. "You and me."

She squeezed his hand and then squirmed in her bed. "These bandages are driving me crazy. They itch like mad."

He sat her up, watching her grimace, and looked at her back. She had bandages covering her from shoulders to hips. Small blood spots had seeped through in a few places. He winced.

"Scratch them for me," she said, wriggling against him. He scratched her gently and she smiled. "Oh, you don't know how good that feels."

He must have hit a sensitive spot, because she flinched and then pulled away. She looked angry again. "I can't believe this happened again."

"I'm just happy you've survived two houses blowing up in your face. You should be proud. Not too many people can claim that."

She grinned then. "Strike three and I'm out? I only get one more."

He laughed and then he heard a knock on the door. It swung open slowly when he answered and Ray, Gil, and Mel came in. Ray carried some flowers in his hand. Mel had balloons.

"I hope we're not intruding," Ray said. "We just wanted to see how you were. Hi. I'm Ray."

Vick reached for the flowers, smiling, and took his hand in hers.

"I'm Victoria."

Gil and Melanie introduced themselves and then they all left. Jaxon said he would be down in a few minutes. Ray nodded and closed the door behind them.

"Your team," she said. "I like them."

"They've been lifesavers."

She nodded and grew thoughtful again. "Have you been to the house?"

"Not yet. I'm going there next. I wanted to make sure you were ok."

"I didn't look for the clue. I got out like you said."

"Not exactly like I said."

She smiled sheepishly. "I know. I couldn't leave without Michael."

He understood and picked up the picture of his dead son. He set it on her nightstand and adjusted it so she could look at him.

"How long will you be in?"

"I should be out of here in a few hours," she said. "They wanted to make sure I didn't have a concussion. I don't."

"Go to the motel we stayed when we first got here. You remember? I won't tell anyone where you are. Especially the police. I talked with the detective on the phone and they still haven't found Fanucci. He hasn't called in or reported for duty."

"He's been too busy."

Jaxon nodded. "I'll stay."

"No. You know you can't. I know you won't. I'll call when I'm out and we'll get this guy. Now go."

He grabbed her hand and she pulled him to her. He kissed her gently, lingering a little longer than normal. He knew she had been lucky and he felt a little like he was abandoning her. She pulled away and let his hand go.

"Go find him. Beat the crap out of him for me."

He closed the door behind him and fought the urge to stay. The cop at the door nodded to him and Jaxon told him to keep his eyes open. He turned and walked out of the hospital.

The asshole was out there and he had to find him. But first, he had a girl to find.

* * *

Jaxon stepped from the Mustang and surveyed the ruined wreckage of his home.

The fire had been mostly contained within the first floor, but the blast had wreaked havoc on the front of the house and the second floor master bedroom. If he had to guess, he would say there were charges left in two separate places inside the house. What Jaxon really wanted to know was how did they get there?

The fire marshal was standing by the front door. Jaxon flashed his ID at the cop by the driveway and approached his ruined abode. He introduced himself to the fire marshal and asked him for his opinion.

"I don't normally discuss things like this before I've made a thorough analysis, but since you're a retired cop and it's your house, I'll tell you what I think."

"Thanks."

"Two incendiary devices were discharged within the confines of the house. One on the second floor inside the master bath. You can see the destruction caused by that unit from out here. Upstairs, it's even more conclusive. The unit downstairs was placed behind the couch in the living room."

He stepped inside the ruined doorway and pointed to the couch. Or what was left of it.

"The piece of furniture absorbed quite a bit of the blast, but not all. The windows and doors were all blown outward from the pressure wave and the fire that ensued was the couch burning and then spreading to the walls. Not much fire upstairs, just mostly blast damage. You'll be able to rebuild."

"What kind of incendiary?" Jaxon asked.

"Unknown at this point. I haven't tested any residue. If I had to guess, I would say C4."

"Plastic explosive? Pretty edgy stuff."

"Somebody wanted damage without a lot of material. Didn't take much to do this. It would be easy to hide that way."

Jaxon wandered into the kitchen and saw it was mostly intact. The window over the sink was gone, but most of the appliances and dishes remained in good shape. The fire marshal followed, keeping quiet. When Jaxon entered the family room, the man spoke up.

"Don't know what that means, but it was drawn on the walls with some kind of heat reactive material. Do you know what it is?"

Jaxon nodded.

On the wall, brown and ugly in three foot letters, was a set of lat/longs written in a looping hand. Probably lemon juice. More invisible ink.

Jaxon did not like the idea that this guy had the time to plant the explosives in his house, and then write his message in lemon juice on his walls, all while either Vick was asleep or out of the house. The problem was, Vick hadn't left the house in almost two days. She had been busy helping Jaxon with the investigation. He must have done it when she napped or slept. That was not good.

"What does it mean?"

"It's a message. For me."

Jaxon walked out of the house and left the fire marshal behind shrugging his shoulders. The detective in charge of this investigation stood with Ray and the kids next to the Mustang. He watched with a wary eye as Jaxon walked up.

"You Jennings?" he asked.

"Yes. You?"

"I'm Detective Tate. The sheriff would like you to come down to the station and answer a few questions."

"I don't have time right now. He should know that. Has he found Fanucci?"

"No. And you'll have to make time. It's not a request."

"Am I under arrest?"

"No."

"Then it can wait."

"The sheriff isn't going to like this."

"I don't care." Jaxon turned, ignoring him, and he walked away. "Gil, give me the GPS."

Gil handed it over and Jaxon punched in the numbers from his smoke damaged wall.

"Where did you get those?" Gil asked.

"They were written in lemon juice on my wall. The heat of the blast and fire activated it."

"How did he get in there without your wife knowing?"

"That's what I want to know."

Jaxon watched as the waypoint centered on the map.

Well, at least it was back here in Jacksonville and they hadn't wasted too much time coming home. The only problem was it was smack dab in the middle of Naval Air Station Jacksonville off US17 on the Westside.

"Looks like we get to hassle with the military," he said and handed the GPS to Ray.

"Anybody ex-military?" Ray asked.

"I am," Jaxon said and opened the door to the Mustang. "I'll need to drive. Let's go."

They made good time to the entrance and pulled up to the security building.

The Mustang did not have a sticker and could not get in without clearance. Jaxon would have to get passes for them all anyway. As they stepped from the car, Jaxon noticed the extra

Marines at the gate and watched as cars were being turned away. "Shit," he said. "They're on lockdown. Dammit!"

"What does that mean?" Gil asked.

"It means they're going to give us a hard time."

"But you're prior military."

"There's some kind of security alert. When that happens, only active military are allowed. We'll have to see. Come on."

They walked in to the building and stepped up to the counter. The room was small and painted an ugly off yellow color that Jaxon always associated with the military. They must have bought tens of thousands of gallons of the stuff and were using it until it ran out.

A Marine sentry stood guard at the door. He had an M4 rifle slung over his shoulder and a Kevlar helmet on his head. A computer screen sat on the counter and a security camera pointed its lens at them from the other side of the desk. The sergeant behind the counter looked them up and down and said, "Base access restricted to active duty personnel only."

"I figured as much," Jaxon said to him. "But I have a special situation and I need to gain access." He pulled his ID and showed it to the man. "I'm investigating a case and it's very time sensitive. We need to get in right now."

"I'm sorry, sir. That is not possible."

Jaxon pulled out another form of ID and flashed it to the man. "I'm also ex-Army. MPs. I need a favor."

The sergeant looked him in the eye. "My hands are tied. I can't let you in. You'll have to come back tomorrow."

Jaxon lost it.

"Tomorrow? Didn't you hear me, sergeant?" He spoke in his command voice from his days as a captain in the Army. The man reacted slightly, then regained his composure. He stood stoic and did not budge. "I'm on a time sensitive case and there is evidence located inside this base. A girl's life is at stake."

"Authorized personnel only, sir."

"Dammit!" Jaxon slammed his hand on the desk.

He knew it was not the thing to do, but the exhaustion and frustration he felt was taking its toll. The Marine standing guard at the door came to a ready position and lowered his weapon. He stepped toward Jaxon and placed a hand on his shoulder.

"I need you to leave, sir," the Marine said.

Jaxon shrugged him off, violently, and pointed his finger at the sergeant across the counter.

"This girl's life is on your head," he shouted. "If she dies, I'm personally going to come down here and have your ASVAB Waiver revoked, then I'll see to it myself you find your way to the hospital."

Ray touched his arm. "Easy, Jaxon."

The sergeant's face turned an ugly shade of red and he nodded at the Marine sentry. Another Marine appeared, slinging his rifle, and grabbed Jaxon's left arm while the first, his right.

"You need to come with us, sir." They held him tightly and he fought for a second, then pointed at the sergeant.

"You'll regret this."

The sergeant was on the phone as the Marines escorted him to another room.

Ray, Gil and Melanie followed all looking shocked.

They sat Jaxon down in a chair that was bolted to the floor and handcuffed him to it. They motioned for Ray and the other two to sit in the remaining chairs. They were not restrained.

"What now, Marine," Ray asked.

"The local police are on the way. You'll be taken into custody."

The Marine closed the door and remained standing guard inside.

Ray turned to Jaxon, "Well, it looks like you're going to get to talk to the sheriff whether you like it or not."

Ten minutes later, Detective Will Tate showed up with a patrolman. He looked at Jaxon and shook his head.

"Looks like you're going to get to talk to the sheriff after all."

"So I've heard. Listen. I really need to get in here. I need a favor."

"You should have thought of that an hour ago. You haven't made me want to jump through any hoops for you. I had to go back to the station and explain why the small task I was given hadn't been completed. Now, you want me to go to bat for you?"

"It's not for me. A girl's life is at stake. I'm running out of time."

"Let's go talk to the sheriff and you can explain it to him."

He nodded at the Marine who unlocked the handcuffs and Jaxon was free. Tate gestured to the other three and they all walked out of the office.

Jaxon paused at the desk. He pulled out his cell phone.

"Let's go, Jaxon," Tate said. "These guys have had enough of you."

"Just a sec."

He punched his own cell number into his cell phone and made sure it showed up in its display. He held the phone up close to the security camera for a second then leaned down in front of it so his face was seen. Tate pulled on his sleeve.

"Come on."

"What the hell are you doing?" The sergeant asked.

"Trying to communicate."

"With whom?"

Jaxon didn't answer as he was led away.

His phone rang just as he reached the door. Tate stopped and the sergeant paused what he was doing. Jaxon looked at the display and grinned. It showed no number. Just the words 'Private caller.'

"Your security system has been compromised," Jaxon said to the sergeant. "You better have it checked."

He grinned and walked out of the door. Outside, he answered the cell.

"Jaxon."

"Hello, Detective. So nice to hear your voice. I was wondering when we were going to get to speak."

The voice was high pitched, not quite feminine, but still up high in the register. Like the son-of-a-bitch had no balls. It also carried a slight southern accent. He didn't remember Fanucci sounding like that, but it didn't mean his voice wasn't disguised. Tate and the rest stared at him, but let him talk. They could tell it was something out of the ordinary. Ray moved closer and nodded at Jaxon. He nodded back.

"You know me. I don't know you."

"Oh, I wouldn't say that. I know what you used to be. And you definitely know me."

"I'm at a loss. Help me."

"Later. I'm sure that's not what you got my attention for, Detective. If so, I'm hanging up now."

"I need some help."

He hated admitting it to this asshole, but he didn't know what else to do at the moment.

"That can't be," the voice mocked him. "You've been doing so well. You and your little gang." It grew angry then. "Why should I? You're not playing by the rules."

"I can't get into the base. It's on lockdown. I can't get to the next clue."

Laughter filled the speaker and Jaxon had to pull the phone away from his head. It went on for a few more seconds and then stopped abruptly. "I don't remember telling you I would help you solve your dilemmas. Figure it out."

"You aren't playing fair…"

"Neither are you," he shouted.

"Tell me the next waypoint."

"Consider this your punishment for cheating. Oh—and your wife too."

"I'm coming for you. You know that, right? I won't stop. Ever."

"I wouldn't expect anything less, Detective."

The line went dead.

CHAPTER 21

Jaxon sat in the sheriff's office alone. Ray, Gil, and Mel were out in the station sitting, twiddling their thumbs. The door opened and a bull of a man walked in and sat behind the desk. The name on the plate that sat on the desk, trimmed in gold, read James Guest. He glanced at Jaxon over wire rimmed glasses and put the papers he was holding down on his desk.

"I'm not sure what to do with you Mr. Jennings."

"Jaxon."

"Excuse me?"

"The name's Jaxon. Everybody calls me Jaxon."

The sheriff pursed his lips and looked at the paper on his desk.

"You've created quite a dilemma for me. You and your little posse out there."

"That's not my intention, Sheriff. I'm conducting an investigation and I appreciate all the help you have given me."

The sheriff sat back in his chair and studied Jaxon.

"I don't know what you're used to where you're from, but here in the south we don't like it when someone blows sunshine up our ass. Just an hour ago you told my detective to basically shove it and then you threaten a member of the armed forces of this United States. Now you sit there and shine my ass on the so called 'help' we've provided you. I don't like it. Not one bit."

Jaxon smiled. He didn't think he'd be able to smooth talk his way out of this, but he had to try.

"You're right Sheriff. My apologies. I'm just in a tight spot and I don't have much time to find this girl."

"Then why didn't you involve us in the first place? You should know this. You were a detective in DC for God's sake."

"I was instructed to not involve any law enforcement or risk the life of the girl. From what I observed, he seemed capable of determining whether I had in fact done just that or abided by his request. In my opinion, involving you would have been a mistake."

"So you think. How, pray tell, did you determine that the man was able to know every move you made?"

"He is very adept at manipulating recent technology to his advantage. At the site where I found the severed finger and first note, he was monitoring the spot with a remote camera. He knew when I found it and his game began. He has also been able to hack into just about any public and so called private security service and learn of my whereabouts and who I am interacting with."

"Sounds like a superman. I don't buy it."

"Did your detective inform you of the telephone call I received as he took custody of me from the Marines?"

"Yes."

"That call was the result of me displaying my telephone number into the lens of the security camera at the naval base. He was monitoring it."

The sheriff considered this and then stood up.

"I understand why you've involved us now since you believe the perp to be one of my own men. Robert Fanucci, who has been conveniently unavailable. Your wife explained to my men how you came to this conclusion. What I don't understand is why he would pick you?"

"I'm still not convinced that I wasn't just some random player in his game. The first person to discover his little cache."

"Your wife seems to think otherwise."

"We've discussed the possibility but have not yet discovered any conclusive evidence pointing to that."

The sheriff sat in his chair again.

"All right. This is how it's going to go. This investigation is now under my jurisdiction…"

"I don't…"

"I don't care what you think. It's now under my jurisdiction and you will only be allowed to participate as a consultant. I have no doubt of your ability, but your recklessness and this man's disregard for the lives of those involved and also those of innocent bystanders necessitates our involvement…"

"He'll kill her."

"…and our expertise. If he contacts you again, or gives you any evidence of the whereabouts of this Bethany Hope, whether directly, or in the form of some kind of puzzle, you will turn that evidence over to Detective Tate immediately."

"I won't agree to that."

The man's face turned red.

"I make it a point to know every private investigator with a license to operate within my jurisdiction. You're new here and I don't know you. I made a call to your chief up in Washington and he had some exemplary things to say about you. I find that hard to believe." He paused to judge Jaxon's response. "He also informed me that you were a hot head. A loner, and you didn't like to abide by the rules. That I find easy to believe." He leaned forward and pointed his finger at Jaxon. "I will not tolerate you acting on your own, nor will I allow you to continue to be even a consultant on this case if you do not cooperate. I will have your license revoked and your ass thrown in jail until I can find something that will stick to you. Do I make myself clear?"

"Crystal," Jaxon said.

The sheriff took a deep breath and leaned back in his chair. "Now, get out of here."

Jaxon stood and walked out of the office. He glanced at Ray, who stood and followed. Gil and Mel caught up as quickly as they could. When they were outside, Ray said, "I heard it all. Looks like we're out of business."

"Bullshit."

"I don't know about you, but if a sheriff threatened to throw my ass in jail and revoke my ability to earn a living, I'd listen to him."

Jaxon ignored him and pulled out his cell phone. He dialed from memory. The phone rang at a desk a thousand miles away and was answered on the second ring.

"FBI."

"I need to speak with Emory Holt."

"Please hold." He listened to canned music for a minute or two then the line picked up.

"Holt."

"It's Jaxon. I need a favor."

CHAPTER 22

Jaxon stood in front of the sergeant at the counter again. The man did not look pleased. He asked for Jaxon's ID and the IDs of the rest of the group and he filled out some paperwork. Producing a badge for each of them, he slid the clipboard over to Jaxon.

"Sign here."

Jaxon signed and slid the clipboard back. He looked at the security camera on the counter. "Did you get the security problem fixed?" he asked.

"It's shut down right now."

"Sounds like you need a new security company."

"We manage it within the Navy."

"Like I said, it sounds like you need a new security company."

The man glared at him and handed him the badges.

"You will be escorted while on the base. Do not wander away from the escort or you risk being subject to apprehension with deadly force. You have thirty minutes."

"Thank you." Jaxon couldn't help but grin at the man.

"I don't know what you pulled to get in here, but I hope it's worth it."

"Me too," Jaxon said. "Me too."

The same Marine who had handcuffed Jaxon to a chair a few hours before was their escort. He walked them to a waiting Humvee and he signaled for them to get in. Jaxon rode up front with the Marine and he pulled the GPS out and looked at the display.

"Where to, sir," the Marine said, emphasizing the word 'sir.'

"The Navy base."

The Marine gave him a look and put the Humvee in gear. He pulled through the gate and headed down the main thoroughfare.

"What's the lockdown all about?" Jaxon asked.

"I can't discuss that with you."

"Let me guess. You had an intruder."

The Marine slammed on the brakes and pulled over. He looked at Jaxon and then the three in the back.

"What is it you four are looking for?"

"Someone has left us a message of some kind here on the base. We have a GPS coordinate that gets us within a few feet. Then we have to find it. A woman is relying on us to continue on this kind of scavenger hunt to save her life."

The Marine sat back absorbing this information. "Why is she in danger? Is someone trying to kill her?"

"We believe she hurt someone in his family in the past and this is a payback."

"Why you?"

Jaxon paused. "We don't know that. My wife thinks he knows me somehow. I thought it was just some random thing."

"How could it be random? He had to contact you, right?"

"Sort of. I was GeoCaching and found the first clue in his game. It was her severed finger, along with a note."

"GeoCaching?"

"It's like a scavenger hunt. People do it as a hobby for fun. Only this time, somebody's life is at stake."

The Marine thought about this for a minute and then put the Humvee in gear. "Keep this to yourself. You didn't hear it from me. We had a breach a few days ago."

"Who?"

"We don't know. We caught it on a security tape. He was dressed all in black and wearing a mask. He gained access through a sewage pipe on the other side of the base."

"He made you guys look bad," Gil said. "Didn't he?"

The Marine didn't even acknowledge Gil. "We don't know what he did, so we're searching right now."

"We can probably find what you're looking for. He's left this for us."

"Seems like an awful lot of trouble for all of this. He must really hate this girl. Or you."

Jaxon thought about that and couldn't agree more. He already decided the guy had been harboring this grudge for a long time and it had built to something he could no longer contain. Like a vat of acid boiling over. It had to spill on someone and that someone was Jaxon. And Bethany.

The GPS started to track to the left.

"What's over there?" Jaxon pointed. "We need to head that way."

"It's the airfield. Nothing but hangars and runways. If you hand me your tracking device, I'll follow it to the spot."

Jaxon handed it over. He turned to Ray, Gil and Mel in the back. "Everybody ok?"

He realized he hadn't really talked to them much over the last hour. Too much bullshit going on and they had been along for the ride.

"I'm tired," Mel said, leaning up against Gil. "And I know he's exhausted."

"I'm fine," Gil said, but the look on his face told Jaxon otherwise. The kid was a trooper and if Jaxon had gotten bitten by the Mamba, he didn't know how he'd be fairing right now.

"I'm sorry Mel," Jaxon said. "This has been a nightmare for everybody. I can't tell you how much I appreciate all you've done so far and how much I admire you for helping. You didn't have to do all this. I know curiosity got the better of you two, but you've really made a difference and I wouldn't have gotten this far without you."

Mel smiled and touched his hand.

Cache 72

Ray said, "Any warm and fuzzies for me?"

Jaxon laughed and nodded. "I owe you. I have a tendency to get off track. Thanks for keeping me on the course."

"Seems like you do whatever you want anyway. I'm just here for the ride."

"I hope that's not what you really think."

Ray didn't say anything else.

"Looks like this is as far as it will take us," the Marine said.

They had stopped in front of the airport control tower and the runways themselves sat a few hundred yards beyond. An F-18 was spooling up on the runway and then it blasted down the length of it, pointing its nose to the sky and climbing almost straight up. The jet blast was deafening. Even inside the vehicle.

They all got out of the Humvee and Gil headed directly for a small door that stood at the bottom of the control tower. It was only half the size of a regular door and Jaxon thought it either an electrical access hatch or a small storage area. Gil was reaching for the handle when the Marine yelled, "Don't touch that!" Gil froze and turned with his hand on the handle. He let it go and stood there.

"This is where the cache is probably located," Gil said as they all moved toward him.

"You need to let me open it," the Marine said.

Gil moved out of the way and shrugged.

Jaxon stood next to him and watched as the Marine grabbed the handle and turned it slowly. The door popped open slightly, as if it was on a spring and Jaxon yelled for him to stop.

"Look," Jaxon pointed.

The Marine peeked inside and saw the red wire that Jaxon had seen as soon as the door sprung open.

"Move back!" he ordered and slowly let the handle go.

The door stayed in place and he backed away. Herding them all back away from the tower, he got on his radio and called for assistance including the EOD, the military's equivalent of a bomb squad. He told Jaxon to keep his people back and then ran for the door to the control tower and entered. A few minutes later, all the personnel within the structure came streaming out and running for cover. Jaxon heard sirens in the distance. They were growing closer.

"We need to evacuate to this hangar," the Marine said and nudged them toward the hangar door. Jaxon heard one of the air traffic controllers talking on a portable radio instructing some aircraft to abort its landing, that there was a possible bomb on the airport surface. Jaxon heard a garbled response and then the controller was on his cell phone calling other air traffic facilities to inform them they had an emergency and had evacuated the control tower. The airport was temporarily closed to all military and civilian aircraft.

The navy firefighters showed up and shortly afterward a squad that dealt with mines and booby traps made their way to the small door to evaluate the situation. They grew excited quickly and moved back away from the area.

A few minutes later, a guy dressed up in a suit that resembled the Michelin tire man approached the door with a blast shield and a long tool with a grasping hook on the end. He kept his body behind the shield and the door. Jaxon could not see behind the door. The device, or whatever was there, was hidden behind it.

Michelin Man worked the door open wider and then used the long hook and pulled the device clear of the building. When he stepped to the side, Jaxon got his first good glimpse at it and was surprised how small it was.

About the size of a softball, it sat on a wooden board, wires protruding from various places, a small block of some compound sitting at the center. Probably C4.

Michelin Man knelt behind his shield and took a tool from his belt. It was another grasping mechanism but much shorter and much more adept at closer, more subtle work. He extended it toward the device and held it steady as he positioned the jaws of the device to sever a red wire. He activated the cutter and the wire was severed.

Nothing happened for a second and then the device started to smoke.

Michelin Man jumped back with the shield held in front of him and everyone else on the squad yelled and took cover. Jaxon moved behind the wall of the hangar and he pushed Melanie and Gil back behind him.

The device smoked on the tarmac for a few more seconds, but did not detonate.

When the smoke cleared, the device looked different. Michelin Man approached warily again and knelt next to it with the shield held in front of him. He bent to get a closer look, then sat back. He pulled his helmet off and stood up, moving around the shield to the device. He bent to it and grabbed something off of it. He turned and held it up.

"We're clear!" he said and smiled. "It's a joke. We're good." The rest of the squad moved toward him.

Jaxon stepped out from behind the hangar wall and started walking toward the EOD squad. Their Marine escort caught up to him and grabbed his arm.

"We haven't been given the all clear yet, sir. Please. Move back behind the wall."

Jaxon yelled at the EOD squad. "What is it?"

Michelin Man held up his hand and waved a piece of paper in the air.

"It's just a scrap piece of paper with a message on it."

"What does it say?" Jaxon shouted. The Marine was pulling on his arm.

"'Jaxon sucks pricks.' That's it."

The Marine stopped pulling on him. "That's your name, right?"

Jaxon nodded and started to move toward the EOD squad again.

A blinding flash erupted in front of him, and Jaxon and the Marine were tossed backward onto the ground. Jaxon stared up at the blue sky not sure exactly what happened. There was a ringing in his ears and the brightness of the blast remained burned into his retina for a few seconds more. The Marine was over him yelling if he was all right and Jaxon felt déjà vu. He'd been here before.

He sat up and checked himself but didn't find any injuries. Mel was next to him with a worried look on her face and she knelt there on the tarmac and hugged him. He heard her ask if he was ok. Gil stood above him extending his hand.

Michelin Man took the brunt of the blast from behind and his body had shielded his other squad mates from most of it. He had been tossed forward into one man and the third member of the squad sat bleeding from his head.

Michelin Man was working himself back up into a sitting position and the squad mate who had landed underneath him squirmed to his feet and helped him up.

The fireman ran up to the wounded EOD squad guy but he waved them back and Jaxon thought he was yelling it wasn't safe yet.

"Stay back!"

The firemen halted in their spot and then moved back again. The Marine pushed Jaxon, Gil, Ray, and Mel back behind the hangar wall and then inspected himself. Jaxon looked him over and pronounced him ok.

After fifteen minutes, it was determined that everything was safe.

There were no more devices and the one that had detonated had done little damage beside knock a few people down and scorch the tarmac. The EOD squad member who had been bleeding was being attended to by the paramedics and would be fine. The bleeding had even stopped. Michelin Man was out of his suit and Jaxon approached him.

"Do you still have the message that was in the device?"

The man nodded and produced a plastic baggy with the note inside. Jaxon looked at it and noted it contained his name just as the man had said. Nothing else. The letters were consistent with a set of lat/longs but it was going to be another puzzle to solve.

"Thanks." Jaxon said and started to walk away.

"Do you know who did this?"

"Yes and no."

The guy looked at him, puzzled, but let Jaxon walk away toward his group.

"We need to go," Jaxon said to the Marine. "I've got what he wanted me to have."

"This guy is psycho," the Marine said. "I can't believe he did this just to give you a message."

"I don't think I was meant to survive," Jaxon said. "I don't think I've been meant to survive any of this."

"We got lucky. Glad you were able to lead us to this and you saw the booby trap. Who knows what would have happened if that door was opened by some innocent maintenance man."

Jaxon thought somebody would have had to be scraped up off the tarmac with a shovel.

* * *

It was daytime again in her prison and the little box was starting to heat up.

The water had risen again during the night and she was still wet from it filling the container almost halfway. If she had still been tied to the floor, she would have drowned. Maybe that had been the plan.

She wandered the small box again, trying to find anything that would help her get out of this thing, but she found nothing but trash and little skittering crabs that dashed out of her way as she approached. She watched them scatter and then crawl under cracks where the floor met the wall and she wondered where they went.

She pushed on the walls near the deteriorated sections that were separated from the floor, but they would only flex a little. The remaining metal held. She banged on the sides and even kicked them with her bare feet, but she only succeeded in bruising her heel and making the crabs run around in a panic. When she stopped, they found their hiding place again and did not return.

She was down to her last two bottles of fresh water and as she stared at them, she grew thirsty again. She had to ration them or she would become so thirsty she risked drinking the seawater which she knew would kill her. Not right away, but she'd fall into delirium, and finally lose consciousness. Then she would die of dehydration.

The picture of Danielle sat atop one of the bottles. She had held it during the tidal surge that had flooded the compartment and it had stayed mostly dry. She glanced at it again. A single tear fell down her cheek and she looked away, trying to push the memory from her head. It was hard to do, trapped in this little dark space with nothing to think about but death. Danielle's death, her death. It all seemed to merge and she knew she would probably perish in this place, holding on to the picture and staring into the face of the one she had killed. It only seemed fitting.

She felt so weak, her legs shaking, so she sat on the floor and cried. She knew she needed to stop, she had to conserve as much moisture in her body as she could, but the tears kept coming.

The wave of grief and guilt overtook her and she remembered everything that had happened after Danielle's suicide. All the scorn, and the pain. Her family devastated in the eyes of the community and the torture she had put her own parents through.

The press had been especially bad and they had stalked her relentlessly, to the point of her staying home from school for weeks on end. She had almost failed her junior year. They camped out in front of her house and shouted things at her all through the day and night. The police had been little help in controlling them. They were responsible for keeping the peace, she knew, but when even they scorned her and gave her looks she caught out of the corner of her eye, she knew they would not put forth their best effort. It would take over an hour for a car to arrive after the crowds became unruly in front of her house, and her father would have to shout into the phone at the dispatch officer until he nearly collapsed. She had been worried he would have a heart attack.

The people of the community came out in droves to condemn their actions and they carried signs pronouncing them as evil and vile creatures on whom God would surely dole out his own punishment in time. The religious zealots had been especially bad and even though they spouted their righteous ways, they had been the first to condemn and the last to forgive.

The worst had been the ones who had supported the teens in their actions against Danielle and her lover. God had condemned anyone who could commit such vile actions against their own sex and used Bethany and her friends to punish the sinners. Bethany had been so angry at those people, she had even started shouting back at them through her window. They had not understood why she did not appreciate their support.

Rocks had been thrown through the windows of her house and smashed the windshield on her father's new car. Her dog had been fed some kind of poison and the vet had barely been able to save it. A fire had been started in her front yard and the house had been spray painted with the words "KILLER" in huge red letters. It went on for weeks.

Danielle's family had been devastated, of course. Her mother had been the one to find her and Bethany swore she had awakened early the morning Danielle had died and heard a voice wailing in the distance. Of course, that could not have been. The family lived on the other side of town.

For weeks afterward, Bethany would wake in the middle of the night, a noise like that of small fingernails scraping along the thin glass of her bedroom window pulling her from her sleep. She would sit up in her bed, thinking the girl had come for her, but it had only been a dream or her imagination. As she slowly drifted back off to sleep hours later, the soft mournful wail of Danielle's mother led the way to her dream world and she would relive that morning over and over again as the rest of the night bore on.

Danielle's mother had been the worst. She had not fixed blame on anyone or any group. She had barely said anything afterward. The funeral had been held a week later and Bethany heard Danielle's mother would not even move during the ceremony. She had remained silent and mournful, tears quietly streaking her face. Her husband tried to console her, but it had been futile. She had taken a bottle of pills in the night on the fourteenth day after her daughter's suicide and followed her into that blackness that had enfolded her only little girl.

Bethany and her friends had destroyed not only the lives of a mother and daughter, they had destroyed many lives close to them and in the community. The pain with which many had suffered for the carelessness of their acts could not be measured.

After the death of his wife, the husband refused to talk to anyone in the press. He shuttered the house after the funeral and Bethany had not been surprised to find it empty a few weeks later. She had heard he moved, but did not know where. He had never said one word to her or her friends.

Bethany tilted her head back and let the heat of the compartment wash over her. Her tears dried quickly and were replaced with a light sheen of sweat covering her face. She tried to take a deep breath but the sauna-like conditions inside the container made it hard to expand her lungs completely. The darkness inside the container seemed less today and she was surprised to find she could see to the other end of the box. Maybe her eyes were adjusting to the darkness or there was more light coming in.

Something caught her eye and she stared into the far corner trying to see what it was. She stood and walked closer as she kept her eyes on the upper corner opposite her. A small shadow seemed to seep from the darkness up there and as she walked closer, it turned into a shape. Standing under it, her mouth open in astonishment, the anger swelled within her and she screamed. Jumping back so she was in front of it, she waved her arms and cried at the camera that was mounted above her head in the darkness. Its dark lens seemed to mock her.

CHAPTER 23

The phrase 'Jaxon sucks pricks' had been easy for Gil to decipher.

Two things bothered Jaxon as they headed for the next destination with Ray driving the Mustang. The first was that his name had been so prominently displayed in the message. He could understand that after all the times he had been seen in the lens of various security cameras and him supplying his cell phone number over that last two hours, he would be ID'd by the perp. But when Vick had been injured in the bombing of his house with the perp somehow gaining access to the house with Vick in it, and planting a bomb at the naval base before Jaxon had even found the severed finger, he could not discount the fact that the guy had somehow known he was going to find the severed finger first and had even planted it there for him. This also meant that Jaxon was some unwitting pawn in the psycho's game and had not been some random GeoCacher stumbling on the cache find from hell. It could also mean that he knew Fanucci somehow. That did not jive.

The other thing that was nagging at the back of his mind was the fact they were heading for Gainesville. And not just some new spot in Gainesville, but the same spot they had been given over a day ago. The one they had skipped. Jaxon wondered just what they would find there and now that it had been given to them again, what they had missed by skipping it. If he were a betting man, he was sure the cache in Gainesville would not contain the GPS position in Lakeland, but a new position and that if they had gone to Gainesville first a day ago, they would have skipped all the other stuff in between. They would be way ahead of the game.

Jaxon could almost hear the killer's laugh in his ears as Jaxon cursed himself for the mistakes they had made. It was as if the asshole could read his mind and control their actions and thoughts like tugging on the strings of some sick marionette puppet.

Mel must have seen his face because she gave him a pitiful look and said, "How could we have known? He made it look like it was easier to skip."

"He played into my training. He knows all about me and I've refused to accept it. I'm running down the Psycho Serial Killer Apprehension Checklist and he's one step ahead, laughing as he checks off the traits one at a time."

"I'm not following."

"Most criminals are dumb. It's a known fact. That's why they get caught most of the time. Even murderers are mostly stupid in what they do and act with passion as opposed to thought and planning. I assumed he was a dumbass loser and when he presents me with these puzzles that seem stupid, he's set me up. He knew I would underestimate him and think I could take advantage of his supposed lack of intellect by skipping ahead. He planned on that and that makes him one smart mother. He's played me this whole time and all I keep telling myself is I'll find something to get ahead of the game, but I'm falling farther and farther behind while Bethany lies somewhere waiting to die. Who knows? She may already be dead and I'm running around chasing after her while his real purpose is fulfilled somewhere else."

As the words left his lips, Jaxon realized he may have just stated the obvious. The killer had some other agenda and he was being led away from it. Or was it another ploy? Like the

Gainesville point, or the Power Run cache on Kingsley. Jaxon cursed to himself again and felt like he was losing his mind. Mel only looked more confused.

"I can't think like him," she said, "so I have no idea. If we could think like him, we may be able to figure him out."

"Easier said than done, but I agree."

Vick had called, while they drove, with the news she was being discharged. Jaxon was sorry he couldn't be there, but she said she understood. It was more important to find the girl at the moment than to hold her hand. Besides, she said she was fine. He wasn't so sure about that. He knew she was tough, but anybody who's had their home invaded knows what they were both feeling. Even if they both carried guns and knew how to use them.

"I'll be there as soon as I can," he had said.

"I know. I'll get on the computer and keep digging."

"You get some rest. I'll call you if I need something."

"Don't baby me, Jaxon. You need my help. She needs my help."

He couldn't argue with her there so he said he loved her and he'd talk to her soon. She sounded tired already.

Jaxon sucked on the soda in his hand trying to get some more caffeine into his system, but it was doing little good. Gil was in the front passenger seat passed out and that was good. The kid had been through a lot and really needed to rest so he could heal. His hand was still swollen and looked like it was causing him pain. At least it wasn't so painful he couldn't sleep.

Twenty minutes later they were at their destination. The University of Florida. Home to the Gator Nation.

Jaxon sighed and realized nothing was going to be easy. They pulled on to the campus and Mel woke Gil. She looked excited. Apparently both she and Gil had attended the university a few years back. Gil was a graduate. She had never finished.

Gil sat up and looked around.

"I knew it would be here," he said and smiled. "Turn left up here, Ray. I bet I know where it is."

Ray directed the Mustang to an area near the main campus park. They found a spot and stepped from the car. Gil had the GPS out and pointed toward a statue in the center of the park. They started walking.

Classes were in session for the summer term and the park was moderately full of students eating an early lunch and generally goofing off between classes. A few were even throwing a Frisbee around and it glided in front of Jaxon who caught it and flung it back to the closest Gator. The guy waved and passed it on to his buddy.

Otherwise there was nothing remarkable about the campus or any indication that anything dangerous might occur. Jaxon kept his eyes open just the same. This guy was capable of anything.

They came up to the statue and Gil stopped.

"It's around here," he said and started looking over the statue. Mel wandered over to a water fountain and searched while Ray and Jaxon looked around in some of the nearby bushes. A guy walked up and stared at them.

"You guys GeoCachers?" he asked.

"Yeah," Jaxon said. "You?"

He nodded. "This one's been getting quite a bit of activity lately."

Jaxon stopped what he was doing and asked, "Do you know where it is?"

"Sure."

"Tell us."

The guy frowned. "That's not supposed to be how it works."

Gil walked up and said, "I'm Gatorcache. You?"

"You're Gatorcache? Man, I follow your stuff all the time on the boards. You're a legend. I'm DelFuego."

Gil nodded and shook his hand.

"I know there are standards for this stuff, but we're on a different kind of hunt and we need to be as fast as we can. If I were to guess, I would say it's in that tree, since it's not the statue. Am I right?"

DelFuego frowned again and Jaxon could tell the kid was struggling with the ethics of GeoCachers worldwide. You weren't supposed to give the locations away. It was like cheating.

"You're not what I expected," he said to Gil. "I can't believe you're asking me this."

"I know it goes against all you know about caching, but this is important. You know I wouldn't be asking if it wasn't. Am I right?"

He nodded and pointed to the tree just behind them.

"It's wedged in the crook of that first big branch."

"Thanks. We owe you."

Ray volunteered to climb the tree, and while he was making a fool of himself, Jaxon asked DelFuego if he had seen anybody unusual paying attention to this GeoCache spot.

"That's weird you ask because you guys are acting a little weird. But yeah, there was a guy a few days ago who climbed the tree and then spent a while up there. I eventually yelled at him to see if he was in like a diabetic coma or something and he said he was fine and to bug off. He was a prick."

Ray yelled from the tree. "There's a set of lat/longs carved into the bark of the tree."

Jaxon took out a notepad and pen and told him to call the numbers out. Gil yelled up to Ray, "That seems awfully easy. Look around more and see if you see anything else weird."

Ray wedged himself in the crook a little better and leaned out and around the main trunk of the tree. He then looked up under another big branch and stood up examining something. "You're right," he yelled. "There's another set up here hidden under this branch. It's very small. My eyes suck. I can't make it out."

"I can," DelFuego said. "I've got great vision."

"Come down, Ray," Jaxon said. "Our friend here is going to look for us."

Ray climbed down and DelFuego went up to the spot and leaned in close.

"They are small," he shouted, "but I can read 'em. You ready?"

"Yes," Jaxon said.

DelFuego called them out

"Got it."

DelFuego moved down to the lower branch and then stopped. "There's something else up here."

Jaxon walked up under the tree and looked up. "What is it?"

DelFuego poked at something on the trunk and his finger disappeared inside the tree. "There's a hole bored into the trunk covered with camouflaged paper. My hand won't fit all the way in. It looks just like bark. Does anybody have a pencil or pen?"

Jaxon held his pen up and then tossed it up to DelFuego who caught it deftly. He pushed it into the bored hole and worked it around. Jaxon heard a pop and then DelFeugo screamed, putting his hands to his face.

The kid lost his balance and fell from the tree landing with a horrific thud on the grass below it. He writhed around on the ground, his hands covering his face. Jaxon bent to him and tried to pull his arms away, but the kid was strong. Ray came over and grabbed his other arm and Gil started talking to him, trying to get him to calm down. Mel stood out of the way crying.

A small crowd had gathered from the commotion and Jaxon told somebody to call an ambulance. A handful of cell phones went to their owners' ears and calls went out.

Jaxon was able to coax the kid's hands from his face and was shocked at what he saw. Somebody screamed. The kid's eyes were bleeding and his face was covered in blisters.

"Don't touch his hands or face," Ray said. "It looks like some kind of acid."

Jaxon kept the kid's hands clear of his face and did his best not to touch them, but some kind of liquid rubbed off on his palm and it started to burn. He ignored it.

Sirens could be heard in the distance and the University's security showed up and made an attempt at some kind of crowd control. The regular police and then the fire department showed up next and took over.

Jaxon looked at Ray and Ray nodded.

They backed away and grabbed Gil and Mel.

"We need to get out of here now," Jaxon said.

They moved away from the crowd and headed for their car. Jaxon felt horrible leaving the kid, but he could do nothing else for him. The paramedics would know what to do more than he could help. Mel was still crying and kept looking back over her shoulder at the crowd.

"We can't stay, Mel," Jaxon said. "They'll detain us too long."

"We can't just leave him."

"He's in good hands. Come on."

He pulled her along and she went reluctantly. No one stopped them.

When Jaxon got in the car he got on the phone and called the Clay County Sheriff's office and asked for detective Tate. He answered and Jaxon came right to the point.

"We've had a few developments and there are a few things you can track down for me."

"For you? If I'm not mistaken, I believe you were told to act in a consulting capacity only."

"All right, you're consulting me now."

Tate sighed. "What have you got?"

Jaxon explained the situations at the Navy base, his house, and what had happened here in Gainesville.

"Check on the kid for me. We had to evacuate the area."

"You just left him?"

"No, the paramedics and the locals are here. He's in good hands. I just want to know."

Jaxon could hear him scribbling things on a pad.

"What else?" Tate asked.

"I need you to chase down a lead in Orlando. Specifically Disney World."

He explained the GeoCaching site in the lagoon and that people had to reserve in advance if they wanted to access the site underwater.

"Have them check their reservations for Fanucci."

"I know Fanucci. Between you and me, it isn't him."

"I know how you feel, but it sure is pointing toward him. You haven't found him yet have you?"

"No."

"Just check the Disney lead and if you don't feel good about it, track down who else has visited that site in the last thirty days. It can't have been that many."

"What are you going to do?"

"I'm still consulting. I'm going to consult."

"Keep me in this, Jaxon. The sheriff's watching this. And you."

"Will do."

Jaxon hung up and saw Gil with a grin on his face.

"You were right. Neither of these lat/longs is for Lakeland. They're both new. We should have come here first."

Jaxon nodded. He wasn't happy about being right. "So, where are they?"

"That's the bad news. One's in Palm Beach. The other, in Tallahassee."

"Shit. Which one?"

"Exactly. We have to think like him."

"I don't understand the acid," Ray said. "Why put that there?"

"It was a booby trap," Jaxon said. "Like the snake, and the bomb. He's hoping we'll fall prey to one of his tricks."

Ray nodded. "It seems awfully convenient that nobody but us finds these things. How can he be so sure somebody won't stumble on to his games and then we're shit out of luck?"

"He probably doesn't care. He'll win one way or another. He's amusing himself with this scavenger hunt, but it's just a way to kill time. He's planning on killing her, and me, no matter what. I know that now."

"Then why the hell are we playing his game?"

"We have no other choice," Gil said.

"Gil's right," Jaxon said. "We don't have any other way to find the girl at this moment. We stay on the path and hope something breaks. We have no other alternative."

"Which one, then?"

"The closest," Jaxon said.

"Tallahassee it is."

Ray started the car and pulled out of the lot. As they left the campus of the Florida Gators, an ambulance pulled ahead of them, its siren wailing and lights flashing. Jaxon hoped the kid would be ok.

CHAPTER 24

"They're interrogating him now," Vick said. "They won't give me any more information than that."

Jaxon was about an hour out of Tallahassee and his cell had woken him from a brief nap. He had been irritated at first, but when it turned out to be Vick, he felt a little better.

"Where did they find him?" he asked.

"That's the weird thing. He just showed up for work at his normal shift time. Just walked right in the building like nothing was wrong."

"What did he say?"

"He was sick."

"Did he have an excuse for why he wasn't home or answering his phone?"

"He said he was at his brother's. He had gotten drunk and didn't want to drive, so he called in sick and stayed over there."

"Seems like Tate and the sheriff would have checked there."

"That's what I said and they didn't have a good excuse. Tate kind of skated around the answer. I don't think they take him as a serious suspect."

"He's the only one we've got," Jaxon said. "I guess I need to 'consult' with Tate again."

She laughed. "I heard about that. Apparently they aren't appreciating your interpretation of consultant."

"We're almost to Tallahassee. I have a bad feeling this time it's a wild goose chase."

"Hasn't this whole thing been a wild goose chase?"

He had to agree with her.

This little adventure had turned out much worse than he had expected. They were supposed to have found Bethany by now. Hell, by yesterday. Jaxon was beginning to worry that they may never find her or Fanucci would only spill his guts after the fact.

"How are you feeling?"

"I'm sore," she said. "But I'll live. I can function. They gave me some pills for pain, but I'm not going to take them. I don't need them."

"Where are you?"

"Where we discussed. I got here about thirty minutes ago. It's not the same without you."

He smiled to himself. She knew just how to make him feel like a human again.

"I'd be there if I could."

"I know. Just been missing you a bit."

"Me too. Call me if something else develops."

"Always."

He hung up and called Tate. "I hear you have our boy."

"He's not your boy, and yes, we've got him in interrogation."

"Has he given us anything yet?"

"No, and I don't expect him to."

"You do know that things point his way, right?"

"He's not the guy."

"What? Is he your best friend or something?"

Silence.

"I don't think you need to be working this case," Jaxon said.

"You don't have any say in this."

"Listen, Tate. You're too close to this. An innocent girl's life is at stake and you're jerking things around because he's your buddy."

"Are you saying I'm not doing my job?"

"I'm saying you can't in this situation. You're working with blinders on and you don't know it. Take it from me. I know."

"From what I hear, you couldn't work yourself out of a wet bag. Why don't you keep working on your 'consulting' and let us handle the important stuff?"

"If she dies, you won't be able to handle anything. You won't even be able to piss without help."

"Is that a threat?"

"What do you think? Do your damn job."

"Screw you, Jaxon." And he hung up.

"That went well," he mumbled to himself and he caught Mel looking at him. He could read her expression and he really didn't need to be judged right now. Especially by her. He sighed and then dialed another number. The sheriff of Clay County answered.

"It's Jaxon. You've got a problem."

"I've heard. It's you."

"Then you're hearing has gone bad. Tate is too close to this. You need to put somebody else on the case."

"Tate is the lead investigator. He'll stay on it."

"He and Fanucci are friends. He doesn't believe it's him and he's not operating in the most optimal manner."

"And just what would be the most optimal manner? He's a friend of everyone in this office. We'll do our jobs and we'll do them correctly."

"Have you forgotten about the girl?"

"What did I just say?"

"What have you learned so far in the interrogation?"

"Nothing. He knows nothing and has a solid alibi. And frankly, I'm inclined to believe him."

"He has the motive and the opportunity. You can't take this lightly."

"Dammit, Jaxon. Don't tell me how to do my job. And besides, you're only in this as a consultant. You do not have any authority to tell any of us what to do."

"How would you like the FBI all in your face? That can be arranged. And rather quickly. I would think the Feds would have some concerns in this case especially since it involves one of your deputies. I would call that a conflict of interest."

"My patience with you is wearing thin. If you want to continue to have a working relationship with the local law enforcement in this town you'll think carefully about your actions."

"Are you threatening me, sheriff?"

"Just stating the facts. Stay out of it and let us do our job."

"That's my problem. If you would do your job and your detectives would do their jobs, I wouldn't be having this conversation with you."

"This conversation is over. And stay out of this, Jaxon."

"Not on your life, Sheriff. You couldn't drag me away."

Jaxon hung up and looked at Mel again. She was smiling at him.

"It doesn't seem to be going your way," she said.

"Those pricks don't know what they're doing. Sorry."

She shrugged.

"Fanucci is our best opportunity to end this and they won't put any pressure on him because he's one of theirs."

"How would you feel if it was one of your fellow policemen you worked with in DC? It would be hard to overlook all the years of trust just because of some suspicion."

"Still, I'd do my job. That's all that matters. If they cross the line, then they have to be dealt with."

"I've seen you cross the line."

He smiled at her. She was right, he knew, he just didn't want her to know that.

"I'm a civilian now."

"That's kind of lame."

"True."

She smiled back at him. "Why is this so important to you? You don't even know the girl. I just want to hear it from your lips."

He hadn't considered this. It was just something he did. He didn't want to analyze it, yet here she was, wanting just that.

"I just don't like bullies. This guy Fanucci is bullying her, and us, and it drives me nuts. She doesn't have a fair chance against him and I'm trying to even up the odds."

"But she bullied someone herself. Remember?"

"She was just a teenager. Kids do stupid stuff."

"Adults do stupid stuff."

"Why are you on his side?"

She looked shocked. "I'm not. I…you just seem…I don't know…very determined. Especially for someone you've never met. Most people would've given up by now."

"Up in DC, it was my job to stay in the fight. I still feel like it's my job. This guy thought he was having some schmuck play his little game and I'm glad to disappoint him. She may not have had a chance with just anybody."

"You're different, Jaxon Jennings. I would hope to have someone like you if I was in trouble."

"You are in trouble."

"Oh yeah. See? You made me forget."

"Why these questions all the sudden?"

She shrugged. "Just trying to figure out what makes you tick I guess. We only met a short time ago and I feel like I know you. Then you surprise me."

"Don't base your judgment of me on this experience. I'm half out of my mind with fatigue and this guy gets me going."

"People's true selves usually show through in times of extreme stress."

"Great."

"I like your true self. It suits you."

She smiled again and touched his hand. He took it in hers and squeezed. He didn't know what to say, so he didn't say anything. He let her hand go after a second and turned to look out the window at the passing trees. He hoped he would be able to live up to her expectations. He had a feeling things were going to get a lot worse.

*　*　*

Tallahassee proved to be a non-event. They arrived at the waypoint and found the situation very similar to Gainesville. It made Jaxon think there was some kind of connection but it was escaping him at the moment.

The waypoint was located in a park-like area on the campus of Florida State University. Home of the Seminoles. In fact, it was also in the shadow of Bobby Bowden Field at Doak S. Campbell Stadium. The statue of Bobby Bowden was in the area of the cache point, but they ignored it and concentrated on the trees. Some of the students looked at them strangely, but nobody questioned them or made a point to even talk with them. Jaxon was glad. He didn't want to have another DelFuego incident. If something was going to happen, he didn't want an innocent bystander suffering the consequences.

Mel found it in the third tree they checked and she called down the lat/longs carved into the tree. There were no others hidden and no fake bark with a hidden explosive acid booby trap. In fact, it was probably the easiest one they had located. The lat/longs, unfortunately, were the same ones they had found in Gainesville. The ones for Palm Beach. This trip had been a waste of time.

"We guessed wrong again," Jaxon said.

"Seems like the norm," Ray said.

He gave Jaxon a look, but Jaxon couldn't read him. If he had to guess, he assumed his impression of him was not as glowing as Mel's. And Jaxon agreed with it. He was blowing it, and it pissed him off.

It was time to change things up. "We need to split up," Jaxon said back at the car.

"Split up how?" Ray said.

"I need to go back to Orange Park. I want you guys to continue on to Palm Beach. I need to talk to Fanucci and see if

I can get anything out of him, but we need to keep at the search in case I can't."

They looked a little sober at this news, but he could see they were all in agreement.

"I'll join you wherever you are after I have my little talk with Fanucci. Can you three stick together?"

Gil and Mel nodded their heads. Ray said nothing. Jaxon motioned for Ray to walk a few steps away and he joined him out of earshot of the other two.

"Can you keep them safe?"

Ray nodded. "That's the plan."

"You don't agree with this?"

"Yeah. I think it's the right thing to do. I just don't like being a babysitter."

Jaxon nodded.

"I know how you feel, but they've become something I want to protect. I'd take them with me, but this will be strictly police work over there and their strengths lie in this GeoCaching and puzzle solving. You've seen Gil at work. We'd be a whole day behind if it weren't for him."

"I know. I just don't like it."

Jaxon slapped him on the back.

"At least you'll have company. I owe you man."

Ray grinned. "I like Crown Royal."

"Me and you and two shot glasses when this is over."

He shook his hand. Jaxon couldn't help feeling it might be the last time he saw him.

They dropped him off at a car rental place and then he was on his own, making good time on I-10 heading eastbound. A couple of hours and he might have some answers. Or he might be wasting his time. Time would tell and that was not a luxury he had much of.

CHAPTER 25

Bethany braced herself against the roof of the container and struggled with her other arm to keep herself afloat. It was a battle.

The water had risen well above any previous level and she prayed the container would not completely fill. At this point, she realized that this would eventually be her demise, unless she was able to find a way out of here, or somebody came to her rescue. It must have been their plan all along.

The terror that filled her slowly subsided and she began to resign herself to her fate. It wasn't that she was giving up, she was just so tired and thirsty. The bottled water was gone and she hadn't had a thing to eat in days. She didn't know how long she'd been in here exactly, but she could tell it was at least three days. Maybe four.

The picture was clamped in her teeth and she struggled to keep it dry.

The water was up to her neck now with her head bumping along the ceiling. She held on to a loose piece of metal that protruded from the weld at the roof joint and the sharp edges were cutting into her palm. The hand with the missing finger was now infected and the fever she was running made her shiver in the cool water. She knew her temperature would be higher if she was not submerged.

She could see Danielle staring at her just out of focus at the end of her nose and it seemed as if she were laughing. It was her imagination, she knew, but she couldn't keep from glancing along her nose every few seconds. It was a wonder she had held on to the picture this long, but it was like a life preserver to her. It did nothing to keep her afloat in the rising waters, but it buoyed her mental outlook and gave her strength. She would save Danielle this time and the only way she would allow her to drown was if she drowned herself. They would survive.

The container was tilted on whatever surface it was resting on and she was currently at the high end. The end that was above water.

The other end was submerged and the water crept along the roof, slowly rising toward her. The camera at the other end had shorted out and she had seen the sparks fly from it when the water hit it. At least they couldn't watch her die and that gave her some comfort. Dying was a lonely business and as scared as she was, she didn't want to share it with anyone else. It was hers to experience and no one would comfort her or egg her on.

No one except Danielle.

The water rose to her chin and she sucked air through her clenched teeth around the picture. It wasn't going to be much longer and she wondered what it would feel like. Would it be painful? Would she stay awake until the very last second? Would her life flash before her?

She held on and waited. And waited.

She wasn't sure, but the water didn't seem as high as a few minutes ago. Maybe it was her imagination. She shivered and turned her head toward the crack of light. The level of the water looked just a little lower over there. She giggled around the picture in her mouth and looked back toward the other end of the container. The water was slowly pulling back along the roof. It would recede a bit and then flow back in but each time it receded just a bit more. It was over.

She had survived and the water was not going to take her and Danielle this time. She would live for one more cycle and hopefully she would find a way out. She shivered and waited. There was nothing else for her to do.

* * *

Jaxon walked into the station and was immediately greeted by the sheriff. He must have seen him walking up to the building.

"Afternoon, Sheriff."

"What are you doing here?"

"Good to see you too. I want to see him."

"No way."

Jaxon sat in a chair at an empty desk and looked around the room. He guessed it would hold fifteen people during some peak period or intense investigation. He was disappointed to see it almost empty.

"I take it the whole crew is out working on finding the girl."

"My deputies are doing their jobs. You should be doing yours."

"That's why I'm here. I need to see him."

"I told you no. I cannot allow a civilian to be involved in an investigation of this nature."

"I'm already involved. You know that."

The sheriff took a chair opposite him and rubbed his face. "Why are you making my life difficult?"

"Because you're making mine difficult. I'm closest to this case and I just may be able to get through to him. We could save a girl's life. That should be the most important thing right now. I'm not interested in making your department look bad. I just want to know where she is."

He sighed and shook his head.

"Ten minutes. If you touch him or threaten him in any way, it's over. I will not have one of my deputies, who is presumed innocent, harassed."

"It's funny, Sheriff, when I was a detective up in DC, we never used the term 'presumed innocent.' It's not in a cop's vocabulary. That's not our job. To me, everybody is guilty. And I bet until this morning, it was that way with you and your deputies."

"It's different when it's one of your own."

"It's worse when it's one of your own."

"Damn right about that. Ten minutes. I'll bring him up to an interrogation room."

Jaxon grabbed a cup of coffee while he waited and was not surprised to find it sucked. He thought all police departments must get their coffee from the same supplier. It was all crap. He drank it anyway and relished the warm liquid. His exhausted veins seemed to lap it up like a thirsty dog in the desert. If only it would make him feel better. The dull ache behind his left eye wouldn't seem to let up and the odor coming off of him was barely human. Maybe he could torture Fanucci with the smell.

The sheriff led him down a long hallway to a set of doors that he unlocked and held open for him. Jaxon stepped through and entered another room that served as a prepping area for the actual county lock up. The sheriff led him past a glassed-in booth occupied by one deputy and into another hallway that had two doors on either side. He opened the second one on the right and Jaxon entered. Fanucci sat in a chair on the other side of a metal table and seemed surprised to see him. The deputy from the other morning was with him. Williamsen if Jaxon remembered correctly. He held a bottled water in his hand and then set it down in front of Fanucci.

"Thanks Bro," Fanucci said and sipped the water. Williamsen nodded to Jaxon once and then left the room.

"Are you the cause of all this?" Fanucci asked.

"Where is she?"

"Who? The woman I'm supposed to have kidnapped and hidden away to die? The girl who killed my daughter? Bethany Hope? Good to see you too. Jaxon, wasn't it? Excuse me if I don't get up."

Jaxon took a seat opposite him and the door closed behind him. The sheriff had left him alone with Fanucci but he was sure the man would be observing from another room.

"Let's talk about Bethany."

"I don't have to talk to you about anything. You're not even a cop anymore. I'm only cooperating with my department because I haven't done anything."

"Your department believes that too. They seem very supportive of you. You must have a lot of friends."

"I get along with all of them."

"You have to look at this from my point of view. Take a step back and put yourself in my shoes. When everything is laid out, who would you be talking too?"

Jaxon watched his face as he worked it out. It betrayed nothing.

"Me. I know how bad this looks. Hell, I wanted to see all those girls dead after it happened. That was a long time ago. I've moved on."

"It's been eight years. I don't think you've moved on at all. I think that wound has festered inside of you all this time and finally come to a head."

"You don't know shit."

Jaxon leaned forward.

"I know exactly what it's like to lose a child. I wanted to kill anything and everyone who had anything to do with his death. Even myself. I know that you feel a part of you has been amputated. Cut from your body without anesthesia. The pain intolerable and the aftermath impossible to live with. The itch of that missing limb is something you can never scratch and the world is never as sunny as it was before."

"It still doesn't mean I did all this. Yeah. I hurt. It's never gone from me. Not one day goes by I don't think about her and her mother, but I've forgiven them. I can't carry that burden too. It would be too much."

"That's exactly right. It would be too much. You've kept your silence for too long and it finally got the best of you. I know you can't let it go, but don't take it to this level. Tell me where she is. She doesn't deserve to die too."

"I'm telling you I don't have any idea where she is. I don't even know who would be doing this."

Jaxon sat back.

"I'm supposed to presume your innocence. You're not guilty until proven."

"As a cop you don't believe that," Fanucci said and looked him square in the eye.

"That's right. You don't either."

"In this case, you're wrong. The only thing I'm guilty of is abusing my sick leave. I was at my brother's, hung over."

"I'm sure your brother will corroborate that story."

"It's the truth."

"What about before? This has been planned and worked on for quite a while. I'm sure you don't have an alibi for all that time."

"Nobody's asked me for it. Look, I'm always here at work, or I'm at home. I don't do anything else."

"Live alone?"

"Yes. I haven't remarried."

"The other day, when you came up on me at the GeoCache site, what were you doing?"

"I told you then, we got a complaint about a trespasser on the property. You. It's in the log. You can check it."

"Why me?" Jaxon asked.

"Why you, what?"

"Why choose me to send on this hunt? My wife thinks it wasn't random."

"I didn't choose you. I didn't choose anyone. I don't have anything to do with this, but if I were to guess, you damaged something in somebody's past and it's returned to haunt you. Maybe you need to look a little harder at yourself."

The door opened and the sheriff stood in the opening.

"Time's up, Jaxon. Let's go."

Jaxon stood and turned to go.

"You know I didn't do this," Fanucci said. "Find who did and get me out of here."

Jaxon turned back and studied the man. "You said it before. I don't know shit."

He walked out and the door closed behind him.

CHAPTER 26

Ray was feeling the lack of sleep now.

He couldn't even remember the last time he had gotten any shut-eye, and he knew he was working on the fumes of his burnt out brain cells. He could hear them frying in his skull. A steady, low hum or crackle that seemed to radiate from the center of his head. He'd never been this tired.

Mel complained it was too cold in the car, but he needed the AC blowing on him to keep him from dozing off. She was curled up in a ball in the back seat with her arms wrapped around herself, shivering.

Gil had asked him repeatedly to let him drive, but he had refused. The kid had a suspended license. He was not legal to operate a motor vehicle in this state or any state. He shook his head again, trying to clear the cobwebs and thought to himself for the fiftieth time why he cared if the kid had a license or not. It wasn't like Ray had remained an honest, law abiding citizen over the last twenty-four hours anyway. Hell, he'd even shot somebody and he had no idea if the guy had survived or not.

His eyes went out of focus and he blinked, trying to clear them. When they remained blurry, he panicked and shook his head violently. The humming in his brain rose in volume and then receded again as his vision cleared up. He looked at Gil who was staring at him.

"Let me drive, man," he said. "You're going to kill us."

"No."

"Come on! It's my car. I could report it as stolen."

"Go ahead. Then none of us will be driving and the girl will be dead. You don't have a license."

"I do—it's just suspended. I drive all the time."

"I'm a law enforcement officer. If I let you drive knowing you did not have the proper credentials I would be in a shit load of trouble."

"You're already in a shit load of trouble. And you're a glorified zoo security guard."

"Gil," Mel said.

"I'll have you know I have the authority to arrest anyone, and I mean anyone, regardless of jurisdiction. Do you know what that means?"

"No."

"It means I'm a 'zookeeper' with the right to kick your ass all over this highway and it would be legal."

"You wouldn't."

"Keep pushing, kid."

"I'm not a kid. And I'm just trying to help."

A horn sounded and Ray looked up to see that he was drifting off the road. He corrected hard and another horn blew.

"Ray," Mel said. "Let me drive then. You need some rest."

Ray considered this and looked in the rear view mirror at her reflection. She had a pleading look on her face and her teeth chattered in the cold air. He was freezing too, but it was keeping him awake. He turned to Gil.

"All right, kid. You drive."

Gil grinned as Ray pulled over to the shoulder and they did the Chinese fire drill thing. Ray climbed in back and leaned up against the door window, closing his eyes.

"You can turn the temperature back up," he said. "It's freezing in here."

"No shit," Gil said and adjusted the air.

As Ray drifted off, he had one other thought. "Don't speed."

"I'm on it…"

Gil's voice trailed off as Ray blacked out.

* * *

Ray woke three hours later as they pulled off the interstate into West Palm Beach, Florida.

The sun was going down. He sat up and winced in pain as his neck protested its new position. Three hours leaning up against a door was not the best thing for one's vertebral alignment. He felt like he'd been through a wood chipper. At least the humming of his dying brain cells had ceased.

"You're awake," Mel said, looking back at him and smiling. "Feel better?"

"A little."

He rubbed his neck and winced again when the car went over a pothole and his neck shifted unexpectedly. She saw his pain.

"You probably have a bad crick in your neck. Here, let me fix it."

She climbed over the seat and put her hands on his neck before he could protest and she manipulated his head in a way that his neck cracked loudly. The pain was immediately gone.

"There."

He looked at her and smiled.

"That was amazing. How'd you do that?"

"My mom was a masseuse and she taught me. She worked for a chiropractor."

"Thanks."

"You're welcome."

She climbed back up to the front and settled back in.

"How far?" he asked.

"A few more miles," Gil said.

"We should eat something."

"Ok."

They stopped for a bite at a fast food restaurant just outside of the main drag on the beach and ate cheeseburgers. Ray thought they were the best he'd ever had. Either they were really that good, or his brain was misfiring. Probably the latter.

They piled into the car again with Ray driving and Gil manning the GPS.

Heading south, they arrived at an address that Ray questioned at first, but then when he thought about it, it made sense. No one would be bothering this cache site.

They parked outside a chain link fence that encircled Nathan B. Forrest High School. The fence was rusted and leaning in places and Ray found a hole at the north end of the school where they entered the property.

The place was a ruin. The fading light made it appear like the haunted remains of some insane asylum. The wind whispering through the broken windows and scattered trash elicited a response from his subconscious he thought he outgrew in adolescence. He was creeped out.

Mel stayed close to Gil, and Ray watched her put her arm around him as they stood outside the main entrance. They all looked up at the three story building. Not a single soul was around and even the rundown neighborhood they were in seemed deserted. Maybe this one was going to be easy.

"Are we close?" Ray asked, and his voice, sounding suddenly loud in the silence, made Gil and Mel both jump. Gil held the GPS in his good hand and indicated with his bandaged one that they were to go inside.

"About seventy-five feet. That way," he said.

Ray placed his foot on the first of five steps overgrown with weeds, and made his way toward the main door.

One half was still intact, but the other stood ajar, hanging crooked on one hinge and blocking the way in. Ray grabbed one end and lifted. The old hinge that was still hanging squealed in protest and then gave way. The door dropped to the concrete with a thud. Something shifted inside the gloom of the building and Ray heard it skitter off. Mel leaned into Gil and held onto his arm.

Ray pulled his flashlight out and turned the beam on.

The entrance to Nathan B. Forrest High School beckoned them inside and Ray stepped over the door and into the dilapidated institute of once mediocre learning. He wondered what had happened to cause this place to fall to ruin. School budget cuts? Neighborhood gone to hell? Space invasion? He decided it really didn't matter.

He panned the light around inside and it flowed across dusty green and yellow tiles that were probably once white. Trash, leaves, and other detritus littered the floor and spread out in a fan from the entrance.

As the light penetrated deeper, the trash thinned out and was replaced with graffiti. It plastered the walls, floors, and even the ceiling. He wondered how the hell they got up there. To the right, an old counter stood sentinel over a faded door that read 'Main Office.' An old sign hung sideways on it that read 'All Absences Must Be Excused.' Under it in black marker were the words, 'Fuck you.'

Ray moved in deeper as Gil and Mel stayed close behind. Their shuffling feet echoed in the silence. Somewhere in the distance they heard the tinkle of glass fall or shift. Ray froze. He shone the light around down the halls that were now on their left and right, but nothing moved. They waited a beat, but no other sound could be heard except their anxious breathing.

A stairwell led upward to the next floor directly in front of them.

"Which way?" Ray asked, his voice loud in the silence.

"Left," Gil whispered. "About fifty feet."

Ray moved to the left and entered a long hallway that used to house lockers and posters on the walls, but now only supported old wire, holes, and more graffiti. The remnants of a small campfire sat cold and dusty against the scorched wall next to an ancient water fountain. Above it, an old clock stuck out from the wall up high and the hands were forever frozen at 3:31. He didn't know if it was a.m. or p.m. The glass lens of the clock had been spray painted with purple paint that looked almost as old as the clock itself.

"I wonder how long this place has been deserted?" he said.

"Who knows," Gil answered, whispering again. "It feels old."

"It gives me the creeps," Mel said.

They moved further in and distant music could be heard. The bass thump of a radio grew louder as a car passed by outside. It faded quickly and the oppressive silence returned. They came to the end of the hall and stopped.

"This should be it," Gil said.

There was nothing here. No lockers, doors, windows, shelves, water fountains, nothing. It was just a wall at the end of a hallway. Ray shone the light around as they looked, but it was so stark and bare it didn't take long to determine that it wasn't here. They stopped and looked at each other and then Ray looked up.

"Does that GPS have elevation?" Ray asked, staring at the ceiling. It was stained from a water leak somewhere above but no graffiti had made it this far down the dark hall.

"No. We're not receiving enough satellites to get altitude."

"We're going to have to check all the floors then."

Gil nodded and they moved back to the main entrance and the stairwell.

Ray took the first step and some distant rustle came to their ears from above. Something squealed and then little tiny feet ran off away to their right along the ceiling.

"Rats," Ray said.

"Great," Mel answered and looked quickly around as a shudder passed through her.

"Do you want to stay in the car?" Ray asked.

She shook her head. "I'm not staying by myself around here."

He nodded and started up.

The steps were worn and cracked in places, but the stairwell seemed sturdy enough. It was built of concrete and block and would probably still be standing a hundred years from now. The railing was not in good shape and as he grasped the ancient wood, it broke loose and clattered down the stairs loudly, dust rising up in its wake. Something heavier than a rat shifted above their heads and then was silent. Ray did not like that. He glanced at Gil and Mel and started up again.

The stairs rose to a half landing and then doubled back to the left to reach the second floor. The darkness seemed even less penetrable as the little bit of light that leaked in downstairs through the open door and windows was non-existent up here. Any windows were behind classroom doors.

A feeling like he was being watched came over Ray and he panned the light left and right down the bleak hallway. Nothing but trash and broken furniture made an appearance inside the beam. His Spidey senses were tingling but nothing jumped out at him. Gil and Mel came up behind him and stood to his left. Gil pointed right.

The light from his flashlight led the way down the hall and though no graffiti greeted them up here, the discarded leftovers of a hasty retreat lay strewn around the floor and inside open classrooms. Broken desks and sagging chalkboards left little doubt that this was once a thriving school filled with teenager's voices shouting out their independence while teacher's voices clamored to be heard above them.

Ray imagined it all. His old haunt was so similar to this, that if the lights were on and the halls filled with kids, he just might mistake it for the place of his youth. Were they all the same? It seemed every state had a standard blueprint for education and each institution was stamped from the same mold. He could probably find his way to the cafeteria or the gym, and the clinic was probably in the same place. These old buildings built in the 40s and 50s were all the same. Things didn't start to change until the 70s when everybody's consciousness awakened and the new era of openness and peace reigned. Too bad that had been a load of crap too.

Ray moved off to the right and headed for the end of the hall.

Classroom doors stood on either side of the aisle and even some of the lockers were left up here. Things scrabbled and skittered away inside a few of them. Ray had no desire to look inside. Mel squealed behind him and he turned the light toward them to see a rat the size of a small cat run off and climb through a hole in the floor. She buried her face in Gil's shirt.

"It'll be ok, Mel," Gil said. "It's gone."

"How long do we have to stay in here?" She asked into his neck.

"Just a little longer. When we find the cache, we'll leave right away."

She nodded and pulled away from him but kept hold of his arm.

At the end of the hall they found the same thing as the first floor. Absolutely nothing.

They searched for a minute in what little places they could see that might house a cache, but it didn't take long to realize it wasn't here.

"I guess we go to the third floor," Gil said.

Ray led the way back to the staircase and started to climb. He remembered not to touch the railing. As he reached the switchback at the half landing, an odor assaulted his nostrils and he stopped. Gil and Mel came up next to him and smelled the same thing.

"God, that's rank," Gil said.

Ray recognized the smell of death right away and if it was this strong it was not a rat or dog. Something big was dead up there.

"Maybe you two should stay here," he said.

"No. We'll be all right. And you shouldn't go up there alone. That noise. Who knows who, or what, is up there."

"It's not the boogeyman," Ray joked, but nobody laughed.

Gil shrugged in the glow of the flashlight. Mel looked terrified, but said nothing.

Ray proceeded up the last half-landing and reached the top floor. The smell was unbearable. Mel gagged and then pulled her shirt up to her face and held the cloth over her mouth and nose. She didn't seem to care that her bra was showing. Ray was not excited about what they might find up here.

Ray panned the light around the third floor. It looked very similar to the second. Broken desks and chairs lay littered around the floor and some of the classroom doors were even added to the trash. Classrooms lay in wreckage and most of the glass in these windows was broken out.

To the left, a huge stack of desks and chairs was mounded in a heap blocking the way down that hall. Ray had no desire to try to get through it. He moved right and as he passed the second open door on the left, he paused.

He shone the light back inside and was shocked at what he saw. He stepped to the doorway as Mel and Gil came up behind him.

The classroom was set up just as if it were still in session. The only thing missing was the students. The desks were those combination chair and table numbers with a small storage shelf under the seat. They were lined up in rows facing the front of the class and some even had books and folders shoved inside. The teacher's desk was in its place with a few knick knacks on the desk's surface and a lamp that remained dark.

The chalkboard behind the desk was still attached to the wall and looked to be in good shape. There was even some writing in chalk on it. It said, 'Welcome students. I'm Mr. Shawnessy.' A few maps and posters hung on the wall and even a brief class synopsis hung handwritten on a poster. Apparently Mr. Shawnessy taught history.

The smell forgotten for a moment, Ray stepped inside the classroom and went to one of the desks with books stored in it. He pulled the textbook out and looked at the inside cover. Someone named Thomas Winter had been the last owner and his name and year had been scrawled in some thin shaky hand. 1981. Ray closed the book and put it back.

"This is damn weird," Gil said. His voice made Ray jump.

"You got that right," Ray said and moved to the teacher's desk.

He opened a drawer and saw a stapler and some old pencils. The next drawer held a ruler and some paper. A graded history test sat on the top of the stack. Paula Stamos had gotten a C+. He shut the drawer and went to the windows.

These were not broken. They were dirty, but that was to be expected. Ray could see the Mustang parked outside of the fence. Nothing else moved in the dark.

The smell came back to his senses and he walked to the door.

"Come on."

He left the relic classroom behind and walked purposefully down the hallway toward the end. Gil and Mel followed. The smell grew stronger.

Ray's flashlight shone on the floor a few feet in front of him so he could see what was going to block his path and he periodically lifted the beam higher to see what was further down the hall. He did that now and when it struck the bloated face attached to the bloated body sitting against the wall, he froze. Mel screamed.

Ray covered his mouth and nose with his shirt and moved closer. Flies buzzed around the corpse in a cloud and the noise seemed very loud in the echoing hallway. He was surprised he hadn't noticed it before.

The body was sitting upright against the wall at the end of the hallway. Dressed in slacks and a button-up shirt, it was hard to distinguish whether it was male or female except for the fact it wore men's shoes and its hair was cropped short. It was so bloated the shirt buttons were straining against the forces beneath it.

Mel was crying into Gil's shoulder and then she turned and vomited on the floor. Ray knew exactly how she felt and he was having a hard time keeping his dinner down. He kept swallowing, but every time his throat clenched and his Adam's apple worked up and down in his throat, the greasy, slick stench that encircled all of them seemed to physically slide down his throat. He could taste it.

"Do you know who it is?" Gil said in a weak voice barely above a whisper.

"No idea."

"Does he have ID?"

Ray didn't want to check.

He didn't want to get anywhere near the thing. As a matter of fact, all he wanted to do was run out of this building and never look back. Very uncop-like, he knew, but his rational mind was buried beneath all the revulsion he was feeling.

He knelt in front of the corpse and the smell seemed to hit him like a living thing. It crawled across his skin and lips, and his eyes could feel the stench lingering in the air like a mist. Even his hair felt as if things were crawling through it and he shook his head as if to shoo them away. He gagged.

The arm that was not holding the flashlight dropped the shirt and Ray could see it moving toward the body. He didn't want that arm anywhere near it, but it had a life of its own. He watched in detached amazement as it reached behind and into the body's back pocket. Somewhere in some distant part of his mind, he felt a lump there and watched as a wallet emerged grasped in his hand.

A rat's head popped up from behind the body, and squeaked at him.

Ray leapt backward as shock shot through him like a bolt of electricity. He wasn't sure but he thought he may have cried out. The light fell from his grasp and rolled away. Darkness filled in around him, and Mel screamed again.

He got it together and crawled to the flashlight laying a few feet away. He picked it up and stood. Shining it back toward the body, he watched as the rat, huge and bloated itself, scampered away through another hole in the wall. He cursed at it and grabbed a piece of broken furniture, throwing it after it in a rage.

He felt like he was losing his mind and the physical act of violence toward the thing that had scared the crap out of him seemed to ground him back in reality. He breathed in and out heavily despite the stench. Slowly, he started to calm down.

Ray walked back to where Gil and Mel stood and shined the light on the wallet. He opened it and saw it belonged to Dirk Samuels. The name meant nothing to him.

"Isn't that Bethany's fiancé?" Gil asked.

"I don't know. Jaxon would know."

Ray flipped through it and saw some credit cards, a few pictures and about $12 in cash. A piece of paper was folded and stuffed in one of the slots. He pulled it out and written in looping purple handwriting was a set of lat/longs.

"Thank God," he said. "I thought I was going to have to dig around that corpse more to find the cache."

"Let's get out of here, please," Mel said. "I can't stand it."

Ray nodded and turned to leave. His light shone down the hall and sticking half out of one of the doorways was an arm and leg. It moved quickly back inside the room out of the light. Mel screamed again. Ray pulled his weapon and crouched low, quickly moving toward the room.

"Freeze!" Ray yelled.

Glass shattered and then silence. Ray ran to the room, panned the light around with the gun and seeing no one, ran in and to the window.

Outside, a figure ran off into the distance and out of sight. Ray could not understand how he had gotten down to the ground from the third floor. He leaned out of the window and discovered a rope dangling from it. He cursed and holstered the weapon.

Gil and Mel stood at the doorway. "He's gone," Ray said.

"Who was it?"

"I have no idea. He used a rope to climb down so he was planning on being here."

"Did you see his face?" Gil said.

"No. Come on. Let's get out of here."

Ray led the way to the stairs and when they reached the landing, he smelled smoke over the stench of decay. Shining the light down the stairs, he could see it just starting to rise from below.

"Come on!" he yelled and pulled them down the stairs.

As they made it to the bottom floor, flames lit the walls down the hallway to their right as the fire quickly spread. They ran from the building and stood outside as the left half of the structure became engulfed in flames.

Ray got on his cell phone and dialed 9-1-1. He reported the fire and then hung up when they asked for his name. He knew they could trace the call if they wanted, but he wasn't worried about that now. They needed to get the heck out of there before all the activity delayed them.

They ran to the Mustang, jumped in, and he squealed the tires as they left quickly. The stench of death followed them down the road.

CHAPTER 27

Jaxon drove south on I-95, the headlights from the oncoming traffic like bullets to his head.

The pain behind his left eye had grown to more than an annoyance and he wondered if he was having a stroke or something. Maybe even a brain tumor. He shook four more aspirin into his hand from the container he bought at the gas station and swallowed them with the giant coffee he had poured there also. His stomach wanted to rebel but he wouldn't let it. He had things to do.

He was a few minutes away from West Palm Beach and had just gotten off his cell with Ray. He confirmed that Dirk Samuels was indeed Bethany Hope's fiancé and had gone missing shortly before all this started. He wasn't surprised. He really hadn't expected him to turn up alive. He was beginning to think Bethany wasn't going to survive either. In fact, she may already be dead despite the fact her 72 hours were not up.

Victoria was doing a little better. She was going to take a nap and then check in with Jaxon and see if she could help with anything. He was glad she was going to rest. She was probably in worse shape than she was admitting and he knew she needed it. Being blown up was a lot more traumatic than she was letting on.

Jaxon pulled into a parking lot at a local grocery store and saw Gil's Mustang parked in a quiet part of the lot. He parked next to them and got out. Ray stepped from the driver's seat and Gil and Melanie followed. Mel looked pretty shaken. He walked right up to her.

"Are you ok?"

She shook her head and started to cry. Gil pulled her to him and held her. He looked a little worse for wear too and Jaxon wondered if they were all pushing it beyond what they were capable of handling. He touched Mel's shoulder and tried to comfort her. He felt useless.

He turned to Ray and said, "You look like shit."

"Feel like it too. And you look about to collapse. Do I need to worry about you, old man?"

"I'll run rings around you any day."

Ray chuckled but couldn't seem to muster much more energy than that.

He pulled Jaxon over away from Gil and Mel and spoke in a low voice.

"It was pretty rough in that abandoned school. She took it well while we were in there, but I don't know if she's going to be able to continue. Maybe we should send those two home. We've got your car. I'll turn the other way and let him drive."

"You sure you'll be able to live with that?" Jaxon said sarcastically.

Ray just gave him a look.

Jaxon nodded.

"All right. I agree. Fanucci is locked up and it should be safe for them to go home. I just hope we won't need Gil's expertise."

"I think between us, we'll be able to figure it out."

"We're not leaving," Gil said loudly from where they stood. Either they had overheard them or they could tell what they were talking about. Jaxon and Ray walked back over to them.

"She's been through enough, Gil," Jaxon said. "It's time to take her home."

"I'm all right," she said, but her face betrayed her words.

"I don't think so," Jaxon said. "What you guys went through would be traumatic to me and I've seen a lot in my career. Ray and I will be fine without you. Really."

"We're not leaving," Gil repeated.

Jaxon sighed and looked at Ray who shrugged. "You're a lot of help."

"Mel. What can I do to convince you to go? We'll be all right without you."

She got herself under control and shook her head. "There's nothing you can say. I'm not giving up on Bethany. All I can think is that she's probably going through so much worse. I'll be fine."

Jaxon couldn't argue with that so he just touched her on the shoulder and said, "Anytime you're ready to go home, you tell us. You can leave whenever it gets to be too much."

She nodded her head and even smiled.

"Ok," Jaxon said. "Where to?"

Gil pulled out the GPS and showed Jaxon the map. "It looks like a neighborhood. It's right around the corner from here."

"We'll take both cars and I'll follow you. Hopefully, it will be easy."

"I'm just praying for a nice neighborhood," Ray said.

"This is West Palm. All the neighborhoods are nice," Jaxon said. "I grew up here."

"That neighborhood with the school wasn't nice," Mel said.

Jaxon paused for a beat and then said, "The school. It wasn't Nathan Forest High was it?"

"Yes. Why?"

"That's where I went. It closed down a couple of years after I graduated. I can't believe it's still standing."

"Well, part of it probably isn't. That fire we left burning was going pretty strong."

"The neighborhood was shit?"

"A deserted slum."

"Great. I lived there. Guess things change."

"Always."

Jaxon got in the car and followed the Mustang out of the parking lot. Ray drove slowly and made a right turn into a ritzy neighborhood with a manicured entrance and an award-winning golf course. At least that's what the sign said. Ray was going to get his wish.

The road wound around in the dark and then Ray turned right at a cul-de-sac. The houses lining the street were very nice; brick and stone fronts with lush landscaping, columned entrances, and fancy outside lighting. BMWs, Mercedes, and Audis sat parked in the drives. Screened-in pools could be seen through the sides of the yards and most on the right side backed up to the golf course. The street was deserted at this late hour and nobody noticed two strange cars cruising the neighborhood. That was good.

They came around a curve in the road and the cul-de-sac ended directly in front of them. The house at the end was probably the largest on the street and as Ray pulled up to it, Jaxon noticed smoke wafting up from the roof. He jumped out of his car as Ray, Gil and Mel got out and he pointed.

"It's on fire!"

"Shit!" Ray said. "This is the waypoint."

"Call 9-1-1."

Ray got his cell out as Jaxon ran to the front of the house and banged on the door. His old training took over.

"Police! Open up!"

Gil and Mel stood behind him looking lost and he pointed to the side yard.

"Go around and see if anyone's in the back. I'm going in."

Gil and Mel took off and Jaxon slammed his shoulder into the front door. It shifted but held. He stepped back and kicked with everything he had and it gave way with a loud crack. Ray came up beside him.

"They're on their way."

Jaxon nodded and stepped into the house. It was filling rapidly with smoke.

"Police! Is anyone here?"

He pointed to the massive spiral staircase directly in front of them and Ray headed up shouting. Jaxon went right, into a kind of study, and found nothing. He backtracked and passed the staircase heading toward the back of the house. He could hear Ray shouting above him. Jaxon added his own voice, but no one responded.

He entered the kitchen. It was empty. The smoke was thicker here, but the fire had not shown itself. Jaxon continued through the kitchen into a long hallway with doors on one side. Floor to ceiling windows filled the other wall with a view of the pool and surrounding landscaping. He saw Gil and Mel making their way to it. He waved his arms at them but they didn't see him. Flinging doors open as he moved down the hall, he found the rooms empty of people. Maybe no one was here.

"Police! There's a fire! You need to evacuate the building!"

Jaxon's throat was burning and his eyes were tearing up. He was having a hard time finding his way as the smoke thickened. The place was huge and he would never be able to get to all the rooms before the smoke overcame him. He wondered how Ray was doing upstairs. The smoke was probably worse there.

No one responded to his shouts and he began to wonder if the place was empty.

He came to the end of the hall and tried to open the door. It was locked. He banged on it and shouted but could hear nothing. The door felt warm. He knew he wasn't supposed to open a hot door in a fire, but he had to see if anybody was trapped. He stepped back and kicked the door in.

A blast of heat wafted out as the door flung open. The fire was along the back wall of the room and was contained within it but was producing a lot of smoke from the carpet and drapes. He tried to cover his face and nose as best he could when he entered but it was still difficult to see with his eyes tearing so much. He coughed hard and thought he'd never be able to take a deep breath again.

The room was some kind of game room and bar, as a pool table sat to the right against a wall of windows facing the pool. The bar was centered along the left wall and as Jaxon turned toward it he saw a woman bound in a chair, unconscious. He stepped to her and worked to untie her. It was not going to be easy. He worked a few of the knots, but at that rate, they were both going to die from smoke inhalation. He already felt as if he was going to pass out. Suddenly, Ray was next to him.

"I can't get her untied," Jaxon shouted over the fire. "Let's pick her up."

Ray nodded and went behind her. They lifted her and backtracked out of the room.

Back in the hall it was no better. The black, billowing smoke snaked along the ceiling and began descending along the glass walls lower and lower. The air was so stifling, Jaxon had resorted to holding his breath. He didn't think he was going to make it. He stumbled and almost dropped the woman, but regained his feet and had to take a breath.

The pain was worse than he could imagine as his lungs tried to reject the smoke combined with the panic his body was feeling as the oxygen in his blood stream plummeted. His brain was screaming for it. He started coughing and couldn't stop. Ray was having his own difficulty with breathing and Jaxon could see his eyes bulging from their sockets as he struggled to hold his breath. Just a little farther.

The door at the end of the hall burst open. Gil and Mel came through it in a rush just as Jaxon went to his knees. He was blacking out. Somebody grabbed under his arms and half dragged him along the hallway as he worked through the fog in his head to make his legs move. They didn't want to cooperate. He stumbled forward, trying his best to maintain a grip on the girl, but she was pulled from his hands and he thought he dropped her. He stopped and fumbled around, but then a voice shouted close to him.

"I got her! Come on!"

He looked up to see someone helping him and Gil holding the girl. They wavered in and out of his vision as he coughed uncontrollably. He had never coughed so hard in his life. The air started to clear a bit and he was able to choke in small gasps of cleaner air between his fits of coughing and soon he could walk on his own.

He was guided out of the house just as the fire trucks pulled up and a paramedic put a mask over his face. The cool oxygen blowing past his lips helped but the burning in his throat continued to make him cough. At least he was alive.

He held the mask to his face and nodded to the paramedic as he sat on the ground. He coughed hard again and felt as if his lungs would rip from his chest. He hacked up black phlegm and then seemed to be able to breathe a little easier. He glanced up and saw Ray, Gil, and Mel all with oxygen on their faces and the firemen trying to free the woman in the chair. They were administering oxygen to her with some kind of bag they squeezed as a mask was pressed to her face. The rest of the firemen were working to get the fire under control.

Jaxon stood and wobbled on his feet. The paramedic came up.

"You need to stay off your feet, sir."

Jaxon waved him away and walked over to the group working on the woman. In a voice he could barely recognize as his own he said, "Is she dead?"

One of the firemen looked up and shook his head.

"No. We're just trying to get her some oxygen. Her blood is saturated with the byproducts of the smoke. She can't absorb the oxygen as well as we can yet."

She moaned and then started coughing.

She wasn't quite free of the chair, but she could move enough to roll to her side and vomit all over the paramedic's boots. This made them all grin in relief. Apparently, she was going to be ok.

Jaxon went back to his spot and sat on the grass. He grabbed the oxygen mask and sucked on the cool stream of air blowing through and gave a thumbs up to Ray who grinned. They had almost died, but in the end, had saved this woman.

One of the local cops came up to them and asked what had happened. Jaxon explained as best he could through the mask who they were and what had happened. The cop seemed to take it all in stride, but he had a look that betrayed his true feelings. He thought this all bullshit. Jaxon produced his ID, as did Ray, and he seemed to show a little more respect.

"How did you know she was in there?" He asked.

"We didn't," Jaxon said. "We just saw the fire."

"Good thing you came along. She may not have survived much longer."

"Is her name Bethany Hope?"

The cop looked at his notepad.

"No. Rebecca Levesque. Her husband is Jim Levesque. He's on his way from the hospital. He's a doctor and on call at the moment. No children."

"That name sounds familiar," Ray said.

"It's Bethany Hope's friend," Jaxon said.

"Who's Bethany Hope?" the cop asked, looking confused.

"She's the woman we're looking for. Shit! If this is Rebecca's house, the others might be in trouble too." Jaxon stood up. "I need you to try and track down a few people, and quick. They may all be in danger."

He gave the officer the names and he went to his car and got on the radio. Jaxon called Tate in Orange Park and woke him up. He told him what happened.

"Sloan Upton is here in Orange Park," Tate said.

"You better get somebody over there."

"On it. You sound funny. Everything ok?"

"I'm talking through an oxygen mask. The fire."

"Got it. Be careful."

"You too. He's set up all kinds of booby traps for us, so there's no telling what's waiting for you."

"Great."

"And Tate?"

"Yeah."

"I believe you."

"About what?"

"It's not Fanucci. How could he be doing all this from jail?"

"True. Glad you're finally convinced."

"Don't get all warm and fuzzy. This guy is still out there and he's killing people."

"Right. I can take care of myself."

Jaxon hung up and the cop came back over.

"The firefighters say there is something written on the walls in the house. A bunch of numbers. Does that mean anything to you?"

Jaxon nodded. "Am I allowed back in? I need those numbers."

"The fire is out, so I don't see why not. Are you all right to go back in there? You look like shit."

"I'm just tired, but I'll be all right. Lead the way."

Jaxon followed the cop and entered the house through the front door. The smoke scent that hung in the air was heavy and wet and it made him wheeze and cough again. He had to stop for a second until the coughing subsided.

"Maybe you should wait outside and I'll get the numbers for you."

"No. I got it. Lead on."

The cop looked at him sideways but said nothing more.

He led the way through the kitchen and down the long hallway to the game room. The firefighters were still cleaning up and the fire chief was inspecting the location. On the wall behind the bar was a set of lat/longs scrawled in what must be lemon juice because it wasn't there when he had been in here before. Or, at least, he hadn't noticed it. The chief was looking at it.

"Was it lemon juice?" Jaxon asked, standing next to the man in the bright yellow chief's hat.

"Either that or some other reagent. It reacted to the heat. Do you know what it means?"

"It's for me. It's a message."

"Looks like some kind of coordinates."

"Exactly. Anything else weird?"

The chief turned to the cop with a questioning look on his face. The cop nodded. "He's cool."

"The fire was rigged to a bomb. It could have been planted at any time. A timer was set to ignite a slow burn to create a lot of smoke."

"How long for it to actually start the fire and not just smoke?" Jaxon asked.

"At least two hours. Could be more."

"So the woman could have been tied up for a while," the cop said.

"Looks that way. Thanks, Chief."

The man nodded and then went back to work.

Jaxon and the cop walked back out of the house and he joined Ray, Gil, and Mel out front.

"Another set of lat/longs," Jaxon said and showed them the numbers. Gil plugged them into his GPS.

"They're close," he said. "Just a couple of miles away."

Jaxon's cell rang and he didn't recognize the number.

"Jaxon."

"It's Tate. Sloan Upton was there and her husband was injured. She was tied up to the bed, a bomb set to go off in an hour. The bomb squad is here now trying to diffuse it."

"Be careful. Is she ok?"

"Fine. Except she's pretty traumatized. She said the guy wore a mask. Stabbed her husband when he tried to fight back."

"Were there any messages there? Numbers on walls or mirrors?"

"Not that I can see, but I haven't been through the whole house."

"Go look now. Is there a good sized wall where the bomb was planted?"

"Yes."

Jaxon could hear voices as Tate passed men doing their jobs in the house.

"Do you have a lighter?"

"Yes," Tate said, a little out of breath.

"Find something to burn, like a piece of paper and run it along the wall. We're looking for invisible ink."

"You're kidding, right?"

"Just do it."

Jaxon waited a couple of minutes as Tate put the phone down. Ray was staring at him and Mel looked a little anxious. She was still holding it together ok, but the fire had been scary. For him and her. He only just now realized she was the one who had supported him as they tried to escape the smoke. He owed her his life. His face must have conveyed this because her eyes changed and then she smiled.

Tate came back to the phone.

"There are a bunch of numbers."

"Read them to me." Jaxon listened as he read them off and confirmed they were the same as the ones here in Palm Beach. "Thanks. Glad you made it there in time."

"It was close. How about the others?"

"Haven't heard yet."

"Keep me posted."

"You bet." Jaxon hung up and went to the patrolmen. "Any word on the others I told you about?"

He shook his head no and then got on his radio. He listened for a minute and then said, "They've gotten to Taylor Swenson's house and no one answers. They're entering the property as we speak. The others are still en route to Ellie Fountain's."

"We're going to take off. Here's my cell number. Call me if they find numbers anywhere in the house like the ones on the wall here. Can you do that?"

"You got it."

Jaxon signaled Ray, Gil and Mel and they all got in the Mustang and headed out. They left Jaxon's rental for later.

"Where to?" Ray said.

"To rescue Bethany."

CHAPTER 28

The water rose again and Bethany waited.
There was no light in the compartment and the pitch black made her that much more afraid. She was exhausted, thirsty, and hungry, yet all those things faded from her mind as she felt the first trickle of water brush against her shin. *Time to die*, she thought.
A tear trickled down her cheek and she thought of Dirk. She wondered if he was ok and if he was thinking about her. It felt like a lifetime had passed since she had seen him and her despair at never being able to look upon his face before she left this life for good, made the loneliness of the box she was trapped in that much more stifling. If the water didn't drown her, her sorrow surely would. She was at the end of her endurance and she could fight no more.
She waited as the water lapped against her thighs, a little shiver running up her spine. Her fever was probably high and her hand throbbed from the infection, but those seemed distant annoyances compared to the fate which she awaited. She wished she could look at the picture again. Danielle's smiling face would give her strength, for she was sure that Danielle had forgiven her.

Sometime over the last twenty-four hours, she had made her peace with the dead girl and knew in her heart that forgiveness was something she could allow to enter her soul.

The thirst that burned her throat returned stronger, and she touched her damp fingers to her lips and tasted the wetness. Salt. She knew she couldn't drink it, but her thirst was so strong she found her mind trying to convince itself it would be all right. Maybe if she went crazy or delirious from it, the pain of drowning wouldn't be so bad. Her rational side knew there would not be enough time. The water was rising faster than it would take her to go crazy from the salt.

She stood slowly in the rising water and steadied herself against the metal of the wall. She was so weak. She stepped to her right and tried to find the small crack in the roof that she knew was there. If only she could see a little light, it would bring her some comfort. The moon, the glow from a streetlight, even the dimness of the stars would be reassuring, but she could not find it. Nothing showed itself and she sank to her knees in the water and hung her head. The darkness would take her in its arms and there was nothing she could do about it.

* * *

They raced east as the moon rose full and Jaxon felt little comfort from it.

He had a feeling they were going to be too late. He didn't know where it came from, but it was strong. He also felt that this was it. These coordinates were going to lead them to Bethany and her prison. Somewhere up ahead, she was waiting, and hopefully, still alive.

He pushed the Mustang to its limits and the engine screamed as they flew down the empty streets. He could see Ray in his peripheral vision glancing his way, but he ignored him. Gil grinned in the reflection of the rear view mirror and Jaxon knew he wished he was behind the wheel. Mel was silent.

"Make a left ahead," Gil said. "Then it should be in front of us. It looks like it's near the ocean."

The tires squealed and lost their purchase as he rounded the turn, then found the grip of the road again and the car shot forward as if flung from a slingshot. Ray grabbed the dash and Mel made a little sound of distress in the back seat. The car vibrated beneath them as it churned up the gravel.

The sign for Palm Beach Harbor flashed past as they shot through the gate, a sleepy guard barely moving from his nap as the engine woke him. Jaxon could see him standing in the guardhouse looking around not sure what had just happened. It didn't matter. The police knew they were here and should be showing up themselves in a few minutes.

Jaxon could see the water of the harbor up ahead and the stacks of containers on a huge cargo vessel looming above the warehouses to his left. Lights shone bright on the ship and a crane was moving crates and containers onto it even at this late hour.

To the right was an abandoned section of the docks and if Jaxon was a betting man, he was sure that would be their destination. He turned the wheel slightly right and headed straight for it.

Jaxon slammed on the brakes just before the Mustang launched itself off the dock into the bay, the car skidded to a stop, and they all jumped out.

"Where?" Mel said.

Gil pointed to the right.

"It should be over there about fifty feet. We're almost right on top of it."

Jaxon ran to the spot and stopped on the edge of the pier.

The bay spread out before him with lights twinkling in the distance and the sound of the crane's engine coming to his ears as it hoisted its burden on a thin thread of a cable, depositing it somewhere in the bowels of the only ship berthed at the moment.

Beneath him in the water, five or six derelict cargo containers sat in the silt and trash of the bay, the water just brimming over the top of two and approaching the rim of the others. They bobbed in the high tide of the full moon and he cursed. She had to be in there.

Which one though? They were running out of time.

* * *

Bethany clung to the piece of metal at the roof and thanked God for the light.

The moon must have risen and when she saw its glow winking off and on through the crack in the roof, she cried. She would not have to die in the dark.

The container rocked gently in the tide as the water continued to rise and she was certain it would cover her head this time. The moon was full and the tide would be at its apex tonight. There was no denying it. She would drown in this metal pit and no one would know she was here. Except the bastard who put her here.

She pounded her fist on the roof in frustration as her teeth chattered from her fever and the chill water. She was determined to use her last bit of energy in defiance of whoever had done this to her. She had spent the last few hours in this world trying to figure out who, but it really didn't matter now. She would never know, and even if she did, it would change nothing. The water was going to rise higher and her mouth was going to sink below its cool surface where she would finally drink of the moisture she so longed to feel on her tongue. Too bad it would be the last thing she felt.

The water was at her neck and the panic began to rise in her throat like before.

She took back her request to die alone now, and wished she had someone to comfort her along in this journey. Somebody to hold her hand. To tell her it would be all right and it would not hurt. That all the pain and suffering she had born out the last hours would be over. She wished for Danielle to be with her, but knew it would not be.

A voice floated out of the gloom and she froze, unsure of what she was hearing. Had Danielle come to comfort her in her last minutes? Was she delirious from exhaustion? Who would be calling her name?

"Bethany!"

It was clear, now. No mistaking it.

Her name was shouted from the lips of some woman and if Danielle were here, then it must be close. She shook her head, trying to clear it and heard her name again.

"Bethany Hope! Where are you?"

She cocked her ear. Could it be coming from the crack in the roof? She heard it again and was sure. It was outside. It was not Danielle!

She pounded on the metal roof with her fist and shouted at the top of her lungs.

"Here! Here! I'm in here!"

Suddenly a great pounding could be heard on the roof and then a face appeared in the crack. A face she did not recognize. But she cried aloud anyway and yelled as loud as she could.

"I'm here! I'm here! I'm here!"

The face smiled and turned to someone else outside.

"She's here!"

* * *

Gil motioned to the top of the container he had jumped to and yelled, "She's here!"

Jaxon rushed over and jumped to join him. He could now hear a voice yelling and was elated to see a face in his flashlight beam on the other side of a rusted out section of the roof. The water was almost over her head. They had to hurry.

"Bethany! Stay calm. We're going to get you out of there. We're right here."

"Hurry!" she said. "The water."

Jaxon looked around the roof and could see no way in. Gil was searching along the edge and yelled as he pointed.

"It looks like the doors are here. But they're under water."

Ray had joined them on the roof while Mel stayed on shore. Jaxon could hear sirens approaching. He went to where Gil was and looked over the edge.

The surf sloshed along the top but he could see the levers that released the doors a few feet below the surface. He didn't even think. He jumped in.

The water was cool, and the surf was building as it tossed him against the container, painfully.

He gagged a mouthful of water and choked as he sputtered and tried to tread water. He grabbed the side of the container and caught his breath.

"Shine the light down here!" he yelled up to Ray who obliged.

He dove down under the water, pulled himself to the door latch, and tried to release it. It moved a little but wouldn't unlock completely. He grabbed the second one and it wouldn't budge at all. It must be rusted shut. He surfaced and took a huge gulp of air.

"Hurry!" Ray yelled. "She doesn't have much time."

"I can't get them open."

He dove down again and worked on the one lever that would wiggle, but it wouldn't release. He felt along the length of it and discovered why. He surfaced again and reached his hand out. Ray pulled him up. He knelt on the roof as the water rose and said, "It's got a padlock on it."

"Shit!"

He nodded. He stood and went to the opening where Gil knelt and looked inside. The water was almost completely over her head. She had to tilt her face up and gulp breaths between the small wakes of the tide. She was panicking.

Jaxon saw the police arrive and he looked around frantically trying to find a way to get her out. Nothing came to mind. They needed a torch, or cutting tools, and that would take time they didn't have.

The crane's motor droned on as it worked and drowned out the sound of the sirens. He could hardly think with the noise.

The crane!

"Tell the crane to swing over here and we'll hook the container up! It's the only chance."

Ray nodded, jumped to shore, and ran over to it.

Jaxon looked at the jagged edges of the rusty crack in the roof and bent to the hole.

"Bethany! Move away from the opening. We're going to try and make it bigger."

She didn't hear at first and he had to repeat himself, but she nodded and disappeared in the gloom.

He and Gil kicked at the rusted metal and it bent and gave way a bit. A small piece broke off and it made the hole a little larger. It might buy them more time.

Bethany came back into view and pushed her face up to the hole where her nose and mouth were able to stick up through it into the air. She gasped and breathed it in. The water had reached the roof. Her fingers locked onto the edge of the hole and she kept her face pressed up against it. The jagged metal had cut her, but she didn't seem to care. Gil grasped her fingers and held on.

Jaxon looked and could see Ray up next to the cab of the crane gesturing wildly toward them. The crane operator shook his head and Ray grabbed his shirt and shook him. He then pulled his pistol and shoved it in his face. The operator got the point.

Jaxon looked down and saw water sloshing around his feet and Bethany's lips and nose were just above the water. She was breathing raggedly and he could see her eyes, wide and fearful just below the water.

The local cops ran up to the edge of the container and one jumped on.

The weight of him actually pushed the container a little lower in the water and Bethany became fully submerged. Her fingers splayed out in panic and she pushed her face around trying to find air.

"Get off! You're pushing her under the water."

The cop nodded, jumped back to the shore, and her mouth and nose resurfaced. She sucked a ragged breath in and then gagged. She tried not to breathe the seawater in, but she was having a hard time.

"Gil, you go too. Maybe we can lift it a little higher."

He nodded and let go of her hand. Jaxon grasped it in his and watched Gil leap to the shore. The container rose up another couple of inches and bought her a few more minutes. Her eyes came out of the water too and she looked pleadingly at him.

"Please," she said. "I can't take much more."

"Hold on, Bethany. The crane is coming."

Mel yelled, "Give her this!"

It was the snorkel. Leave it to Mel to think of the obvious. He grinned at her and she tossed it over. He grabbed it and showed it to Bethany. She nodded and he held it to her lips. She opened her mouth and took the mouthpiece in as he held the upper end up out of the water. She breathed loudly through it and nodded her head. It was helping.

The crane rolled closer with Ray and a cop riding on either side. The operator understood the urgency now and was pushing the machine to its limits. The engine roared as black smoke poured out of the exhaust, the metal wheels that rode the tracks, screeching over the engine. Jaxon watched the crane arm lower as it approached and four cables dangled above him.

If he let go of the snorkel it would sink under the water. He waved at Gil again who jumped to the container and took over keeping her airway clear of the ocean. The cables lowered to where he could reach them and he grabbed one as it swung. The hooks were huge. Bigger than his head.

The container had welded points attached at each corner and the crane operator yelled for him to attach a hook to each one. The points were basically big, metal circles. They were corroded and in bad shape. He hooked the first cable to one and ran to the other, sliding its hook into the hole. He continued to each corner attaching the hooks. The crane operator took up the slack and when it was taut, slowly applied power as he tried to pull the container out of the water.

The cables groaned as they stretched and the weight of the container filled with water was probably more than the crane could handle. The operator inched the machine closer to get a better angle and the engine roared again as it increased the tension. The container shifted under Jaxon's feet and the water started siphoning off the sides. It was rising.

The group of officers cheered on the shore as it continued up out of the water and Jaxon could hear and see the water draining from within the container. Suddenly, one of the weld points broke free and that end of the container shifted.

Jaxon went to his knees as his world tilted and then the other weld broke on that same side. Jaxon slid down the length of the roof and plummeted to the ocean below. Gil followed right behind.

The crane operator swung the container hanging by the remaining two cables toward the shore and Jaxon watched as it touched down. He wondered if Bethany was all right. Maybe the water inside the container cushioned her fall as the welds broke.

One of the cops came to the bulkhead side and helped Jaxon and Gil out of the water as a fireman pried at the doors with a big metal pole. It took two of them to break the padlock off and then the door swung open, water pouring out in a rush. Jaxon stepped to the opening and looked inside. Bethany was kneeling in the remaining water smiling. She stumbled forward and threw her arms around the first person she could get to. It just so happened to be Jaxon.

She was safe.

CHAPTER 29

Jaxon lay on the hotel bed with the phone pressed to his ear.

He was having a hard time keeping his eyes open but he had to hear Victoria's voice first. Gil and Mel were next door getting some rest. They were all in pretty beat up shape and he didn't want to risk driving until he had a little sleep. Ray didn't want to wait. After a handshake and a promise to stay in touch, he took Jaxon's rental car and headed back to Naples. Jaxon wondered if he'd ever see him again.

Vick answered the phone. She had been asleep. She didn't seem to mind.

"We got her."

"I heard. Feels good when things work out, huh?"

"How did you hear?"

"Tate. Just a little bit ago."

"Are you feeling any better?"

"I'm sore as hell, but I'll live. You?"

"So exhausted I probably won't be able to sleep."

"Somehow I doubt that," she said. "You get some rest before you drive home."

"That's the plan. They put us up in a hotel. Gil and Mel are next door."

"How's the girl?"

"Dehydrated and weak. She's in the hospital overnight so they can get some fluids in her. Cop's outside her door."

"That's good. I bet she was glad to see you."

"I got a hug."

"I'm sure you did."

A little silence played out between them and Jaxon always liked the fact they didn't have to say words to convey what they were feeling. He could tell she was smiling.

"Sleep," she said. "I'll see you soon."

"Can't wait."

He hung up and closed his eyes. He was out before the next thought could enter his mind.

* * *

Bethany lay in her hospital bed and cried.

The I.V. in her arm was pumping much needed fluids, electrolytes, and antibiotics into her depleted body, but she didn't care. All that time on the brink of death, her life playing out in her mind, the horrible thing she had done to that poor girl, and all the good things in her life, everything that had enabled her to hang on, were now shattered and broken. Dirk was dead and it all seemed such a waste.

She had endured hell, gotten out and wanted nothing more than to be held by Dirk, and when she learned he had been killed because of her, it was just one more blow to add to all the other injuries. He had not deserved it and she hated herself for it.

The door to her room opened and a male nurse came in wearing a mask and blue scrubs. She wiped her eyes and tried to compose herself, but it was difficult. The nurse noticed her appearance and said, "It will be better soon. The trauma you've been through can create all kinds of emotions. How are you feeling, physically?"

"I'm tired. I know I'm running a fever, but I'm sure I'm not infectious. You don't have to wear the mask."

"Instructions from your physician." He was carrying a syringe on a small tray and he set it down on the bed, reaching for her I.V. "This will help you feel better too."

"What is it?"

"It's a sedative. Help you sleep."

She nodded and a tear trickled down her cheek. She wiped it away quickly.

"Anything else bothering you?"

She didn't know why, but she decided to open up to the man.

"My fiancé. He was killed because of me. I'm just having a hard time dealing with that."

"I'm sure you will see him soon enough."

"What? No. He's dead. Killed by a horrible man. The same one who put me through that torture."

The nurse swabbed the I.V. port, slipped the needle in, and pressed the plunger. He looked at his watch.

"It's horrible to lose a loved one. I know."

Bethany nodded and felt the medication course through her veins. It would be good to sleep. Forget about everything for a while. Her vision began to cloud over and she welcomed the calm that overtook her.

Then a pressure began to spread across her chest and she opened her eyes in surprise. She couldn't seem to catch her breath. She tried moving her hand to grab the nurse, but it didn't want to move. It felt numb and the numbness was spreading. Pain flared in her chest and spread to her arms as the drug took effect. Something was wrong. She tried to speak, but her body wouldn't respond. She couldn't even turn her head. The lights on the ceiling began to dim and the world faded as the pain spread throughout her body. The last thing she heard was the nurse whispering in her ear.

"For Danielle."

* * *

Jaxon drove the Mustang the speed limit and drained the remainder of his coffee.

I-95 was moving along nicely for a Monday morning and if that didn't change, he'd be home in thirty minutes. St. Augustine had just passed them on the right and Gil offered his opinion on the caches in the area.

"I've found every cache they have in St. Augustine. Some pretty tough ones too."

"I don't think I'll be caching ever again," Jaxon said.

"I don't blame you, but for me, I can't stop. I want to find a cache in every country in the world."

"Pretty ambitious. Where are you going to get the money?"

"Not all at once. Over my lifetime. You know, maybe a couple a year."

"Still. Pretty expensive."

They had gotten up late, all of them sleeping well, and grabbed a quick breakfast before hitting the road. Jaxon enjoyed the banter between him and Gil, and even Mel chimed in periodically, though she seemed somewhat subdued. He didn't blame her. They had all been through a lot and she was probably a little shell shocked.

"I'll go," she said.

Gil turned to her in the back and smiled. "That's what will make it all so cool. You have to go with me."

She touched his hand and held it for a minute. "We're not going to Africa any time soon. No Mambas."

"Right."

Jaxon's cell rang and he snatched it up. "Jaxon."

"It's Tate."

"Detective. Good to hear from you."

"Bethany Hope is in ICU."

"What? Why?"

"They found her unresponsive in her hospital bed and had to revive her. She's on a ventilator."

Jaxon had to hold on to the wheel tightly as the news sank in. He couldn't believe what he was hearing.

"Aw dammit! What happened?"

"The officer on duty recalled a male nurse entering the room about 3:30 a.m. He was carrying a syringe. He left shortly after and did not return. At shift change a few hours later, another nurse discovered her with no pulse."

"A male nurse?"

"Yes. Employee records show only female nurses clocked in at the time. We're pretty sure he was involved somehow and they're pulling surveillance recordings as we speak."

"There won't be anything on them."

"Do you know something I don't?"

"He was able to hack into a number of other systems and manipulate them. I'm sure he's done the same there."

"We'll see what we get. There's more."

Jaxon felt the whole last few days slipping away.

"What?"

"The other four are dead. Rebecca Levesque, Sloan Upton, Ellie Fountain, and Taylor Swenson."

"How?"

"We don't have particulars on those yet except that all four were shot in the head from close range."

"Does Fanucci have anything to say about all this?"

"Why would he?" Tate's voice grew angry. "He's been cleared. You know that."

"He's the closest to all of this. He might have some theories. Have you thought of that?"

"He would tell us if he knew anything."

"Why don't you ask him?"

"You're not making many friends around here are you?"

"I don't care about friends. I care about catching this guy."

"He's played you all along, Jaxon. Haven't you realized that yet? He sent you on a wild goose chase and has planned this all along."

Jaxon knew he was right and it made him even angrier.

"Talk to Fanucci. He might know something."

"He's spending time with his brother. I'm not going to bother him, and his brother was good enough to take time off to be with him."

"Do you know his brother?"

"Of course. He's an officer at this station too."

"What? Why wasn't I aware of this?"

"I don't know. It isn't important. He's a stepbrother anyway."

"Tate, have you talked to this brother?"

"No. And I don't plan to."

"Where are they?"

"I have no idea."

"You don't know where he lives?"

"Yes. But they're not home. They left to get away from things here for a while."

"What's the address?"

"I'm not giving you that."

"Dammit, Tate! You're too close to this. Don't you see? What kind of relationship did his brother have to Danielle?"

"I have no idea. He's talked about her before, but I wouldn't call him a killer if that's what you're getting at. What is it with you? Everybody in this department a suspect to you?"

"No. Just ones with a motive to kill. What's the brother's name?"

"I don't know if I want to tell you. I don't want you bothering them. Fanucci's been through enough."

"His name's not Fanucci is it?"

Silence.

"Tate. This is important. What is his name?"

"Collin Williamsen."

The name hit Jaxon in the chest like a blow from a prize fighter. He should have known. How could he have been so stupid?

"Jaxon? Still there?"

"Yeah. I need you to do something for me?"

"What now?"

"I need you to go to a hotel and check on my wife."

* * *

Ray woke up and looked at his watch. "Shit."

It was 10:00 a.m. and he had slept too long. His body had needed the rest, but he really hadn't wanted to take the time to get it. His chief had wanted him back earlier this morning and he had tried his best to drive through the night, but after he almost wrapped the rental car around a tree at 4:30, he knew he was going to kill himself if he didn't stop and sleep. He pulled into the first place he saw and paid for the remainder of the night. The motel office attendee had been asleep himself and it had taken repeated ringing of the bell to get the guy up. Even with him sitting right in front of him passed out in a chair. Ray could smell alcohol on him.

Michelle had told him she didn't want him driving so tired anyway and even though he told her he could handle it, she had been relieved when he woke her to tell her he was stopping.

"I'm glad. I wasn't sleeping very well anyway," she said. "I was worried."

"Sorry to give you a restless night. Go back to sleep and I'll see you later today."

"It is 'today' already, isn't it?"

"Yes. Get some sleep."

"I will. You too."

"Easily."

That had been what seemed an eternity ago though it had only been a few hours. He sat up and looked around the room. It was just that. A room with a bed, chair, and TV. He had been too tired to even look last night. He went to the bathroom and flipped on the light. He groaned. He'd wait to shower until he got home. No way was he getting into that tub.

He splashed some water on his face and then pulled the door closed as he left. The motel looked worse for wear in the daylight. His car was the only one in the lot and he could see weeds growing up through cracks in the asphalt. He had made a great choice in his haste to sleep. At least it had been better than sleeping in the car.

He walked to the office, found the manager, and checked out. The guy hadn't moved from his chair. At least he hadn't been asleep again.

Ray grabbed a quick bite at a fast food joint just off the highway and then he was on his way home. Three hours on the road and this nightmare would all be over. He felt pretty good about the outcome, yet he had this nagging thorn in his side that he never should have gotten involved. Too late now, that was for sure. He just hoped he hadn't jeopardized his job.

He pulled his cell phone from his pocket and dialed Michelle. She'd probably be worrying again, and he knew she wouldn't call him for fear of interrupting his rest. He'd better check in so she could relax.

After the tenth ring it went to voice mail and he looked at the number to make sure it was her. He hung up and tried again. When it went to voice mail for the second time, he left a message and hung up. Maybe she wasn't as worried about him as he thought.

His phone rang and he saw it was from her. He hit answer.

"You were still sleeping weren't you?" he joked.

"You should have kept your nose out of it," a male voice said.

The line went dead.

* * *

When Jaxon had been sixteen and attending Nathan B. Forrest High School in West Palm Beach, Florida, life had been good. As good as it could get for a teenager in the 70s and early 80s.

He played linebacker on the football team, was getting good grades, (not great, but good) and had a girlfriend who would let him get to second base most nights and had promised more for the prom. His stepmom stayed at home and took care of him while his dad worked for the government doing something he had no clue what. The man was rarely home.

Jaxon had been liked. Not popular, but liked. Nobody messed with him because of his size and his group of friends all stuck together. Most of them were football players like himself.

Collin Williamsen was a loner.

One of those kids who always seemed to end up in the wrong place at the wrong time. Small, thin build, lank brown hair and black rimmed glasses. The typical geek of the 80s. He liked the band Air Supply, wore colored denim jeans, and drew pictures of dragons and wizards all day. If Jaxon had really given a crap about the guy, he would have noticed the talent the kid had for art. But, like most his age, Jaxon couldn't care less about drawing.

Collin also had some kind of genetic defect, and Jaxon saw it for the first time in the locker room after gym class.

Jaxon was goofing off with some of his teammates, snapping towels, and joking around when his best friend and fellow linebacker, Rocky Menlose, saw Collin come out of the shower with towels covering his whole body. He had one towel around his waist, another over his shoulders and a third wrapped around his head, twisted, like girls do when their hair was wet.

Rocky pointed and said, "Hey, dork. What's up with all the towels?"

Collin ignored him and went to his locker. Rocky was not the kind to be ignored and this usually made him angrier. The room had gotten quiet as the boys could sense the tension. Everybody was watching.

"Hey, dork. I'm talking to you. What's up with all the towels?"

Rocky had walked over to Collin and stood over him. Jaxon followed. He thought this should be funny.

"I'm cold." Collin said, but did not look at Rocky.

"That's 'cause you don't have any meat on you. You need a cheeseburger or two."

Jaxon laughed with the rest of the boys and he could see Collin flinch at the sound.

"I heard things about you," Rocky said. "I bet they're true."

Collin said nothing and seemed to shrink into himself a little more. Jaxon had heard rumors too, but he had ignored them. He wondered what Rocky was getting at.

"What's wrong with you?" Rocky asked.

Collin said nothing and pulled the towel off of his head. His normal lank, brown hair was gone and in its place was skin. He was completely bald. A few gasps from the group and even a chuckle of laughter.

"I heard you don't have a single hair on your body. Like a baby. That true, Dork?" Rocky reached out and tugged at the kid's towel. "I bet if I pull this towel off, you're as bare as a newborn babe."

"Don't," Collin said.

"You gonna stop me?"

Collin tried to pull away, but Rocky was going to have none of it. He looked at Jaxon and Jaxon shrugged. He went to the other side of the boy and held his arms as Rocky yanked the towels off. Collin stood up and tried to fight back, but Jaxon and his friend were too much for him. He was not getting away.

The towels fell free and Collin stood there, stooped in the chilly air, his hairless body shivering from cold and fear. The boys in the room pointed and burst out laughing. Jaxon couldn't help it. He laughed too. Rocky had been right. The kid didn't have a single hair on him.

"He's like a girl," Jaxon said and laughed in Collin's face.

"Told you," Rocky said, and let Collin go. "Maybe you should dress and shower in the women's locker room."

"What's going on?" a booming deep voice shouted from the coach's office. It was Mr. Shawnessy, the history teacher. The regular coach had the day off for something and Mr. Shawnessy was filling in for him.

Everyone scattered.

Jaxon let Collin go and took one last look at the kid as he went to his own locker. The teacher stood with his hands on his hips in the doorway and waited for everyone to disperse.

When he was satisfied nothing needed his attention, he went back into the office as if nothing happened.

Jaxon glanced over at Collin and saw he was crying. The kid dressed quietly, putting his wig on and left without another word or a glance back. Jaxon never saw him in the locker room again.

Hearing his name again from Tate had brought back the flood of memories and as Jaxon thought about what they had done to the kid, he knew it was not his proudest moment. He hadn't given it much thought over the years and in fact had completely forgotten about the incident until the name had been dropped by Tate.

Collin Williamsen. Stepbrother of Robert Fanucci. Uncle to Danielle Newsome. Angry cop with a score to settle. A kid in a man's body who had apparently never gotten over being bullied. Maybe his niece's death had tipped him over the edge as the anger built over the years. He couldn't put himself in Collin's shoes and no matter how hard he tried, Jaxon could not fathom the despair the guy must be feeling. And Jaxon had helped.

Collin was paying it all back.

Paying it back for his niece and paying it back for the jocks who had tormented him in school. Rocky Menlose was dead. Jaxon had heard he died of some kind of brain tumor a few years back, so Jaxon was the only logical target of Collin's anger.

Things made some sense, and he could get the motive for his actions against Jaxon, but going crazy over a niece seemed a bit extreme. He could only guess at their relationship. Maybe he had been a favorite uncle or in one of those families where blood ties meant everything, but as far as Jaxon knew, they weren't even blood related. Fanucci was a stepbrother and not even Danielle's real father.

A lot of his whole game was clicking in place in Jaxon's mind and many of the blanks he had about all this fell into place as he thought it through. Collin had been planning this for some time and that's how he had been able to pull all of this off. Weeks, maybe even months to coordinate it all. Hell, he'd probably broken into Jaxon's house and planted those bombs way before this all started.

Jaxon tried to narrow it down to a specific event, but his mind couldn't wrap around it just yet. How had Collin known he would be at the original cache spot when Jaxon had found the finger? Hell, Jaxon had just started GeoCaching only a few months ago. It must have given birth in Collin's mind since then. Yet, there was no way he could force Jaxon's hand on that.

Or was there?

PBIStalker.

Jaxon had forgotten about that. "Stupid!" he said aloud and Gil and Mel glanced at each other.

PBIStalker. The handle meant everything now, but Jaxon had thought nothing of it when the person had befriended him on the GeoCaching forums. Everybody had weird names and most meant nothing, but now this one did. PBIStalker had been the one to tell Jaxon about the "really cool cache" he had found in Orange Park. The brand new one that no one knew about yet. The one with the really funny trackable item.

PBIStalker. It had meant nothing then. PBI was the federal government's official acronym for West Palm Beach. Jaxon's home town. Collin's home town. The place they went to high school. Jaxon should have seen it. He should have seen it with his eyes closed. He balled his fist up and punched the steering wheel.

Jaxon dialed Vick's number and listened to it ring. Gil and Mel were quiet in the car and waited for some kind of explanation from him. He didn't have any to give.

As the phone continued to ring unanswered, he pressed the gas pedal further to the floor and the car accelerated as the urgency rose in Jaxon's blood. He could not get there fast enough.

CHAPTER 30

Ray had the rental car floored for the last hundred miles and as he pulled into the apartment complex, he saw the lights of the local police he had called and a few officers standing around. He slammed on the brakes, skidded to a stop and jumped from the vehicle, running to the apartment. Someone shouted for him to stop, but he didn't listen.

He burst into the place and found it a wreck. Furniture tossed about and lamps shattered, pictures broken and appliances smashed. The officers inside asked if he was Rayford Maningham and he nodded.

"Where is she?" he said, his voice sounding as if from some far off place. He was like a zombie. He could hear and see things happening around him and he even knew his own voice when he heard it, but he could feel nothing but an electrical buzzing coursing through his whole body.

"Who?" An officer asked.

"Michelle. My fiancée. Where is she?"

"There's no one here. The place was empty."

Ray sank to a chair as he felt his legs give and he seemed to come out of his shock. If she's not here, then she must still be alive. But where?

He jumped back up and climbed the stairs to their room. Pushing the door open, he saw that this room had remained mostly untouched. Everything was in its place. Dresser drawers were closed, pictures were still on the walls, the bed was made. Everything was normal except for the huge numbers scrawled in red on the wall. Red that looked like blood as it dried. He touched the wetness and smelled. Paint. Thank God.

The numbers represented a position somewhere on this planet. A global position that held answers for him. A place he must go. And those numbers seemed strangely familiar.

* * *

Jaxon's phone rang as he was crossing the Buckman Bridge from Mandarin over to Orange Park and he picked it up quickly. It was Ray.

"She's gone," he said.

"Ray? Who's gone? What are you talking about? I've got my own problems right now."

"Michelle. My fiancée. He took her."

"What the hell are you talking about?"

Ray explained what had happened and Jaxon cursed.

"Give me the lat/longs and I'll plug them in."

Ray gave him the numbers and he repeated them to Gil who shook his head.

"What?" Jaxon said.

"We've been there already," Gil said. "It's the high school."

"Nathan B. Forrest High School?" Jaxon asked.

Gil nodded.

Figures, Jaxon thought to himself, and as he realized what that meant, he held little hope he would find Vick at the hotel.

"Gil says it's the high school in Palm Beach. My alma mater. You've been there before."

"I thought I recognized the numbers. I'm getting in the car and going there now. I need you."

"Wait just a bit, Ray. I know you feel like you can't, but I have to see if Vick is ok. I'm only a few minutes away. And anyway, we need to do this together. He's expecting us and the only chance we'll have is if we work together. Can you give it a few minutes and hold tight?"

"I guess I'll have to. Dammit! Why did he do this to her? She's done nothing to him."

"This isn't about her. It's about me. And you helped me. I don't have time to explain right now. It's all making sense."

"Not to me."

Jaxon pulled into the hotel parking lot with the tires squealing. He could see Tate standing in the parking lot looking his way.

"I have to go, Ray. I'll call you back in a few minutes." He didn't wait for Ray to respond.

"What's going on?" Mel asked.

Jaxon didn't answer. He jumped from the car as it stopped and ran to Tate who stood there with an unreadable face.

"She's not there," he said. "The place has been ransacked."

"I need to see."

Tate led the way as Gil and Mel followed. The room was down about halfway along the main stretch and the door was open. Jaxon stepped in and stared. On the wall in red were some numbers.

"They're the same," Gil said. "It's the high school."

Mel gasped as she saw her name on the wall. It was part of the message.

Come alone with Ray Gil and Melanie or they die.

* * *

They pulled into the run down neighborhood and drove slowly toward the remains of Nathan B. Forrest High School. Ray was leading.

They had met up at a diner just off the interstate and briefly talked about how they would handle it. Every plan they came up with had flaws, so they decided no plan was best. Collin was expecting them and there was no element of surprise and no tactical advantage they could come up with. They would just have to see what he wanted.

The street was deserted and Jaxon stared at the ruins of his old neighborhood and high school. This was home to so many good memories and it was hard for him to associate this run down slum and abandoned buildings with anything he remembered.

His heart sank at the sight and he was sure Collin was laughing at what had become of the place of such torture for him. He felt sure the man was gloating at the irony.

Jaxon pulled up to the school behind Ray and parked. He stepped from the Mustang as Gil and Mel followed. The night was quiet but bright as the full moon shone down on them. A siren could be heard in the distance and they all paused. It passed without incident.

Jaxon stared up at the ruin of his school and saw nothing but blank and broken windows staring back. One half of the building was scorched from the fire that had been set during Ray and the kids' last visit. Police tape was strewn across the front, but some gaps had been broken through already.

Ray led the way through the hole in the fence and they walked to the front steps in silence.

Gil finally spoke. "Shouldn't we go in the back or something? I mean we're walking right in through the front door. He'll know we're coming."

"He already knows we're coming," Jaxon said and walked on.

Jaxon climbed the overgrown steps and almost tripped over the door as it lay in the opening. Something skittered away into the darkness of the building and Mel gasped.

"Rats," Ray said and Jaxon nodded.

He pulled his gun and watched Ray do the same. He didn't think they would do any good, but it felt good to hold it in his hands anyway. The place was just like Ray and the kids had described and as the litter of his youth laid spread out before him, he felt nostalgia for the building that seemed out of place.

"It's on the third floor," Ray said and headed for the stairs.

Ray had told him about the weird classroom re-creation and they both felt confident that that was the place they needed to be. Mr. Shawnessy's room. The teacher who had turned his back on Collin that day in the locker room.

As they headed up the stairs, Ray turned on the flashlight and led the way. Jaxon noticed that the smell of smoke and wet, burnt, wood grew stronger as they climbed. A lesser scent hung just under that. The smell of death. He knew the body of Bethany's fiancé had been removed, but he also knew that decay and decomposition lingered for a while.

At the third floor landing, Ray doused the light and pointed to a classroom door about halfway down the hall on their right. The windows up here were letting in enough of the moonlight to see, though it was gloomy. Broken furniture and trash hung in the shadows. The silence was pronounced and the air held a tension that he could feel.

Jaxon stepped to the door, pushed it open, and entered with his gun leading the way. He was shocked at what he saw.

The room was immaculate. Desks were all lined up in rows with books and notebooks shoved underneath. Posters hung on the wall with sayings like, 'Hang on' and 'There's no I in we'. An old TV stood on a wheeled cart in the corner. A globe sat undisturbed up front by the chalk board. The teacher's desk had pencil holders and trays for homework assignments. The chalkboard even had Mr. Shawnessy's name written in a looping hand. Jaxon recognized that writing and concentrated on the task at hand.

Danger was in this room. He could feel it.

He stepped further in and turned to the back of the class. A man stood in the shadows and his silhouette did not hide what he was holding in his hand. A gun was pointed at two figures in chairs to his right. In the moonlight he could see Vick bound and gagged next to another woman he assumed was Michelle.

Jaxon turned his gun toward the man and the man spoke.

"Don't be foolish, Jaxon. Put it down."

The voice he did not recognize.

He didn't know why he thought he should, but for some reason, he expected it to match his memory of Collin Williamsen. The weak, frail, boy from his youth. This man was almost his same height and was definitely well built. His outline displayed a bulk that betrayed strength.

A lantern was switched on next to the man, and Jaxon was not surprised to see a much older Collin staring back at him. He must have been wearing a blonde wig back in Orange Park, but now he was bald. The body had aged and changed, but the facial features had not. Jaxon lowered his weapon but kept it in his hand. Ray did the same.

"Hello, Collin."

"So you do remember. You flatter me. I see you obeyed the rules this time and only brought your friends like I instructed. Good. Maybe things will turn out for the better in the end."

"Let them go," Jaxon said. "This is between you and me."

"It is, isn't it? But I also remember many others who laughed along with you. Others who brought me down just as easily as you and Rocky. These others," he briefly waved the gun toward Ray, Gil, and Mel, "they're laughing now, just as the ones did so long ago. I can't allow it. They must be punished, just as surely as you."

"You're full of shit," Ray said and Collin turned the gun toward Ray and pulled the trigger.

The shot was huge and booming in the quiet room and Ray spun and went down, his gun clattering to the ground and sliding under a desk, Mel screaming. Jaxon crouched reflexively and brought his gun up again. Collin quickly turned the weapon back to the women.

"That's a warning," he said. "One more outburst and I'll finish these two off right now. Put the weapon down."

Jaxon lowered the gun again and slowly stood. Ray writhed on the floor as blood leaked out of his wounded shoulder. At least he wasn't fatally hit. Mel clung to Gil who held her slightly behind him.

"On the floor, Jaxon."

He knelt and put his gun on the floor by his feet.

"Kick it away."

Jaxon kicked it with his foot and it slid a few feet from him. Collin did not move.

"What do you want with me?" Jaxon said.

"What do you think I want? I want you to die. Apparently my little scavenger hunt was not as deadly as I had hoped. At least for you. So now you leave me little choice but to deal with you here and now."

"Then deal with me and leave these others out of it. Their only crime is they know me. Let them go."

"No."

"Let them go, Collin."

The voice came from the open door and Collin's face fell briefly and then he grew angry. Robert Fanucci stood in the door, a gun pointed at his stepbrother.

"Let them go, Collin. We can figure this out without all this bloodshed."

"What the hell are you doing here?" Collin said, his calm composure ruptured by the unexpected entrance of his stepbrother.

"I knew something must be up when I woke groggy and hung over. You drugged me."

"I needed you out of the way."

"I see that. But it wasn't hard to figure out when I put two and two together. All that time off the last few weeks. You disappearing while I was visiting. The multiple requests for access to surveillance equipment and camera usage. Why?"

"Why do you think, brother? To give those who hurt Danielle a little payback."

"That's not the way it works. You know that."

"Oh, that's right. The brother who doesn't even care enough for his own stepdaughter to avenge her death. I don't think you even cried when she took her life. Well, I did. She was the world to me!"

"I know you cared about her. Of course I wept. I just never showed it. You were the best uncle a girl could have, but this is way beyond anything a loving relative should display. You need to stop."

"Bullshit! And I was more than just a good uncle. I was her father. And you let them take her from me."

Jaxon watched Fanucci's mouth drop open and the wheels turn behind his eyes. He couldn't seem to work out what he had just heard.

"That's impossible. Why would you lie? You can't be her father. David Newsome is."

"You're a fool," Collin spat. "You're gullible and an idiot, and I can't believe I've called you brother all these years. You never knew, did you?"

"Knew what?" The gun wavered in Fanucci's hand slightly and Jaxon saw his edge slipping away.

"Me and Renee. We had a thing. She loved me even though she was married to that idiot, Newsome. We were in love and she was going to leave him, then she got pregnant. She got pregnant with Danielle, my daughter, and everything changed. She wouldn't leave him and refused to admit Danielle was mine. But I knew. I knew. You could see it in her eyes. Danielle was my daughter and no one else's."

Jaxon watched Fanucci work this out and he could see the truth surfacing there.

"Then you came along," Collin said. "After the asshole died, you came along and took everything from me. You took her, made her yours while I was in the Philippines. I returned home to find you married to the woman I loved and you calling yourself the father of my daughter."

"I never knew," Fanucci said in shock.

"Then you couldn't even protect her. They teased and bullied my little girl and you let them. You killed her just as if you pulled the trigger yourself. Both of them. You let my loves wither away and die. You son-of-a-bitch."

Fanucci stood there. The shock on his face complete.

The gun in his hand sagged as the strength left him and he leaned against the wall, unable to hold himself up. A man whose whole life had been a lie had just told him his family was not what they seemed. His whole world had changed in a blink of an eye and he couldn't absorb it all.

"That's right, brother. Take that all in. You weak piece of shit."

Collin turned the gun toward his brother and as Fanucci realized he was about to die, he did the only thing his reflexes allowed. He fired his weapon at the man he no longer knew.

Collin spun backwards and his gun fired wildly, hitting the ceiling.

Jaxon dove to the floor for his weapon as Mel screamed again. Snatching the gun up, Jaxon rolled up to a kneeling position and fired his weapon into the reeling Collin Williamsen, hitting him in the chest, and slamming his body back against the wall.

As silence returned to the room, Jaxon watched Collin's eyes roll back into his skull and his body sink to the floor. Jaxon sprang to Vick's side and pulled the blindfold and gag from her head. She saw Collin on the floor. She sagged into Jaxon's arms and wept.

"I've got you," he said, rocking her there in his arms. "I've got you."

EPILOGUE

Bethany stood in front of the grave and wept.

The marker for Danielle Newsome was a little weathered and worn, but the picture of her set in the stone was clear and bright and one that Bethany had never seen. It was from a school play. She had been the lead and she looked so happy playing the part of someone who was not her.

Bethany remembered how all the other kids had made fun of the play. Nobody who was anybody went to the three performances, but it must not have mattered to Danielle. She still smiled and probably did her best. Bethany wished she could go back in time and see that play. Maybe things would have been different.

She knelt next to the marker and looked at the picture she held in her hand one more time. It was a little worn, but Danielle's face remained untouched. It had been through a lot. She leaned it up against the tombstone, put the flowers she had bought next to it, and stood. Glancing at the fresh grave next to her, she felt a shiver run through her body. She tried not to feel anything negative toward the man who had put her through hell, but it was difficult standing in the presence of Danielle's father. Even if he was dead.

She felt someone next to her and was surprised to see the man who had saved her life standing right there.

Jaxon Jennings stood tall and strong, yet she could see a sadness in his eyes and knew a little about what he was feeling. She had read the story of him and Collin Williamsen in the papers and had felt sympathy toward his plight. She and Jaxon shared a common mistake in their lives and would forever be connected by it.

He turned to her and smiled. She reached out her hand and he took it in his as they stood quietly over the father and daughter whose lives had so tragically ended. The pain was immense for Bethany, but she knew it would ease with time.

She stood holding the hand of the man who had saved her life and let the healing begin.

ABOUT THE AUTHOR

Richard C Hale has worn many hats in his lifetime including Greens Keeper, Bartender, Musician, Respiratory Therapist, and veteran Air Traffic Controller. You can usually find him controlling Air Traffic over the skies of the Southeastern U.S. where he lives with his wife and children.
Drop by his website and give him a shout. He'd love to hear from you.
www.richardchaleauthor.com

Printed in Great Britain
by Amazon